A Little Death by Chance

Kimber Swan

ISBN: 978-0-615-87473-9

This book is dedicated to my family and friends who helped me on this wonderful journey.

CONTENTS

ACKNOWLEDGMENTS

To my husband- Thank you for always supporting me in all my dreams. If it was not for you, I may not have had the courage to write this. I'll love you always. "Now put that in the book."

To my boys- Mommy is almost done with her "homework." I love you two.

To mom- Thank you for reading every single version of this book and taking care of us all. I don't think I would have been able to do this without your constant help with the boys.

To Ilene- If I did not have your honest first reaction, I don't think I would have written more. Thank you for supporting this and being a good friend not just a co-worker.

To Deb- Where do I start? Thank you for your honest reactions (and you know what I mean) to the book and being not just a good friend but a great one.

To Lennys and Tami- Thank you for the last minute read and invaluable input. I started the next one earlier than expected because of you two.

To Jessica- Well I don't know what to say. You have been a constant friend who has always told me the truth. I'm glad you like the book and I thank you for reading it along with me.

CHAPTER ONE

Kaitlyn

Finally! Its closing time at the candy store and just as I start to rush out from behind the counter to lock up, the tinkling of the bell from the door alerts me there is one more last minute shopper. This always seems to happen when I have plans. Why should this time be any different? But tonight should be different. It has to be different.

My name is Kaitlyn Daniels and I finally graduated college yesterday and am ready to start the next stage of my life. Tonight the biggest party this town has ever seen is planned by one of the more affluent families. They are throwing the party for their son, a friend of mine since middle school and fellow graduate of the same university as me, located here on Long Island in New York. He and one of my best friends have been dating since junior year of high school. Normally attending parties is not my thing but this party is the rare exception. I have finally achieved a major milestone in the plan for my future. *Hello medical school.*

The town I grew up in is a small prosperous town with a right side and wrong side- very "Pretty in Pink," one of my more favorite movies. It's located on the north shore of Long Island in New York. Everyone knows everyone's business and my family's business is no exception. I am the oldest of four children. My father is a typical blue collar, middle class worker, who likes to go to the bar in the next town over. While my stay at home mother likes to have her "hidden" drinks at home. When the two of them get together in a drunken state, the arguing starts and does not stop until things are broken or worse someone develops an injury.

Having been lucky enough to receive a full academic scholarship to Hofstra University, I majored in pre-med and graduated Magna Cum Laude. Having patience and diligence, pre-med was not as difficult as I was

1

led to believe. However, I did sacrifice a social life for maintaining a perfect GPA to keep my scholarship. It was an easy sacrifice to make because besides my two best friends my social life was almost nonexistent.

Even though I applied to colleges out of state, going away to college after high school was not a realistic option for me. Turning down Duke and their scholarship was very difficult but staying at home and helping to care for my younger siblings, Thomas and Serena, was the priority. Bethany, my other sister a few years younger than me, is entering her senior year of high school. So between the both of us, we have been able to care for the two of them. If I had gone away to school, someone could have, most likely would have, been seriously hurt, maimed, or worse. My parents have already scarred me, unbeknownst to them, and the thought of them inflicting these scars on my younger more vulnerable siblings was too much to bear. All my parents, specifically my mother, see is the daughter who makes dinner, cleans up around the house and can be relied upon to help care for my siblings.

If I had not made the decision to get a job after high school, my life would have been much different from what it is now. I shudder to think what it would have been like. Work was part of my social life and it allowed me to escape the demands of my dysfunctional family. My best friend since pre-school, Sophia, was able to talk to her boss and get me a job at the candy store. Since there was no extra money around and bills were always in jeopardy of not being paid, the money I earned was needed to pay for my gas and other incidentals. Most kids in my town relied upon their savings for spending money but my savings had long been depleted to help keep a roof over our heads.

Ralph, the owner of the candy store, is more like a father to me than a boss. He worries about me incessantly. Knowing my home situation, he has at times increased my hours or called me in last minute-despite not really needing the help in order to get me out of the house. I quickly caught on, but my parents never did being as self-absorbed as they are. Work has been always been fun because Ralph always made sure it was lighthearted and entertaining, an escape for me. When I was there I was able to forget home and attempt to be the young adult I was supposed to be.

I am hidden by the display cabinets when the customer strode into the store. This hiding spot affords me the opportunity to focus my attention on the customer and notice his distinguished build and long legs currently clad in leather. I try to glimpse his face but a motorcycle helmet and his position hides his facial features. *Helmet?*

The tight fitted black tee shirt partially reveals a tribal tattoo around his left bicep muscle and an intricate tattoo starting mid right forearm. This guy screams trouble to someone like me.

2

He walks with indecision looking for something, acting as if he doesn't have a care in the world. Unfortunately for me, he has not noticed the store closed fifteen minutes ago. Normally this would not bother me, but I need to leave! Knowing I have to leave causes my irritation to grow exponentially. Then he turns around and I glimpse his eyes very briefly before he turns around again looking for help.

And when he finally speaks, "Do you have any milk chocolate covered marshmallows?" my heart soars. *A guy after my own heart.*

Relieved I won't need to help him but saddened he will be leaving shortly, I answer his question. "Sorry, we're sold out."

As he turns to leave the store and our eyes make contact. In that transitory moment the whole world stops. The earth has tilted more on its axis and stopped rotating with this look. Even though logically I know only a few seconds have gone by, it seems to have to lasted hours. Crazy, I know! In these few short seconds it feels like it is only him and I. *Well yeah idiot it is only him and me.* Then he nods curtly breaking the contact and leaves abruptly, as if a fire just set flame to the building.

Glued to the spot unable to move and still floored by my reaction to him, the tinkling bell from the door sounds like a fog horn calling a ship home during a storm finally awakens me. Even after a few seconds has elapsed, my legs are still lead weights rooting me in place. This sort of reaction has never happened to me before. My lacking social life needs improvement pronto, hopefully decreasing the chance this type of reaction will occur in the future.

Sophia's talks of taking risks and going out on limb venture forth from the deepest recesses of my mind. So when I finally come to my senses, I jolt into action and rush to the door in time to see a sleek, powerful motorcycle drive away. Frustrated I took so long to react and realizing I'm too late to take the risk and chance speaking to him, I rub my head in thought. It is now that I realize my appearance resembles nothing that could pass for a woman with my hair tied in a ponytail and no make-up applied. Groaning to myself remembering all the times Sophia and I argue over my lack of make-up and hair styling. Never will I admit this to her, but today I wish I had done something to my appearance. It may have made a difference now.

Once I am done speculating about what ifs, I return to earth and close the shop for the night. "We are Family" is playing muffled in my messenger bag. Habitually I look at the caller id but I already know it reads #1 BFF, Sophia. We set the ring tone when I first got my phone and she would tell me we were closer than friends that we are family.

Oblivious to my surroundings, I rush to the car while talking. "I know I'm late. I'm leaving now. It should only take me fifteen minutes to get home and change. Then-"

Sophia cuts me off. "No just come here and get ready. I have an outfit for you and I don't care what you say, you're wearing it. This is your night." Her tone brooks no room for arguing, so I forgo a comment. "We don't have a lot of time to do your hair or make-up properly, so it will have to be simple."

"Okay, I'm on my way. Hey wait. Have you spoken to Lara yet?"

"Yeah, I just got off the phone with her. She was wondering where we were. I told her you still hadn't gotten here. Is everything okay? You should have been out of there thirty minutes ago."

"I know. There was a last minute customer who seemed to know then not know what he wanted. When he found out we were out of what he wanted he left." I explain juggling the keys, phone, a travel mug of hot tea and messenger bag to open the car door.

"I'll see you soon. I want to get this night started. Danny Rocks' band Sexual Encounter is going to be there tonight," her excitement screams through the phone, "and I have to meet him. You know they only perform at large gigs now. This is a favor for Tyler's cousin. Hurry!" Danny's band is the newest band to hit the radio. Being from around here, he knows many of the same people as Sophia. He rarely does small house parties since they started performing at bigger venues. Sophia has had a crush on him since before he made it big. The brief encounter they had a few years back has never been forgotten by her.

The phone lands on the passenger seat, bounces then disappears between the seat and car door, forgotten once I start the car. Backing out I notice a sleek, black motorcycle stopped across the parking lot, appearing to be watching me. *Creepy.* Trying not to pay it more attention because I am too late to think about it, I continue on my way but curiosity causes me to look in the rear view mirror once more. The driver has not moved. *Hmmm…freaky.*

Five minutes later, motorcycle forgotten, I am in front Sophia's house, a beautiful center hall colonial on half an acre of land with perfectly manicured lawns and gardens. Her mother loves to garden and it has rubbed off on me, despite her attempts to get Sophia interested in it. There is a beautiful rose garden in the backyard which I hope to replicate one day. Gardening helps me relax. I tried to garden at my house but everything I plant there dies. I have often wondered whether or not my mother kills them somehow.

I sprint to the front door and open it without knocking. Normally I would never be this forward, but Mrs. Duncan, Sophia's mom, has long since told me I am like her daughter. Sophia and I have spent more time here than anywhere. In the last couple of years I have probably had more meals here than my own home. Recently though, if I was not home to cook my mother would order take out, making me feel guilty that my siblings were not getting nutritious meals.

"Hi mom!" I yell out winded from the sprint and rush up the stairs.

"Hi honey. How was work?" She laughs back.

"It was fine except for the last customer. He didn't seem to realize we were closing."

"Mom we're late. Talk to her later. Lara's waiting." Sophia yells from her room.

Rushing into Sophia's room, the outfit is out and ready on her bed. Her room is about the size of my parent's living room and kitchen combined. She is buried under clothes in her vast closet and tossing out clothing unfit for tonight's party.

"You have five minutes to take a shower."

Her bathroom is a girls dream. She is an only child, not spoiled exactly but she usually gets anything she asks for. No guy she has dated has been able to keep her in the life style she has become accustomed to. Starting to strip as I hustle into her bathroom, she sticks her head out of the closet and hoots at my retreating backside. "Go baby. Take it all off. Those stripper dance lessons are paying off. I have a few dollar bills for you somewhere."

I flip the bird from behind but can't help shake my non-existent ass at her while I drop my shorts and toss them at her head. She is the best friend a person can ask for. She has never judged me or my family. Sure we have arguments but I know where they come from. When most people would not have given me the time of day, she always stuck by me. She has been like this since we met in pre-school. I still remember that day; I was so shy, not that that has changed much, when she came over to me at nap time and asked if she could nap with me. From that day forward we have been inseparable.

We are polar opposites. Sophia is small and petite with red wavy hair. Whereas I am tall, slim, runners build and mousy brown pin straight hair (we've tried in the past perming it, but it only lasts about a week). Sophia has amazing green eyes as opposed to my almost all grey eyes with brown flecks. Where she is outgoing, I tend to be shy and reserved. She dresses sophisticated and I dress plain. I am more athletic and she hates sports or anything that requires her to sweat too much. I excelled at sports in high school. Hey what can I say, the more I did the less time I spent at home. Sophia's only sport was the cheerleading squad. While I love to get lost in a book, Sophia likes to get lost shopping.

We are and have been two peas in a pod. I know her thoughts and she finishes my sentences. We always look out for each other. Although her life appears almost perfect, she has a past as well.

She has seen me at my worst, red faced and puffy eyed from crying because my parents were fighting again. Scared because I didn't know if I could handle life any more. So angry at my father, mother, myself and life in general. But she has also seen me the happiest I have ever been, like when I found out I was granted the full scholarship for college and then accepted to medical school. We celebrated both those nights with her family because my family's reaction was "well how are you going to help us and go to college?"

When my parents aren't drinking they can be fun, great people. However those days are getting farther and farther apart to the point where I may not be able to say that much longer. I do not think I have ever known the love of a parent. My father's coldness is understandable because of his up-bringing but not my mother. Her parents, my grandparents are the best. They have always loved and supported me in everything. No questions asked. It was hard on me when they moved to Pennsylvania. If it were not for Sophia and my siblings, I would have asked to move in with them a couple of years ago.

Starting to rinse my hair of conditioner, I realize I have been in here for more than five minutes. Just like that Sophia shrieks. "Times up witch. I'm going to flush the toilet and run the hot water if you don't get your ass out of there now."

"Evil bitch." I mutter knowing she would follow through with the threat.

"I heard that. Love you too." She sweetly responds.

As I rush to get out, I trip over my own feet and fall flat on my ass. Hearing my graceful shower exit, Sophia comes to see what the ruckus is. The minute she sees me sprawled out naked on the floor she bursts out laughing.

"Wow that's going to really hurt tomorrow." She is laughing so hard, she has to grip her sides. "I think I may have just peed myself."

From my vantage point I tease, "Yeah I can see the wet spot." Which throws her into another fit of laughter and I wipe the tears streaming down my cheeks. Not sure if they are from embarrassment, pain or laughter, hoping for the latter.

"Get out so I can pee." She walks over me doing the pee dance towards the toilet bowl.

"Geez, can you give me a minute to get up?"

When she calms down enough to offer me her hand, I grab it grateful. Once I have established my footing, we bump shoulders both reaching for my towel on the floor.

"If I didn't love you already and have been scarred by your naked body before, I may have been blinded by the full moon." She snorts. "We're hitting the beach this weekend to work on your tan. I won't have you scaring off potential suitors." Haughtily stated, as only Sophia can.

"You know I hate the beach." I scowl at the bathroom door. "Why can't we just lay out by the pool?"

"Because you need to get out and meet some hot guy that will totally rock your world."

"Maybe I already have." I secretly whisper to myself. If she knew she would ask a million questions which I have no answers for. All I know is he had soulful eyes, a deep voice and had me reacting to a look. Again she is right about getting out more, but starting a conversation with anyone, let alone a hot guy is too terrifying. *Shell, Kaitlyn.*

She continues as if she didn't hear me. "Lara's dad is opening the house in the Hamptons next week. She wants us to go with her. She says many of our friends will be out there next weekend as well. There's sort of an informal end of college party."

"But I have to work next weekend and-"

"No you don't. It's already been taken care of with Ralph. He said he would cover that weekend. He also offered the next couple of Friday nights and Saturdays off."

"Sophia, you had no right! You know I need the money. What about my sisters and brother? I need to be there for them should something happen with my parents."

"Let Bethany keep an eye on them. She graduates next year. You need to start living your life." Sighing, she tries a different tact. "Ralph said he would pay you vacation time."

Eyeing her skeptically I remark, "But I don't get vacation time."

"Whatever. Just don't ask questions?" She brushes me off.

"Okay, fine. But you don't have to always remind me to live life for myself." I answer back icily. This is a subject her and I disagree on, even though I know she means well. It is my life and my family.

"I know that. I don't want to argue with you about this tonight. I'm sorry. Okay? I just want you to live and not feel any obligations. Your parents have never done anything for you besides give birth to you. I wish you would act your age and not always the parent." Her smile is repentant. "Anyway we don't have time to argue, Lara's waiting and she'll most likely be pissed we're late."

"I act just fine. It's your behavior I'm worried about." I say with mock indignation. She ignores my comment, so I continue. "Lara can wait a little while longer. I'm surprised she isn't there helping to set up. The two of them have become inseparable. Have you noticed?"

"Jealous much?"

Yeah! My goals are so set I don't have time for a boyfriend right now but it does not stop me from dreaming. Between my plainness, inexperience and family life, no guy would want to be involved with me. I scramble to get dressed before she emerges from the bathroom. The outfit she picked out should be illegal. It's a black, fitted skirt too short for my legs with a button down, light grey, silk shirt cut so low it almost shows my boobs.

After eyeing me in the outfit, she starts on my make-up and hair. When she's finished, I don't recognize the pretty face or hot body in the mirror staring back at me. She hands me a pair of heels, eyeing me skeptically probably thinking she's pushing it. I look at them thinking they are the devil but put them on anyway. Cautiously, I stand and realize they feel comfortable and confirm it by walking around the room. When I do not bitch about the heels, Sophia smirks at me like she's saying "told you so."

"You're hot!" She claps her hands pleased with herself.

"Okay, ready?" I ask.

"Yeah, let me touch up my lipstick." Once done, we head downstairs saying good bye to her mom.

"Wait let me see." Mrs. Duncan shouts from the other room.

"Hurry up mom, we're late!"

"Okay, okay. I'm coming." She smiles at me when she comments on the outfit. "Wow, is that you Kaitlyn?"

Sheepishly I smile and look at my feet knowing my cheeks redden because of her compliment. "I know it's not me. Do I look okay?"

"You look pretty and will turn the guy's heads tonight." She helps ablate my insecurities but all I do is shrug. We hug goodbye and leave.

Sophia tosses me her keys. "We're taking my car but you're driving." I am always the designated driver because I rarely, if ever, drink and probably never will.

We climb into her sports coupe and I have to adjust the seat back. The radio is playing Adele's "Someone Like You" loudly. Sophia belts out a verse of the song and my mind wanders back to the parking lot at work from earlier tonight. Was the guy on the motorcycle there looking at me? Who was he? Before I know it, we are in front of Lara's house. *I'm losing track of time tonight because this guy has muddled my mind.* Lara comes stomping out of the house.

"Is everything okay?" I ask tentatively.

She looks at me in the mirror and sighs. "Yeah, my dad's new girlfriend thought she could tell me how to dress tonight. Who does she think she is?"

Lara's mom died suddenly and suspiciously last June, leaving Lara and her dad alone. Her dad has not handled it well. He always liked to have a couple of drinks at night but after his wife's death he went off the deep end staying in a near constant state of drunkenness. Finally in December something changed and he realized what he was doing to his daughter and changed vices. His newest vice is in the form of women. He has a new woman every month or so, which bothers Lara.

"What did you say to her?" Sophia asks.

"Nothing, I just ignored her and started to walk out when I heard my dad tell her to be quiet and mind her own business."

"Wow, what did she say to that?" I questioned.

"What could she say? She's not my mother and is only warming his bed."

"Ewhhh." Sophia and I chimed at the same time.

Lara laughs at us. "What took you guys so long?"

"I had a last minute customer who didn't know the store was closed."

"Lara, you had to see when Kaitlyn fell out of the shower naked. It was so funny, I almost peed myself." Sophia wipes her eyes at the memory and Lara chuckles.

"Yeah, I'm going to have some nasty bruises in the morning." I rub my elbow to emphasize the point. I adjust the skirt again and question the outfit. Sophia picks up on my fidgeting and grabs my hand squeezing it reassuringly.

"So what or should I say who's on the menu tonight?" Lara asks in a playful way. We all know where she will be and with who.

"I don't know but Kaitlyn is letting loose tonight. I already told her we're going to the beach next weekend with you. She tried to back out and make excuses, but I set her straight."

What the fuck! I think.

"Great, what time are we leaving? Sophia you're driving, right? My car's in the shop. Tyler is going to meet us out there on Saturday with it. He's staying at his cousin's place."

Ten minutes later, we pull into Tyler's long driveway and our plans for the following weekend are set. There is no room to move on the wrap around porch as people are mingling and drinking on it. The music from the party can be heard in the car despite the radio in the car still being on. As we get out of the car, Sophia and Lara trap me, giving a pep talk and lecture. *This should be good.*

"Kaitlyn, you're going to have fun tonight and not be a wall flower. You'll talk to people you normally wouldn't." Sophia starts the pep talk while Lara continues it.

"You'll at least kiss someone tonight. This is your goal tonight."

Great short form fitting clothes, beach, kissing, what more? I am so out of my comfort zone. Shell... Kaitlyn.

"Let's start slow by getting out of your comfort zone." Sophia reads my mind. "If you don't we'll offer you up on a silver platter to any willing guy. All you have to do is start a conversation with at least one hot guy here tonight."

"We'll never be far away. Just follow our lead. Tyler promised me there would be a lot of hot guys tonight and knowing your goal for tonight he even offered himself. But I don't share." Lara chortles.

"Really, you told Tyler!" I shout exasperated. "I can't believe you would speak to him about something like this. Now every guy will think I'm easy. I'm out of here. You guys can call me when you're ready to leave." I start to walk away, anger and embarrassment oozing from my pores.

"Don't even think about it." Sophia says in a no nonsense voice. "In order for them to think you're easy, you have to actually put out. I will pull the bitchy best friend card if you take one more step." She is quiet in her demand and I know that tone well. *Shit! Shit! Shit!* I resign myself, turn around and start walking briskly to the front of the house ignoring them as I pass.

There are people hanging out on the porch of Tyler's huge house. The house is an older remodeled Victorian with the classic colors of the era it was built. Tyler sees us, jumps off the porch and grabs Lara, swinging her around.

"Hey honey. How's it going?" Lara asks Tyler seductively.

"Better now that you're here." Tyler leans into her, kissing her passionately.

"Get a room," someone yells. Wishing I had something like they have but knowing I cannot afford it right now, I look on uncomfortably.

"Shut it! You're just jealous." Tyler comebacks, his hands still wrapped around Lara. "Tristan came and I want to finally introduce you to him." Every time Tyler has planned for them to meet something always comes up.

"Oooh, I can't wait. Please tell me he isn't going to act like the douche they say he is in the papers. Is he?"

"He's not like that. You know I told you not to believe any of those rags. He's my cousin." Tyler retorts coolly.

"Sorry honey, but he seems so crazy in the papers but he's hot so it's hard to not read them. His eyes, those lips-"

Tyler cuts her off disgustedly. "All right, I get it, he's hot."

"Right Sophia, isn't he hot?" Lara remarks.

"Sorry Tyler, he is." Sophia responds dreamily.

"Well do me a favor and don't hit on him okay. He doesn't need that shit tonight." Tyler responds with resignation. He whispers to Lara but I over hear him. "I think he may be the right guy for Kaitlyn tonight."

"I don't think so." I reply as they turn an assessing eye at me. "Are you kidding me? Really!" I squawk.

"Come on Kaitlyn, just talk to him. You guys may have a lot in common. He isn't looking for anything tonight." Tyler coaxes.

I adamantly shake my head no. Sophia looks at me and says to Tyler, "Of course she will."

"No! No! NO!" *I won't do this.*

Sophia grabs my hand and politely excuses us for a minute. Dragging me away from the crowd, she starts threatening me. "You have no choice. I already told you how this night was going to work itself out. Now is your opportunity. Take it or I make you."

"No Sophia, I can't do this." My plea falls on deaf ears

"Yes. You. Can. I'm not telling you to have sex with him. All I'm saying is to let loose and have fun. Don't think of the consequences."

Shell...Kaitlyn. The stupid voice in my head keeps reminding me to step out of my shell.

"If he tries to take it further than I'm willing to go, I'll hurt him."

"Don't worry. He's not hard up for company. If he wants more and you're unwilling, he won't push. He'll just find it elsewhere from what I hear." We turn around, Sophia smiling sweetly and me like I just sucked a lemon.

"Fine I'll do it, as if I have a choice." My voice rings loudly with acquiescence and sarcasm.

"Thanks Kaitlyn. You're exactly what my cousin needs. No demands, no nothing."

Feeling very uncomfortable with what is about to go down, I question him. "Where is he?"

"I don't see him but I know where he'll probably be. He sometimes likes to get away from the crowds. Come on." Tyler points in the direction behind the house and starts to lead the way.

The grass is soft after the last couple of wet days that I have to walk on my tip toes so the heels don't sink in the grass. We all walk in the direction of what appears to be a secluded section of the backyard behind some shrubbery, unnoticeable from our original spot nearer the house. Sophia stops abruptly cursing to retrieve her shoe from where it was stuck in the grass. Tyler and Lara slow down and lag behind a few feet in order to kiss. So when we finally enter the area where Tyler pointed to, I'm entering first and catch an eye full of what appears to be tangled bodies.

Inhaling sharply and gasping, I flee the sight that was before me. Embarrassment is burning my cheeks as I run toward the front of the house passing first Tyler and Lara who look surprised by my near sprint and next Sophia who looks annoyed with her shoe. When she glances up she sees me coming straight towards her.

"Where are you going?" She says to my fleeing body.

"I'm going up front to see who's here?" Yelling over my shoulder I try again with a different excuse. "I forgot my phone in the car."

CHAPTER TWO

Tristan

There is a candy store near Aunt Michelle's house in a small strip mall where I can get her milk chocolate covered marshmallows as a way to apologize for not helping set up for Tyler's graduation party this morning. I was too hung over. Mom thinks this may help but I don't know if she will forgive me. My family should know by now not to rely upon me for anything. I always let everyone down but I never used to be like this until that devastating night. I am Tristan Chance and that's my life.

As I drive down the narrow road toward the strip mall, I am reminded of that night almost 4 years ago this month on a similar road as this one. Tara and I were fighting in the car after a party. I was drunk and high and she was livid because her best friend had flirted with me and I did nothing to discourage it. Her best friend had made many passes at me in her drunken state and they were not the flirting kinds either. She was saying things like "Tara will never know" or "I won't tell if you don't." She grabbed my dick in the middle of the party. Well Tara did find out and blamed me completely. She thought I was taking advantage of her drunken friend. I told her if Claudine was her best friend, drunk or not, she would not have encouraged me and grabbed my dick. What Tara didn't know was that Claudine kissed me and attempted more before I put a stop to it. Our argument did not end well that night.

I shudder at the memory and push it back down deep in the vault of memories. Recognizing I am about to drive past the small strip mall, I quickly make a U-turn and maneuver the motorcycle into the parking lot. Dismounting the bike, I walk into the store forgetting to take off my helmet because that memory has left me off key, so I flip the visor up. When I enter I don't see anyone around so I take my time looking for the marshmallows. I see other types of candy I would like but not what I need and I do not have the time to waste. I'm late as it is.

"Where are the milk chocolate covered marshmallows?" I ask to no one.

And the most beautiful sound I have ever heard, like an angel's voice, answers. "Sorry, but we're sold out of them."

How can seven words sound so good? I cannot see where the voice is coming from or the face and body to go with the voice. I turn around searching for it but am unsuccessful, but when I turn to leave I see her and am shocked to my core. She has the most beautiful eyes I have ever seen. Nothing exists except for her eyes. The world has just dropped away. If you ask me what she looks like, I could only describe her eyes. For a brief moment I am drowning in her eyes and her voice sounds like an angel speaking to me from somewhere heavenly.

Who is she? My heart's beating like I ran a marathon. The sweat is dripping off me. This reaction scares the hell out of me. I nod and leave as quickly as my feet will get me out of here. I'm too afraid to stay. Once outside breathing heavy, I jog to the motorcycle and drive away. *Pussy!* I quickly glance at the door to the store as I pull out to see if she's there watching. *Did she feel it too?* Not seeing her, I decide it is best to try to forget this crazy feeling and speed away.

However I cannot help but wonder again who she is. The moment our eyes met, I knew she was someone special, different. Tara used to be someone special and look what I did to her. Do not think about Tara, it will only make you crazy and do crazy things. I have changed since that night and the following years. Think of something else, quickly. *Mom and Abigail - they need me.* Who is she?

I have to go back and talk to her to find out who she is. Again I'm making another U-turn, revving the engine and high tailing it back to the store double time, not wanting to miss her. Pulling into the parking lot just minutes later, I see a girl getting into an older car. She is on the phone. *An angel's voice.* The engine to her car roars to life and she backs out of the parking space. And just like that she is gone. *Pussy you froze. That's not like you.* I could follow her but that would be creepy and she may think I am a stalker.

Quickly I look at my watch and realize I am so late that following her is not even an option anymore. Aunt Michelle's house is not far away and I can be there in less than ten minutes. Pissing Aunt Michelle off further would not bode well for me. My cousin Tyler and I are very close-more like brothers than cousins. Our mothers are sisters and very close. Mom is the eldest of the two and has looked after my aunt since they were young.

My mom married my dad very young. He is fifteen years her

senior. Their courtship, according to mom, was a whirlwind romance but my sister and I have never seen that side of my father. Sometimes I wonder what she saw in him. My mom is a great mom and a wonderful person. She always helps others as much as she can. Everyone who comes in to contact with her falls in love with her, it is no wonder dad did as well. I know it upsets her when I act crazy and get so drunk, but what she does not know is that he is the cause. She has tried to intervene multiple times by sending me to shrinks and therapists but it does not help. I cannot open up about my father. He is too much of a public figure for me to bad mouth him.

My father, wow, I do not know what to think of him. I have always felt like a big disappointment to him. Over the years I have tried everything I could think of to earn his approval. As a child I have no memories of his love or kindness. It feels as if he never truly wanted me, that I was an indulgence for my mother and my father still pays for it. He never could and still cannot say no to her. She has always told my sister and me she wanted a big family but God had a different plan for her. Throughout their years of marriage, she has had numerous miscarriages.

Knowing how my father felt, I always strived to be the best I could possibly be. In high school I was a straight "A" student, captain and quarter back of the football team, captain of the basketball and baseball teams. But this wasn't enough. When we found out I was accepted into Harvard, his alma mater, I never received any praise from him. He just expected me to be accepted and attend.

When I started dating Tara in college, his feelings and comments started to worsen changing his tactic. He started to hassle me further about Tara when we heard I was accepted into Harvard Business School. The comments about her character and how she was money hungry started. According to him, she wanted the prestige of being linked to a Chance. One night when we went out to dinner with the family, he laced into me about her in front of her. He said she would only bring me down and more. My mother and I were embarrassed for him- this was probably one of the few times they argued. Later that same night after dropping Tara off at her dorm, he demanded I break things off.

Harvard is where I learned how to deal with my life recreationally. When I realized I could never gain his approval, I started to party with the best of them, so he could really have something to be disappointed in. Although I was captain of the rowing team and had the social life and girls most guys only dreamed of, I still envied my friends' relationships with their fathers. I started to make a name for myself in the elite party circuits and eventually the papers.

My group of friends had more money than they knew what to do with. Recreational drugs were easily scored. I was sent a monthly stipend from my trust fund to live off. Since my friends and I owned our flats, our allowances went towards booze, drugs and girls. Partying hard, socializing and losing control with the best of them caused me to learn early I needed to be in complete control in the bedroom. Once I almost forgot a condom just as I was about to release because I was drunk and high. Needless to say, I no longer have drunken sex.

Initially, the control I sought in the bedroom was my way of coping with the uncontrollable situation with my father and that night long ago. Whoever I had sex with, and truthfully it was only sex to satisfy an urge, never left unsatisfied. My control of them in the bedroom was what rumors were made of. Sex with me has always had just a touch of edge to it. A little spanking, tying up and blindfolding enhance the moment for whoever my partner may be for the night. Very rarely did I have repeaters in bed. Repeaters thought they had a right to me as a girlfriend. *Not what I'm looking for.* Women meant very little to me and still do.

Once a few years back I tried an edgier kind of sex. Some chick and I went to a club which catered to BDSM. Although I liked the control the dominants exerted over their submissive, some of the devices felt off. I don't like to cause my partner pain. This chick happened to like pain. Sex is about pleasure. The things she made me do to her turned me off. That night there was no release for me, however she got off multiple times. I did learn to blend some of the softer aspects of that life style with my dominant side.

Lost in the past, I almost run a red light. Stopping in time, a cop is sitting at the corner and I nod at him causing him to frown. *Join the group of people I have disappointed.* The light turns green and I refocus my attention on my driving. Pulling into the driveway at Aunt Michelle's, the party is underway and Tyler is talking with friends. Parking the bike off to the side of the house, I take off my helmet and rake my fingers through my hair trying to gain same sort of semblance before seeing Aunt Michelle. The girl nearest me hikes her skirt up, licks her lips and lights a cigarette. Girls who smoke are a definite turnoff. *Sorry honey, not a chance.*

"No man you don't want a piece of that. It's been used too many times to count." He hugs me.

"Don't worry I have no intentions of tapping that."

Being at Harvard has been hard on us. Knowing my father expects me to take over the company, our time of hanging out are about to be cut even more. Between juggling a demanding career and social life, I am not sure what I will have time for. This summer will be spent mostly in the Hamptons since I graduate this coming year and real life starts as they say. I will become the next CEO of Chance Industries, a Forbes Fortune 500 company, when my father deems me competent for the position. Who knows when that will be?

Our family is one of the wealthiest in the country. Chance Industries, CI as it is known, was started by my grandfather out of his garage over 80 years ago. It used to be shipping only, but over the decades it has expanded to have investments in everything from engineering to entertainment, agriculture to weapons and more. CI is an international company estimated to have a net worth in the billions. There are offices all over the world but the headquarters are located in New York City at the Chance Building. My father played the biggest part in making it what it is today. But the last couple of months it seems to have grown stagnant.

"Congratulations cousin." I say patting him on the back.

"Thanks man. It feels great."

"Are you expecting more people?"

"The real partiers will be here in a little while." He answers me distractedly. "What happened to you this morning, man? Mom was disappointed you couldn't help. I think she was more worried than she wanted to let on. You haven't been like that in a long time. Is everything okay?"

"No man everything's good. It's just, you know, this month and my father. I'm fine and I keep telling everyone not to worry about me. Where's your mom anyway?"

"As if my mom or yours wouldn't worry. She's in the house doing last minute things. You know her, everything needs to be just perfect. Just like your mom dude." He is looking everywhere but at me.

"Is everything okay?"

"Yeah my girl's late. She was supposed to be here forty-five minutes ago."

"Your girl? You've never mentioned her before. You've mentioned girls but not a girl. What gives?"

"I know you and girls, but I have mentioned her to you on several occasions. We have been dating since high school." I am pissed at myself that I cannot remember him ever mentioning her to me. "I've tried to introduce you two on many occasions but you either failed to show up or something came up with her. Honestly man, I'm actually happy you two haven't met yet. I know I have her heart and you won't be able to snag this one."

"I would never poach on my little cousin's girl. That's sacred man. I may be a douche to other guys but not my cousin."

"Thanks man. I can't wait to introduce you two now."

"Cool, I can't wait to meet the girl who has nabbed my cousin."

"When she gets here I'll find you."

"Great. Let me go find your mom and start groveling so we can get the celebrating under way."

He returns to his friends and grabs a drink. I pass the keg, grab a cup and down it. On the way to the house I notice several people are staring and whispering. I should be used to this by now but it always makes me uncomfortable. As far back as I can remember the cameras have loved me. People have asked if I was a model because of my height and physical appearance. Having gone to prep school in Manhattan, I have always interacted with the kids of celebrities and celebrities in their own right. Always having their pictures taken when we went out, this was often enough that my own "celebrity" status started. Eventually I did not have to be near them to attract the paparazzi.

Cameras and people seem to follow me where ever I go now. They like to catch me at my worse, never at my best like winning a race. Although I have given them enough fodder, I wish when I am attending a charity function with my mother they would print that stuff. There is always a question about who I am dating? I made the mistake once of answering a reporter's question when I was drunk. I told him that I don't date I just fuck. Well what can you expect leaving a club known for its party scene? They would never print the important stuff, so eventually I just gave up on changing my image. When I decide to let someone know me, they will not care what the papers say.

A group of girls are staring at me and trying to get my attention. I look them over and find them passable but young. Two of them will be my companions tonight. I inform them to expect me later. "I'll be seeing you two later."

They look at each and giggle. "Okay we'll be here." They respond in unison and remind me of the fembots from one of the Austin Powers movie. Man I love those movies. But unlike Austin, my mojo is still intact.

I get to the kitchen just in time to see Aunt Michelle trying to lift something heavy. Placing my empty cup in the trash outside the back door, I offer my help. "Hey I got that, Aunt Michelle." Taking the box out of her hands, she turns around with a fake snarl.

Her reply is snarky. "Well it's about time you showed up. Your mom called and said you'd left a while ago." She points me over to the back door. "What took you so long? Put that over there."

"Well I know I flaked this morning and you didn't sound happy with me so I knew I had to get you something by way of an apology. But as it happened the candy store I went to was out of stock on chocolate covered marshmallows."

She reaches over and gives me a hug. "You're forgiven. And thank you for trying. But what would I have done if you had gotten them? Tristan, I'm on a diet. Haven't you noticed how big my butt has gotten?" She smiles brightly at me while turning around to show me.

Not wanting to look at my aunt's butt or touch the topic of my aunt's weight because honestly, she has gotten a little plumper recently, I simply ask her, "Is mom here yet?"

"No something about your father and getting home late from work. She won't be coming." She sighs and continues. "It's okay though. This party is for college graduates not family."

"Where's Uncle Tom?"

"I don't know." It figures he is nowhere to be found. I don't know why Aunt Michelle puts up with him. He is probably off trying to score with one of the co-eds. Maybe it's something in their blood, my mom and her. My mom is the same with dad. They always make excuses for their husbands. Those two women deserve so much better.

"Okay, well I'm going back out to the party. I'll see you later. Oh hey, I'm probably going to crash here tonight. Is that okay?"

"It's fine. Be good. I'll need your help tomorrow cleaning up and I really don't want a repeat of this morning. I'll let you sleep until eleven." This is her way of telling me not to get too drunk and be careful. She knows me so well but unfortunately the stroll down memory lane earlier has me wanting to dull said memories and to do that drinking and girls have always been my way of coping- the more the better. *Hmmm now where were those girls....?*

Let the partying begin. I grab a new cup, fill it, drain it dry and refill it. I search for the girls while working on my third beer. I notice some of Tyler's friends and congratulate them on graduating, shake their hands, and ask what they're planning to do next. In return I'm asked questions ranging from what's my plans for the summer, when am I going to the Hamptons next, whose the new celebrity I'm dating, or my favorite when are you throwing a party.

Whenever I'm in the Hamptons, I usually throw a huge party. All classes of society show up. I tell Tyler's friends I will be out there starting this week for the summer before heading back to Harvard. Many of them offer their cell phone numbers to be invited to the parties. Knowing I won't invite half of them, I tell them to contact Tyler. He will invite the ones he wants to. Excusing myself from them, I head over in the direction the girls were waiting for me.

Before I meet up with them, I refill my cup with more beer. Ambling over to them I start to feel the buzz. No names are exchanged just one question about their age. I won't get sued or trapped by an underage girl's father crying I violated his daughter. Younger girls have a tendency to crash parties I attend, to try to be my newest bedmate and gain notoriety. These girls say their older than eighteen but if they are a day older I am surprised. Their response is very breathy and I think they are trying to come off as sexy but they miss the mark by a mile.

"Great, then let's get to know each other better. Grab a drink." I lead them to the secluded part of the backyard where Tyler and I used to hide from his dad. I notice Tyler has stocked the area with chairs, tables, and candles. Man that kid is always looking out for us. No one can see us from here. I hope he joins me with his girl soon because I don't want to be alone with these two for too long. I walk off knowing they will follow. Hearing the giggling and whispered exchanges of them behind me, I know I'm right. And just like that my night has improved knowing I will lose myself soon and forget the past.

These girls are quick fixes to scratch an itch only. Any girl okay with escorting me to a secluded spot without me asking their name or engrossing them in conversation is looking and ready for a good time and a good time only. They shouldn't have expectations of a date afterwards. Just the way I like it.

"So tell me what do you think we should do here by ourselves in this secluded spot?" I ask innocently but fail miserably with the smirk.

"I know something," the blonde replies reaching over to grab my hand and pushes me to the Adirondack chair.

"Candice likes to blow and I like to be touched," the brunette comebacks.

"Good because I like to be sucked and touched." *Could these girls be any more obvious?* Normally I am not this crass, there is some seduction involved, but these girls started it and I am finishing it.

The one named Candice kneels in front of me, and wasting no time starts to unbutton my leathers, while the other starts on my shirt. Julie- as I find out- lifts her leg across me and places it on the arm of the chair, offering herself up to me like an open book. *I am in the zone.* As I look at Julie, Candice works me out of my pants. *Umm that feels good, her grabbing it like that.*

Julie starts to kiss me and I kiss her back. Man this chick can't kiss, but her friend can grip a dick. I extricate myself from her kissing and start to touch her over her panties, hoping to distract her enough so she won't try to kiss me again. She tries to touch me but I grip both her hands in my one and hold them to the side. I start out rubbing softly and gradually move up to add more pressure to her bud. She starts to move her hips and gyrates against my hand.

Meanwhile my dick is being encased in a warm, wet mouth, but she's not sucking. It is being licked like a lollipop. These girls are inexperienced. What the hell did I get myself into out here? I'm having a hard time staying hard and I need divine intervention like now to get me out of here. Is this pay back for something? I am not a teacher and I don't do virgins. The last and only time I did a virgin was when I was one. God that experience was bad for both of us as a fumbling teenager I did not know what to do.

I hear voices from the other side of the bushes. Trying to free myself again from both girls this time, I hear a gasp and try to see who it is but all I see is the back of some chick's long legs fleeing. Then my cousin and another chick appear none too happy I might say.

"What the fuck Tristan?" Tyler yells as he's trying to shield his girlfriend, I think, from the scene in front of him.

"And you said not to believe the press." His girlfriend is clearly disgusted by me.

"Tristan what are you doing?"

"What does it look like I'm doing? But thanks for the interruption. I needed it." I look to both girls. "Sorry girls but I don't do amateurs. When you actually learn how to blow and kiss let me know. Until then forget about me and don't look me up."

The girls gather themselves together and brush past me embarrassed. Looking to Tyler questioningly, I start chuckling. "Did I say something wrong?" Trying to stand, I realize I'm doing it too fast because I sway a bit on my feet.

As Tyler quickly steadies me he asks, "How much have you had to drink?"

"Not enough yet." I realize because the buzz is gone.

"What did you say to Kaitlyn?"

"Who's Kaitlyn? Is that you beautiful?" I reach for her hand to kiss it, knowing this always mollifies the ladies. She sneers and pulls her hand away.

"I'm out of here Tyler. I have to find Kaitlyn. I'll see you later. I love-"

"Why is Kaitlyn running away?" A small red head questions us and is quick to blame me. "Asswipe, what did you do to her?" Fiery temper this one has. I try to back up away from her but fall on my ass in the chair. This chick is actually scaring me right now.

"I have no idea who you're talking about. I have not seen anyone except for the two that just left here in a hurry."

"Sophia, she walked in on a scene right out of a porn movie. I'm sorry I didn't know he was back here with anyone."

"Let's go Sophia and find her." Lara kisses Tyler goodbye and Tyler rips into me as the girls are out of sight behind the shrubbery.

"You're such an asshole sometimes. Did you have to embarrass me like that? I thought you were over your problems. You told me earlier you were fine. Did you lie to me?"

"Tyler, listen to me. I-"

"No Tristan. Get your shit together. I have to go help Lara find Kaitlyn."

"Wait I'll come. Just give-"

"No haven't you done enough already."

Tyler storms away pissed and I realize I have to fix this for him. I readjust myself and button up my pants and shirt. What the hell just happened here anyway? I was trying to have some fun and forget the past. How was I to know that some chick would walk in on us? But I did ask for divine intervention someone was listening or is fate fucking with me again?

I head back towards the house and notice Aunt Michelle talking to Lara. When they see me, Aunt Michelle just shakes her head disappointedly and Lara storms off. I follow Lara and stop abruptly as she turns the corner to the front of the house and runs into the other girl Sophia. They are talking with another girl, whom I can assume is Kaitlyn but I can't see her face.

"What happened back there, Kaitlyn?" Sophia starts.

"…walked…..two girls….. one kneeling……Oh God…… embarrassed…. feel…… child….. overreacted…" Kaitlyn answers, but I can barely hear her. *You think! Overreacted?* Tyler comes from behind them and I have move back so I am not noticed.

"Are you okay Kaitlyn? I'm so sorry." Tyler tries to soothe her and the wind shifts so I hear more and can smell her. *I know that smell from somewhere. Sweet.*

"Please don't worry, Tyler. I overreacted because I wasn't expecting that. Hey it happens, right?" She appears to be trying to calm everyone down. "He didn't do anything wrong. But wow I was not expecting that."

Turning to his girlfriend Tyler asks, "Lara, are we okay?" The worry is clearly written all over his face.

"Of course, baby." She kisses him and I see how much he loves her. "It's not your fault your cousin is such a male slut." Everyone laughs at my expense.

"I have seen enough for one night and want to call it a night. It's getting late and I have to work tomorrow." Kaitlyn says.

"Okay we'll come with you." Sophia says.

"No way, you two stay. Call me later when you want to be picked up."

"No I'm going to leave with you." Sophia says to her. "Thanks for the entertainment tonight, Tyler. I just wish I could have met the band." *Band?*

"I'll make sure Tristan gets them for his next party. It's the least he can do. He owes me big for tonight and I'm going to cash in."

He's right, I do owe him. He could have gotten lucky tonight with his girl but as usual I screwed that up. It's time to start planning a party sooner rather than later.

"When is it?"

"I don't know but I'll let you know. He's supposed to go out to the Hamptons tomorrow. The house is always open. He spends the summers there to recoup."

"Oh, we'll be going out there next weekend."

"Hey Sophia, you can go when I'm working. I don't have to go. You know I don't feel comfortable anyway at these things."

"No, I'm only going if you're going."

"Whatever? Crazy bitch. You wanted to meet Danny Rocks tonight, so you should either stay tonight or go to the party whenever it is and not worry about me." *Danny?*

Oh so she has a thing for Danny. Okay I can make that work. He owes me for his budding career anyway. Danny doesn't know that CI owns the recording label he signed with. That's my secret gift to him for saving me that night four years ago. He's good, real good. His name will be spoken in every household when we are through with him. Girls will fantasize about him while their mothers will dream about him.

"No, I'm leaving now. Just let us know when the party is and we'll see if we can make it. I hear his parties are awesome. If we can make it, we have to go shopping." Sophia squeals. "Good night Tyler and thank you for inviting us."

"Good night and thank you Tyler. We're out of here."

We're out. It's that voice again; I'm almost positive and sobering instantly. I try to lean a little further out to catch a glimpse of her, but her back is still to me. I can't remember what the candy chick looked like, only her eyes. I will never forget those eyes and that voice, but I can't see Kaitlyn's eyes. It's too dark. What do I do? She didn't actually see me back there so maybe I can pull it off now and try to talk to her. But her friends and Tyler know it was me back there. So they could blow this up for me. I have to plan this just right. I can wait......

CHAPTER THREE

Kaitlyn

Sophia and I drove out to the Hamptons to spend the weekend at Lara's father's house. The house, described by Lara as a beach bungalow, is situated on the beach and to say it is a beach bungalow is insulting to the house. The house is a modern two story Spanish style house with manicured landscaping. Sophia and I have our own rooms each with an in-suite bathroom and balcony overlooking the beach and ocean. The pool is directly below and the private beach with its fine clean sand is not far away.

When we arrive Lara has mimosas for them and a diet Coke for me, waiting to start the weekend. After drinks we change into bathing suits and head to the beach. Once settled, Sophia works on her tan napping while I people watch and read the next book in the series *Fifty Shades* by E.L James. Sophia has been trying to get me to read them for a while now but I had too much studying to do. After graduation she made me promise her I would read it, so here I am reading it. Needless to say I can't put it down.

Tyler arrives unexpectedly from his cousin's house a short distance down the beach. After our greetings, Tyler and Lara discuss plans for tonight when Sophia overhears Tyler mention Danny Rocks and Sexual Encounter. They are performing tonight at a local elite club which Tyler was able to get special VIP passes for through Tristan.

"What time are we going?" Sophia interrupts happily.

"The first set is about ten. We can leave at nine thirty if you want." Tyler looks between Sophia and Lara for confirmation.

"Sounds fine with me. What about you Lara?"

"Perfect. Are you driving Tyler?" Lara questions him.

Wait what about me? Doesn't anyone want to know if I want to go? I am being ignored. "What about me? Don't you want to know if I want to go?" I ask them peeved.

"No." Sophia and Lara reply in unison and continue making plans because apparently what I want this weekend does not matter. I was warned by Sophia on the way out here to let loose and have fun. A word she thinks I do not know. Today however, I think I may do just that and surprise the both of them.

"Tristan is having a car drive us. We can stop by and get you guys if you can be ready?"

"Don't worry about us, we'll be ready." Sophia replies enthusiastically. Knowing her so well, I can see the wheels turning as she is thinking about the perfect outfit to meet Danny in. "We need to get ready then. As it is, we will be pushing it close."

I look at her baffled. It is only three now, still leaving six and half hours until then. What can take six hours? She starts to pack everything up and when I do not follow her she yells at me.

"Move your ass now! I don't want to be late. Don't just sit there."

"I'm staying here for a little while longer. It won't take me long to get ready." I even dare to tell her about going for a swim in the ocean. "Before I head up to the house I'm actually going for a swim after I finish this chapter."

"Are you trying to kill me? We don't have time for you to go for a swim." She snaps.

"Really?" The sarcasm drips from my voice. "Sophia, we have plenty of time. If I don't go swimming than I have to go running. I have to do something active, I ate too much this morning and tonight we'll be drinking."

"Wait, did you just say we'd be drinking? You never drink."

"I know but someone else is driving and I don't have to worry about being on guard when I get home tonight."

"Fine! Go swimming, but if you're not back in one hour, I'm coming to get you. And you don't want to know what I will do."

"Thanks, I'll see you all later. Can you bring my e-reader back up to the house? I can take everything else when I come back." I yell over my shoulder while running into the water.

It still being early in the season, the water has not had the opportunity to warm up but it is refreshing from the unbearably hot sun when I dive in. When I surface and swim out a bit further, I start to turn and swim parallel to the shore. The workout is amazing. A short distance away I notice a guy on a surf board out further than me. Swimming closer and treading water, I watch him catch the wave and notice his physique. The wet suit fits like a glove allowing his movements to appear graceful. The guy notices me and starts to paddle towards me. As he nears me, he is still too far away to discern his facial features.

"Are you okay?" He yells out.

"Yes, I was just admiring your form. It's been awhile since I watched someone surf." I yell back. *Like forever.* "You looked really good out there. Do you surf professionally?" *Stupid question idiot.* If he surfed professionally he would not be here now.

"Nah, it's just something I like to do. I love being in the water."

"Yeah, I know what you mean. Well, good luck. Maybe I'll see you around." I turn around and start to swim back.

When I get back to the house, almost two hours have lapsed. Sophia is perturbed when I enter the house. She starts to rip into me immediately before the door is even closed.

"Where were you? I went down to the beach to find you and you weren't there."

"I told you I was going for a swim. I came across some dude surfing and I couldn't help but watch him. It was a nice sight."

She stops short when she hears me talking about a guy. "Oh really, what was his name? What did he look like?" She starts questioning me.

"I didn't get his name. It was a very brief conversation. I knew you were waiting for me. That's all. Stop reading into it."

She eyes me up and down lingering on my face. "No make-up again? That's it! You have to start wearing make-up daily. You never know when you might run or in your case swim into someone."

"Stop thinking like that. It would not have made a difference." When she refuses to say more, I ask her, "Are we done here? Can I get ready now?"

"Fine, take your shower and when you're done, we'll be up to help with your hair and make-up."

After the shower, Lara and Sophia tag team to get me ready. We decide on a pair of skinny jeans and an off the shoulder red silk blouse. I surprise them by wanting to wear the outfit and matching heels. My hair is partially up and curled. They have painted my nails a blood red to match my lipstick and the blouse. There is a knock on the door just as I put my heels on. I hear Lara and Sophia greet Tyler and then Sophia yells up the stairs.

"Move it Kaitlyn! We're leaving." As she is about to start yelling again, she sees me coming down the stairs and stops herself. Tyler looks at me and smiles.

"Wow, Kaitlyn. You clean up nicely." He looks at Lara apologetically then turns to me and says. "Kaitlyn, you look hot."

"Thanks. You can blame your girlfriend and Sophia."

"Well, they did a great job. Now my night just got more complicated. I have to look out for the three of you." He looks the three of us over. "Tristan better get to the club in time. Babe, don't leave my

25

side tonight unless you are with the two of them." He nods his head towards us. "Can I count on the two of you to not leave each other alone? And whatever you guys do, don't accept drinks from anyone but me or the bartender. Got it?" He is adamant about his last statement. We all shake our heads because we have had this discussion numerous times before.

The air in the car is thick with excitement. Sophia is bouncing out of her seat about her pending meeting with Danny. Lara and Tyler are just excited to be spending time together. And me, I'm just here. Tonight, I am going to try something different and step out of my shell. I have no idea what I am going to do but I have no restrictions here and should be able to act my age. I want to feel the excitement Sophia is emitting and experience the type of relationship between Lara and Tyler. I want that for myself, do not get me wrong I am not jealous of them and don't begrudge them. I am very happy for them.

--- --- --- ----

Tristan

Tyler and I have patched things up. I apologized after everyone left his party last weekend and asked him how I could make it up to him, already knowing the answer. He asked me to throw a party in the Hamptons, which I already started planning. I told him I thought his idea was perfect. He asked that Danny's band play the night of the party, explaining about Sophia wanting to meet him for some time now. So I called Danny on Monday and told him about the party which he agreed to and asked if the band could crash at my place on Friday because they have a gig out here at one of the top clubs. Otherwise, they have to drive back to the city just to come back the next day. There are plenty of rooms in this place unoccupied, so I had no problem with it.

During the conversation, Danny invited me to the club he will be performing at this weekend. Knowing the owner well, I arranged to have the VIP section exclusively. I drove out here last night after picking Tyler up from Lara's house. When we settled in, I told him about the VIP passes for tonight.

"I was able to get us VIP passes to Danny's show tonight. Are you interested in going?"

"Yeah of course. Can we bring Lara and the girls?" *Definitely!* Then I can possibly see if Kaitlyn is the girl from the candy store.

"Of course. Do you know when they are coming out?"

"Providing they didn't hit traffic, Sophia and Kaitlyn should be there any minute. Lara came out last night with her father but he left early this morning. Are we still going surfing today?" My cell phone starts to ring.

"Yeah, go get ready. The boards are out back." I tell Tyler while answering my phone. "Hello?"

"Okay, give me ten minutes." Tyler whispers back and I nod.

"Tristan, I need you on a conference call tonight with the Japanese at nine o'clock. I'm not sure how long the call will take but you need to be a part of it."

"Hi to you too, dad. Why is it so important I be involved?"

"Because starting this summer you're training for your new position."

"What do you mean dad? I don't graduate until next year and I thought that's when we would start?"

"Tristan, don't argue with me just be on the call tonight. I have emailed you the information and the meeting agenda. It's a big contract we are negotiating."

"Fine dad, I'll call in but I don't know how much I will be able to contribute. I'll look over the information and prepare."

"Check the email when we get off the phone. Son, just being on the call will show the Japanese we want to work together." *Son?* He never calls me son. Why the sudden change?

"Thanks, I'll speak with you later."

"Tristan, make sure you're in the office on Monday. This summer you'll be working more than usual."

"Fine, is that it?"

"Yes, I'll speak with you later."

I just hang up. The Japanese do not want me involved in their conversation. They do not know me and what they possibly do know of me is from the tabloids. Dad's the one with the wicked business reputation. This is probably dad's way of controlling me, again. But whatever, he is right I have to start getting used to conference calls interrupting my weekends. Tyler appears in his wetsuit ready for surfing.

"That was dad. I have to take a conference call tonight at nine o'clock. I was having a driver come at nine thirty to drive us around tonight. Why don't you take the girls and then have the car come back for me. By that time I should be done."

"Are you sure? I can wait."

"No man, don't wait for me."

"If you really don't mind? Then yeah, I'll do that."

"Nah, it's no problem. No reason your night shouldn't be as planned. I'll meet up with you guys later." I run upstairs to change quickly.

Twenty minutes later we are in the water catching the waves. After about an hour or so out there Tyler calls it a day and heads over to Lara's house. He plans to spend a majority of the day with her but he is in for a rude awakening when they start working. The water is getting choppy and the waves are increasing. It has to be close to four o'clock now. One more wave and I'll call it a day. Paddling to catch the wave, I hit it and start to crest when I see someone swimming and watching me surf. When I am done, I paddle over to her but not too close.

I swear she looks familiar but I cannot place her and we are too far apart to know for sure. She looks to be barely staying afloat. "Are you okay?'

"Yeah, I'm fine. I was just admiring your nice form. You look good out there. Do you surf professionally?"

"No, I just love being out here on the water."

"I know what you mean. Well okay, good luck. Maybe I'll see you around."

As she swims away, I see Tyler walking back to the house. I guess it is time to get out. Running up the beach with the board, I stop briefly to unzip the wetsuit. I climb the stairs two at a time and place the surf board and wetsuit back in the closet then to the cold outdoor shower to quickly rinse off. Dinner is waiting for us when I come back in. Maria is an amazing housekeeper.

Tyler and I sit to eat the meatballs and spaghetti. When we are finished we place the dishes in the dishwasher and Tyler starts to get ready for the night. In my office, I review the information dad sent over. It looks to be a very profitable endeavor on both parts but I see where we can make improvements. At five minutes before I am supposed to call in, I grab a drink and head back to the office for the call. Tyler sticks his head in twenty minutes later to inform me he was leaving and I just wave him on.

An hour later we are ending the conference call. At first the Japanese dismissed me. But as dad kept involving me in the decisions, they changed their tune. When I made the suggestions for the improvements, everyone was on board. Sitting back in my chair thinking about the conference call, I wonder how dad does it. *Wow that was intense.*

The grandfather clock in the hallway chimes ten o'clock. I rush up the stairs to change into a pair of jeans and tee shirt. While brushing my teeth, I notice my eyes are bloodshot. I better grab my aviators so no one thinks I am high. The doorbell chimes and it is Luke, the driver.

"Hey Luke, just let me grab my keys."

"Hello Tristan, I hope everything is good?" We walk out the front door and he gets the car door for me. Once inside he closes it.

"Yep, everything is good. Did Tyler and the girls get to the club okay?"

"Yes sir, they did. They walked right in."

"Great. How many girls were with Tyler?"

"Three."

Great Kaitlyn is here with them. Finally, I can see if she is the girl from the candy store. The drive is quick and when Luke drops me at the door the line is around the block. I tell him not to bother getting my door that I have it. Damn cameras start to flash when they see me. I forget every now and then about them. But I should have realized since Danny's playing at this club tonight the paparazzi would be here. The flashes are not blinding as the aviators reflect them.

--- --- --- ----

Kaitlyn

The line outside the club is long and winding. The car pulls up to the front and the driver opens our door and escorts us to the front of the line. I feel like a celebrity, it is so surreal. The rope blocking the front door is pulled aside by the bouncer who doesn't even ask for our identification, which I started to get from my bag. The club is a converted warehouse with three floors. The open dance floor allows the moon to shine through the glass roof. The packed dance floor obscures the stage floor but not the instruments.

Sexual Encounter's body guards are at either entrances to the stage and the front. It amazes me that a band from our area has become this popular and requires guards. The devout fans are visible by their tee shirts.

Tyler leads us up to the roped off VIP section and talks to the guard to allow us entry. This area has a smaller dance floor overlooking the stage and is not nearly as crowded as below. The band is here chilling out before their set with a few groupies vying for the band's attention. To the casual observer Sophia's reaction to seeing Danny would not have registered, but to me, her eyes narrow very slightly in Danny's direction. The guys appear happy to see us, well happy to see Tyler anyway.

When Danny tosses a quick glance in Sophia's direction he did a double take. He's snagged and I see the look of triumph on her face as only a best friend would see. Danny calls Tyler over. He and Tyler bump shoulders in that manly way. "My man, how you doing? Thanks for last weekend; we had many calls later for gigs."

"No problem dude. This is my girlfriend, Lara. And this is Kaitlyn and Sophia." He kisses Lara's hand and then mine. He turns to Sophia and stops in his tracks as she looks him up and down. He responds by arching his brow at her and does not kiss her hand. I can't help but laugh to myself. *You go girl.* She has put him out of sorts or he is not playing that way.

"Nice to meet you ladies. This is the band." He points to the guys behind him. At first look the band looks like a bunch of guys having a

29

good time at a bar but upon closer inspection you see the telltale signs of rockers. The biggest one of the group has not stopped leering at me since I arrived. When we make eye contact, he wets his lips as if in anticipation of something. Danny draws my attention away from his look. "Have you gotten any drinks yet?" He asks the group of us but is looking directly at Sophia.

"Not yet, but we can get our own, thank you." She responds tartly. Wow that was cold. She is playing games and he seems willing to play.

"Well okay than, I guess we'll see you later." He nods to her and looks to the band. "Okay guys let's get this show started." They all cheer and start for the stairs. My body shudders as the big guy brushes past me even though there is plenty of room for him to pass. *I feel like I need a shower.*

"Let's go downstairs and dance." Sophia grabs my hand and I nearly trip down the stairs in her haste. She is so enthusiastic this should be fun. By the time we reach the dance floor directly in front of the stage, the band has started to play. Sophia looks up on stage and starts to sway to the music. I notice Danny and Sophia are locked in a staring contest which makes her really begin to dance. He looks away to grab the crowd's attention, when he look back at her, the seductive dance she is performing for him has him moving closer to her to watch and perform from there instead of center stage.

I shout over the music in her ear. "You got him." She looks back at me smiling in her secret way.

--- --- --- ----

Tristan

The bouncer and Luke hold the paparazzi at bay while I pass the rope. Half the line is jeering at me while the other half are trying to catch a glimpse. The band has already started to play. Danny sounds amazing and the acoustics are perfect in here. I am so glad we were able to get his contract. Both he and CI will profit from the contract. I know eventually I will have to tell him about CI's involvement but not now. He has seen me through some very tough times and I don't want our friendship to change. Some of his songs are about the time we first met.

The dance floor is packed. Tyler and Lara are leaning on the balcony watching the band and the dance floor. Sophia is up front by the stage dancing with some guy and a girl. As I look around the dance floor, a woman in a red shirt with one shoulder exposed dances and spins looking carefree and happy. I am floored by her beauty. As she turns back around she appears to be looking for someone. Taking the opportunity while her back is turned, I dance up behind her and place my hands around her small waist pulling her against me.

--- --- --- ----

Kaitlyn

Swarmed by men with Danny looking on unable to do anything, Sophia starts to dance with a guy but another girl is trying to move in on him. We have been separated by about five people but we can still see each other. Sophia leans into his ear and says something to him. As I watch this interaction, a set of hands comes around my waist pulling me tight against a wall of a body. The hands start to wander with the music and I start to let go. I dare not turn around and ruin the image in my head of some hot guy behind me.

He leans down, places his head against the back of mine. One of my hands roam down his leg and the other goes to the back of his head cradling him to the crook of my neck. His hands still have not left my hips and his hips are moving against my backside. I shimmy my way down his front making sure when I rise back up my butt is pushed out slightly giving him a better view of my backside. He grabs my waist pulling me flush to his body and I can feel his growing reaction to me. One hand snakes low cross by waist and the other moves to my ass. Sophia is wide eyed and mouth agape. She shakes her head at me. I smile knowingly at her and she turns back to be swept into the crowd.

It feels as if we are the only two dancing. I turn around placing my arms around my partner's neck as he dips his head to the side of my neck. Both hands are now on my ass and he lifts me up. Feeling carefree, a new experience for me, I grab a fistful of his hair and bring his sunglass shaded eyes to look at me. He looks familiar. Sliding back down his body, I am reminded how much he wants me, filling me with exhilaration. Too soon the song is ending, completing the first set. Without thinking, I turn around looking for Sophia. Her partner seems to not take no for an answer. As I step away, my partner grabs me by the waist and leans down to my ear kissing my neck causing me to shiver in response.

Knowing he can hear me over the DJ's music now I say good bye. "I'm sorry but my friend seems to be having a hard time getting away. I have to go help her. Thanks for the dance." And I walk away. *Coward!* Thinking better, I turn around to inquire if he will be around later but he left. Maybe we will meet again later.

By the time I get to Sophia, Danny is there and they stop talking as I approach them. Sophia looks to me astonished. "Who are you and what did you do to my friend Kaitlyn? Girl you were hot out there. Who was that guy?" She fires off the questions as we head back to our seats stopping at the bar to grab some drinks.

"I don't know." I shrug and mumble ashamed of my behavior. "I don't know what came over me. But I liked it, it was fun."

"Who was that guy Kaitlyn? He looked awfully familiar." Lara questions.

"I don't know. I thought the same thing. We didn't talk. It was weird. Right?"

"Hmpf. It will come to me eventually."

As I search the crowded dance for my mystery partner, the guitarist from the band is staring again which is sort of creeping me out. *He should take a picture it would last longer.* Sophia and I made our way to the dance floor again when the band went on for their second set. By the end of it Sophia is feeling real good and Lara is nestled in the corner with Tyler. My first partner never showed again but I did not lack for one. However the chemistry was not there with any of them. The guitarist followed me the remainder of our time here. Danny and Sophia finally say goodnight and exchange phone numbers. They make plans to talk but with his schedule the only time for sure they can meet is at Tristan's party in a few weeks.

--- --- --- ----

Tristan

When we danced together and she turned around there was familiarity there. The way she danced seductively and erotically had me hardening there on the floor. I buried my nose in the crook of her neck and she smelled like candy making me want to devour her. Instead I opted for kissing her neck and lifting her up against me. That's when she grabbed my hair and would have seen the fire burning in my eyes if not for the aviators.

When she tried to walk away, I was too hard and had to regain control. I grabbed her waist to pull her back to me and placed a kiss behind her ear. She shivered against me but still walked off. *What the fuck?* I quickly catch Danny's attention before he gets lost in the crowd. "Hey dude great set. You guys sounded awesome." I clap him on the back.

"Thanks man. Coming from you that means a lot. We still have one more set to do. Are you sticking around for it? Tyler's here. That girl, Sophia, with him is smoking hot and I want to tap that if you know what I mean."

He is too much a gentleman to do that to a woman. He will flirt with her until he gets to know her. Then all bets are off. I envy him the way he works the girls. It's classic.

"Yeah, she's nice on the eyes but not my type. Who else was with him?"

"Lara and Kaitlyn. I just met Kaitlyn."

"Wait, when did you meet Lara?" Perplexed Danny would have met her before me. Wow that sucks, some cousin I am.

"Duh, they've been dating forever. Where've you been? I know he has mentioned her to you a few times." He pisses me off by what he's saying because I do not remember.

"Yeah, whatever. What about Kaitlyn? What's she like?"

"She seems quiet, not your type at all. She's really beautiful in that classic pure sense but she seems very shy and timid."

"Whatever, douche bag. I was just curious as to what all the hype was about. Did Tyler tell you about last weekend?

"Yeah, I could've met Sophia last weekend. Thanks for that." He shoves my shoulder. "She told me we've met before but I can't place it."

"Can't help you there? I need to find Jim. I'll catch you later."

"Later man."

Maybe I am wasting my time trying to get to know Kaitlyn. Danny knows me very well and thinks she is not my type. The woman in the red was definitely my type. Since I arrived, a past one night stand has been stalking me. She even manages to corner me as I come off the dance floor. When I find Jim and wave him over, he nicely offers to step in and distract her. I would have liked to look for the woman in red but I cannot risk running into this chick again. So I escape. The paparazzi are still here taking numerous pictures and asking toms of questions. Luke opens the door for me and I climb in. He shuts the door.

"Just take me home." I am suddenly tired of this scene and others like it. I just want the quiet. Maybe just chill with a girl. A change of some sort. "You can come back and pick them up when they are ready."

"No problem."

As soon as we get home I shower and climb in bed naked. I'm exhausted and revved at the same time. Exhausted from the day and the conference call but revved from the dance with her. Eventually I fall asleep dreaming of red shirts and hot women.

CHAPTER FOUR

Kaitlyn

It has been almost three weeks since we went to the club in the Hamptons. The girl that came out that night has yet to resurface. She was so carefree. However reality brings to many burdens to allow her free again. Today finds the responsible me working. The phone rings slightly after ten in the morning. I answer with my usual store greeting but am cut off by Sophia.

"Kaitlyn, it's me."

"Hey, what's up?"

"Lara just called. It's confirmed. Tristan is having his party this weekend." She squeals in my ear like a kid opening their Christmas gifts on Christmas morning. "Isn't that great? We both can go to the party. Danny is going to be performing. I'm so excited." They have not seen each other since that night.

"Yeah great!" My voice drips with sarcasm remembering the last party I went to when Tristan was present.

"Hey now don't go bursting my bubble with your bad attitude."

I try again with more conviction. "Yeah great!"

"A little better.. We need to go shopping this week. I have to find the perfect outfit."

"You'll knock his socks off in a potato sack. He's already wrapped around your finger. You don't really need another outfit. I have the per-"

Interrupting me again, she huffily says. "No we're going. You know it's like pulling teeth to get you to go shopping. Are you sure you're a girl? Anyway there's nothing in your closet that's good enough for this party. I'm not even sure there's anything in my closet that's good enough."

"I'm not going there to impress anyone."

"You see that's where you're wrong. His parties have all types of people there. Tyler says there are always high profile people at them. We dress to impress."

"I don't have money for new clothes."

"Don't worry, it's on mom. She has to get you a birthday and graduation present anyway."

"I can't ask her to do that."

"You're not asking she's volunteering. She even wants to come with us and go to lunch. She feels she's losing us this fall. They are taking me to Duke in a couple of weeks."

"Oh." What am I going to do without her? I know we will talk, text, face time and email daily but it won't be the same. She has always helped me out of my shell. Lara is going to Hofstra for her graduate work along with me but we have different programs and a different kind of relationship. I may not see her as much. Sophia has been my constant companion for as long as I can remember.

"Hey, let's not worry about that now. Shopping and fun. Mom isn't busy on Wednesday. Are you working?"

"Yeah, at six."

"Okay, come over about eleven. We'll grab coffee and go."

"Sounds like a plan."

"When you're done today come by and we can go to the beach to work on our tans."

"If we're going to the Hamptons this weekend, then we don't have to go to the beach today. I'd really prefer to just sit by your pool and sun bathe." She knows I'm right and relents.

"Great, come by when you're done."

"Okay, I'll see you later."

When I arrive at her house, she is out back by the pool. It is such an oasis out here. I don't know why she would want to go to the beach when she has this in her backyard. The iPod is playing Maroon 5 and she cannot hear me when I approach her so I grab some cold water and throw it at her.

"What the hell?" She sputters and glares at me.

"That's a preemptive strike for torturing me Wednesday and this weekend." Being too near the pool, she jumps up and pushes me in head first. I come up gasping for air and see her on the floor cackling and snorting, which causes me to laugh. God, I will miss this easiness. She quickly jumps up as I start to splash her. "That's the way you want to play it bitch!" She is soaked within minutes.

"I submit! Stop!"

Not until she jumps in do I stop. But watching her jump is not as satisfying as pushing her. After we calm down, we float on the rafts just relaxing. I hear the doomsday march from my phone, Sophia's joke ringtone for my house, in the distance and I don't answer it allowing it to go to voice mail. A couple of minutes later an incoming beep alerts me to a message. *Great she left me a message.*

About twenty minutes later, Mrs. Duncan comes out with the cordless phone for me. "Kaitlyn, it's your mom." Sophia and I get out and I take the phone from her. She shakes her head at me informing me my mom is drunk and not making much sense.

"Hi mom, what's up?" I try to sound chipper but I fail miserably.

"Where are you?" She slurs. "You were supposed to come home after work to clean the house."

"I know mom but I can do that later. It won't take too long." I sigh. This is why she called. *Really?* "I stopped by here to see Sophia."

"Kaitlyn, I need you home now." She sounds scared.

"Why mom what's wrong?" I ask reluctantly.

"Nothing really, but I seem to be bleeding from somewhere?" *What??*

"What do you mean bleeding somewhere? Where's Bethany?" Where the hell is my sister? I cannot always be the one to rescue them. What about me? Who rescues me? Sophia and her mom's look of concern is about all I can take right now. *Is this really how my life is going to be?*

"She's at the park with your brother and sister. They wanted to go. I thought it was a good idea." So that's why she is drunk so early in the day; no kids to care for. They are old enough to know when she is drunk. Thomas is eleven and Serena is eight but Bethany and I still try to hide it from them as much as possible. "I can't seem to see where all the blood is coming from."

"I'll be right there, mom." As I am hanging up the phone, I grab my bag and toss my stuff in there. I start for the gate but stop to tell Sophia and her mom. "I have to go. Mom's hurt." Getting my keys out, Sophia stops me by grabbing my arm.

"Wait, I'll come with you."

"You should call 9-1-1." Mrs. Duncan says.

"No. She'll be fine. I'll call you later." I am not giving Sophia a choice as I am at the car already.

"You better. If not, I'm coming by." I dearly hope and pray everything is fine.

"Call us, honey." Mrs. Duncan yells with concern.

When I arrive home, I rush to the side door scared then shocked when I open the door. It takes my mind a couple of minutes to register what it is I am seeing. It looks like a murder scene, there is so much blood. "Mom, where are you?" A voice sounds shaky. No answer. Should I have had Mrs. Duncan call 911? Mom did not sound bad when she called, only slurred. Could the slurred speech be from a head injury? Oh crap, what did I do?

"MOM!" I yell. Following the trail of blood from the kitchen to her bedroom, I hear a noise.

"Arghh. Kaitlyn?" It is very faint barely audible.

"Mom!" She's lying in a pool of blood. Quickly I'm at her side assessing her. There is a large gash on the back of her head possibly three inches or more. I need to rinse and cut her hair to really get a good look at it and see how deep. "Mom, I need to get you into the bathroom to see the actual damage."

But before I help her up, I rush to the linen closet, grab a towel and apply pressure to stop the bleeding. Reminding myself a head wound always bleeds excessively, I try to calm down. In mom's case it will bleed more because alcohol tends to act as a blood thinner. The blood takes longer to clot. Remembering this makes all the blood in the kitchen less scary. But how much has she lost? Is she in danger for acute blood loss? Helping her to her feet, knowing this is not a smart move, I risk it anyway. We make it to the bathroom encountering no problems.

"Mom, this may hurt a little." I lie slightly because this is going to hurt a lot but being drunk she probably will not feel it. "I have to clean the area so I can see how deep it is." She nods. I soak her hair with warm water, making a mess all over the place, until I can definitely see she has a three inch laceration and deep, most likely requiring staples. I try to get her attention and keep her from passing out on me. "It looks like you need stitches, mom. We need to go to the hospital."

"I'm not going. You fix it." *What??* Is she crazy? What makes her think I can do this?

"No mom, I can't. It needs stitches."

"No, no hospital." Despite her drunkenness, she is unyielding.

I sigh exasperated remembering we have some butterfly stitches in the closet but I don't think they will hold and will need to be replaced often. "Fine, I'll see if I can get the butterfly stitches to stick. But I have to cut your hair maybe even shave it. We don't have time to do it nicely."

"Fine, do whatever you have to do, but we're not going to the hospital." *Whatever it's your life.* I am so done and over with all this shit. It is making me crazy.

After taking care of her and getting the butterfly stitches to finally stick, I settle her in bed and plan to wake her every couple of hours in order to rouse her. She must certainly have a concussion at least but she refused hospital treatment. Explaining to her the possible consequences of a concussion and more dramatic repercussions of a subdural hematoma, she was not swayed.

Making quick work of the mess in the kitchen and bathroom,

where she hit her head on the corian counter top becomes evident. It's been nearly two hours since I returned home and as I'm finishing my phone rings. Sophia's anger at me is underlined with concern for my well-being.

"You sound exhausted."

"I just want to climb into bed but I can't until Bethany gets back. It's still early but it feels like the middle of the night."

"So what happened?"

"Sophia, I don't know where to begin."

"Start at the beginning."

So I explain what happened and start to silently cry.

"I can't keep doing this. I never know when I come home what it will be like. Or if I will even wake up in the morning."

"I know, honey. It won't be forever. You'll be starting medical school soon and then before you know it, residency. Hold on a little longer."

Ignoring her comments, which are meant to encourage me but they feel empty, I just say to her. "I can't go out tonight. I have to keep an eye on her. It's going to be a long night."

"Okay, just know I'm here for you."

"I know and thanks as always."

I cannot do this anymore… Breaking my plans for tonight is the icing on the cake. As I hang up, Bethany and the kids walk through the door and it's time to start dinner. Bethany and I usher the kids through their nighttime rituals and I tell her what happened.

"I'm glad we stayed away longer. They were having so much fun and happy, I couldn't bring them home to her."

"You did the right thing. I would've done the same. I'm just glad I was able to clean it in time."

We all worked as a team to get the dishes done. When everyone is asleep and I'm going to retire, I check on my mother once more. I set the alarm to wake me in four hours to check again.

Wednesday Sophia and I are shopping with Mrs. Duncan at the Americana in Roslyn, which is an experience not to be missed. Everyone should try it just once but make sure you dress appropriately. I am wearing cut off skinny jeans, a tank top and my converse sneakers. If I do not enter with Sophia and her mom, who are dressed appropriately, I am blatantly ignored by the sales clerks. However when we enter as a group, it is a different story. It looks like I am the lost cousin they are trying to dress properly.

When I have money or really need an outfit I go to the mall, but Sophia would not hear of mall shopping. She says we are attending a high end party so we need to dress high end. Finally, after entering almost every store we find the perfect outfits in Sophia's eyes, my fashion guru, for the both of us.

Never having owned name brand anything before, I feel a little uncomfortable with the small fortune Mrs. Duncan is spending on me. Now I have a complete name brand outfit, names I have never heard of except the shoes. Choking when I see the price tag for a pair of shoes, I keep insisting she does not have to buy me anything more but she is adamant. She purchases me a beautiful red halter top dress and matching stiletto strappy sandals by Jimmy Choo. Sophia is getting a tight fitted green off the shoulder ensemble and matching shoes by Manolo Blahnik. She looks amazing in it. The least I can do is offer to buy lunch but Mrs. Duncan won't hear of it.

When we finally sit for lunch, we are interrupted by my mother making demands that I come home because she still isn't feeling up to caring for my siblings. *Really, can't she do anything?* After finding out Bethany is out with her friends, I apologize to Sophia and her mom and hug them good bye. They are always are so understanding of my family situation. I know they pity me but they never let me feel it. Good thing we have learned to take separate cars where ever we go, otherwise they have to leave with me. As I get to my car, I have a hard time turning it over. Eventually it does start and I'm home fifteen minutes later doing chores.

Thursday morning my car doesn't start. My dad's friend is starting to fix it because I do not have the money to take it to a mechanic. Sophia acts as my chauffer. As I close the front door for the night, an awesome silver Mercedes convertible drives slowly by looking into the store. Maybe they were checking to see if we were open, sorry. I wait for Sophia to come pick me up and I imagine what life would be like to have money. Maybe I will be successful enough as a doctor to not have to worry about money and escape my current life. The parking lot is empty when I take the garbage out except for a small white pick-up truck, which looks to be abandoned. I leave Ralph a note to call the landlord about it tomorrow, if it is still there.

Sophia arrives a short time later. "What time should I pick you up tomorrow?" She asks when we pull up in front of my house. The house is dark except for the light in my room.

"I don't know if I can come. So much has happened this week with my mom and my car that I don't think I can come. I should work. I really need the money. Emphasis on really."

"That's bullshit Kaitlyn and you know it. Stop making excuses. You're coming. It's time for you to cut the cord. You can't always be here for them. They don't appreciate you." She is pissed. "You are the child not the parent. You need to start letting them take care of themselves. You said it the other night."

"Let me talk to mom. I was afraid to tell her we were going."

"You're an adult and don't need her permission to go or not."

"But what if something happens and I'm not around."

"If something happens, then we'll head back home. I promise."

"How about we compromise? You guys go out there tomorrow as planned." She scrunches up her nose at me in disbelief about to interrupt. "Before you interrupt, hear me out. Then first thing on Saturday, I'll take the bus or train out."

"Fine, but you better get the first one out. We will pick you up wherever. If you don't show up, I'm dragging your ass out there."

A silver Mercedes pulls up alongside of us on one side and a white pick-up truck on the other. It feels as if we are being watched but with Sophia's dark window tinting I know it is impossible.

"Agreed."

"I'll see you Saturday."

"Drive safe tomorrow and be good." The house is in disarray with dishes in the sink and food left out. I check on the kids and Bethany is still awake.

"Sorry I didn't get to the dishes but mom was in rare form. We stayed in here most of the night after dinner. When she finally went to bed we were finishing our game and I forgot."

"No problem. Did anything happen?"

"No."

"Okay, I'm just going to take the garbage out. When I come back do you want to watch a movie?" We have not spent any time together recently. This is a big year for her.

"Yeah, sounds great. How about a romance?"

"Whatever, you pick. I'll be right back."

Walking to the garbage to the curb I notice another white pick-up truck sitting midway down the block on the opposite side. It looks similar to the one I saw before. *Weird.* Bethany chooses *Pretty Woman.* I love this movie but it is so unrealistic. Our favorite part is when Julia Roberts goes on the shopping spree and is denied help at one of the stores only to return later with her arms filled with bags. Where ever we are we always repeat those lines and today is no different.

We talk about her upcoming senior year and medical school. Her friends are fighting amongst themselves and she can't stand it. She deals with fighting at home so when she is out with her friends she shouldn't have to face it again. I worry about her. She keeps everything bottled up. Her friends have no idea what happens at home. They are not like Sophia or Lara. I wish she could find friends like them but she is part of the "in crowd."

"This weekend I'm going to the Hamptons with Sophia and Lara."

"Good, you deserve it. When are you leaving?"

"Saturday morning, I'll take the train or bus depending on which leaves the earliest. You'll call me if anything happens? I'll be back as soon as traffic allows us."

"Don't worry about us. We'll be fine."

"You'll call me right?" My tone is stern and sharp with annoyance at her lackadaisical response.

"Fine, fine, yes, I'll call you." Eventually around midnight we call it a night as dad is tumbling in.

---   ---   ---   ----

Tristan

These last couple of weeks has been long. It's Saturday morning and the party is finally tonight. Tyler and I had a pre-party get together last night with a few close friends. Lara and I were finally introduced. She came with Sophia but not Kaitlyn, which was disappointing. Sophia and Lara did offer some meager bits of information on Kaitlyn. I couldn't delve in with too many questions about her without raising suspicion. Sophia is very protective of Kaitlyn but Lara warmed up to me after we spent the day together with Tyler. She may be willing to offer more information if time allows.

It's time to burn off some of this excess energy. Before a party I always get this way. I need to be in complete control when I meet Kaitlyn and see if she is the girl from the candy store. With Aerosmith blaring through the iPod, I begin with stretching. Running on the beach first thing in the early morning is one of my favorite exercises. There are usually only other avid runners about this private beach. The nearest public beach is miles away. Today's run started later than expected because of the late night. The beach is starting to fill with sun bathers as I head in the direction of Lara's house hoping to catch a glimpse of Kaitlyn.

I tried to go back to the candy store all week but something always came up. I was needed in the office until Thursday. Dad and I were at the office until 11 pm most nights, so it was easier to crash in the city at the loft than drive back and forth. The little boy in me is always trying to gain my father's approval therefore I accompanied him to all his meetings. He actually taught and guided me throughout the day. We had many lunches and late nights together. It actually felt good and real for once. I even offered a few suggestions which he considered good and had me present them to the board of directors who appeared to like the suggestions as well. They said they would start implementing the necessary changes.

In order to leave early on Thursday I had to explain, albeit briefly, what happened at Tyler's party. I left with Dad's blessing encouraging me to have fun. *Have fun? Who is this man?* Before I left the office I met a couple of the younger board members in the hallway and invited them to the party. I drove past the candy store before picking up Tyler, hoping to catch a glimpse of her but I noticed her car wasn't there.

Lost in my thoughts, another jogger is running towards me. Despite the sunglasses and hat, I am able to tell the jogger is female by the hot pink running shorts, sports bra, slender legs that go on for miles, waist I can hold between my two hands and perfectly sized tits. Her long strides are eating up the sand, bringing her on a direct collision course with me. She is looking down and has not observed what is about to occur. I have never seen her run this part of the beach before.

At the last minute before we collide, I grab her trying to move her out of the way but as I turn to keep my balance we fall despite my efforts to the contrary. We are both laughing as she lands on top of me. My dick springs to life twitching. *Wait, did she just moan?*

"I'm sorry." I laugh. "Are you okay?"

"I'm so sorry. I wasn't watching where I was going." I point to her ears because she is yelling in my face and she removes the ear plugs, turning a beautiful darker shade of crimson and not just from her run. She is beautiful. "I'm so sorry. I wasn't watching where I was going." She tries again. I catch a whiff of the air and I remember that smell from somewhere. Trying to climb off me rather abruptly she ends up kneeing me in the groin and I cannot help but howl out in pain wondering if I will ever be able to get it up again. Her embarrassment has intensified. Murmuring an apology, she succeeds in getting off of me, turns, and runs off.

"Wait, don't run off." I yell at a higher pitch than normal for me, but she doesn't turn around her ear buds are securely back in place.

--- --- --- ----

Kaitlyn

The Hamptons are beautiful this time of day. The long bus ride out gave me the opportunity to ponder my life again and the changes that need to be made. Lara and Sophia picked me up early this morning and were both tired.

"Go back to sleep. I'll make myself at home and keep myself occupied."

"Are you sure?" Lara inquires.

"Yeah, I have no one to care for, no worries. I just want to enjoy the morning."

"Okay, but we're going to the beach later when we wake up."

"Sounds great." My enthused response has surprised them. "The morning is almost over so I'm going for a run. I'll see you guys a little later."

"Okay, we'll see you later." Sophia says yawning and heading up the stairs to her room.

I change into my running clothes. Afterwards when I am showered, I am going to the beach with a cup of tea to relax and finish Christian and Anna's story.

In the meantime, I shuffle my exercise mix on the iPod and start to run. I think about tonight and how I want to step completely out of my shell, like that weekend a couple weeks ago. My life needs some drastic changes, so a few drinks here and flirting there should be just the ticket to a great night. We are walking to the party after all, no designated driver needed. Although if I told Sophia or Lara I wanted to drink, they would have a coronary but when they recovered, one of them would volunteer to drive. Lara told me Tristan lives only a little distance away. *I wonder which one is his.*

Before I know it, I am being grabbed and fall on top of this hard body. Our bodies are perfectly in alignment. I see his lips moving and realize he is saying something but I can't hear him because of the iPod. We start to laugh and I realize his arms are wrapped around me causing me to feel his warm, wet body. My chest tightens against his rock hard chest and my pelvis is resting perfectly against the hardness in his shorts. When he laughs his hardness pokes me at just the right angle and I cannot help but moan at how it feels.

As I try to wiggle loose I say, "I'm so sorry. I wasn't watching where I was going." He points at my ears and I remove the ear buds, not realizing I am shouting. I feel myself turning a deep shade of scarlet. I try again without shouting. "I'm so sorry. I wasn't watching where I was going." The hardness in his shorts is twitching and poking with the perfect amount of pressure. I lower my head to hide my further embarrassment by being so aroused. I involuntarily moan again. *Holy crap Kaitlyn pull yourself together.*

Did he just sniff me? Do I smell? *Oh God I smell.* I am a sweaty smelly turned on mess that needs to get up and leave immediately before I embarrass myself further. As I try to get up, I lift and bend my knee in one swift movement causing my knee to hit him in the groin. He howls like a wounded animal. Now add mortification and graceless to the long list. When I finally get away, I mutter into my chest my apologies and take off sprinting without looking back.

--- --- --- ----

Tristan

After about fifteen minutes of sitting here trying to catch my breath, I slowly rise to my knees and then my feet. I think of the woman from the club to see if my dick is still able to function. Yep. No problems there. Now to think of something else less sexual like mergers and acquisitions. Okay, no problems there. Continuing towards home, how am I going to approach Kaitlyn to find out if she is the girl from the candy store? This could be tricky because I need her alone. Lara and Tyler should be easy enough to distract. Watch dog Sophia may be a problem, but Danny and she have been getting to know each other so hopefully she will be preoccupied with him. Then I should be able to get Kaitlyn alone by myself.

The mystery girl comes into view as I mount the steps leading up to the house. Grabbing her attention, she walks over and I have the opportunity to look her over leisurely and appreciate the view. She has high cheekbones, full and open lips as she inhales slightly that make me wonder what delights she can bring with her mouth. I notice her ogling me so I blatantly return the look.

"Do you like what you see?" I roguishly ask.

"As a matter of fact I do." She answers impertinently in a sing song voice but glances down toward my groin. "But a certain area seems to be lacking."

Oh no! She did not just make a comment about my dick. I'll show her lacking and speaking of it, it twitches to life. Hardening at her hungry look, I can't help but laugh.

"Oh God you are too much. I can see we're going to get along just fine." I lean over to her and whisper. "I'll let you in on a little secret, there is nothing lacking there sweetheart."

She snorts at me! "Did you like what you saw or is something lacking?"

"Abso-fucking-lutely nothing. I garner to say I can lose myself in you." *Oh baby you have no idea how much I want to sink myself so deep in you; you'll be screaming my name to the ends of the earth.* I need to rein it in before I scare her off. "Hey, we're having a party here tonight. You should come stop by. Let me make it up to you for trampling you earlier? Better yet, you owe me for almost castrating me."

She playfully answers. "Maybe, we'll see what the night brings and sorry about that. I guess you could say it was a knee jerk reaction to getting grabbed and trampled." Again she turns crimson at the mention of kneeing me but she's having fun at my expense. I like her more because she's not trying to impress me.

"No really come by. It's going to be great. I would like to get to know you. What's your name?"

"Now why would I tell you that? To me you're a stranger. My mother actually told me to never talk to strangers." She playfully responds causing me to bark out a laugh. Her smile would light up the shadows if given the opportunity. "Trying to figure out who I am is part of the fun." I like her coyness. Normally coyness bothers me but she is totally different from any of the girls I have ever met. Again, she isn't even attempting to impress me by blinking her eyes or adjust her non-existent clothing.

"I'm trying to make friends here so we won't be strangers. Then you wouldn't be disobeying your mother." Still she shakes her head no. "You know what happens when you disobey? A spanking." Her pupils dilate slightly with, I think, hints of desire. Her skin flushes more. The thought of spanking that perfect ass is causing me to harden more, if that's possible. *Definitely no problems down there.* "Come on if I agree to play your game, will you come tonight?"

"Only fate knows the answer to that." She smiles and starts to turn away. "I have to go my friends are waiting. I also don't want to disobey my mother." Her smile is erotic and knowing. "Maybe I'll see you tonight, maybe I won't."

"I'll see you tonight." I yell to her. If she turns around I know she's into me. *Please turn around!* She turns around and jogs backwards. *YES!!! She will be mine.* I watch her as she jogs away.

--- --- --- ----

Kaitlyn

On the return trip to Lara's I think about my encounter and how I could have handled it differently. A strange guy, happy to run into me, was turned on by me, plain Jane. I need to step out of the comfort zone I have known for so long and start to socialize more with the opposite sex.

Mystery man is waving me over. No time like the present to step out of the shell. *Play it cool, confident, in control.* Walking over to him I cannot help but ogle. He arches an eyebrow in response and quite blatantly eyes me up and down.

His face is perfection and his hair is no longer concealed by the hat. Shaggy blonde hair, shaved short on the sides, disheveled from the run and hat. Hair I could easily put my hands through and hold on to while he explores me with his mouth. *Wow where did that thought come from?* His lips are kissable. Bands of steel for arms. A woman could fall asleep in those arms feeling safe. The black running shorts fit his muscular thighs but hang low on his hips. His grey shirt is made of a light weight material, clinging in all the right spots. I can venture to say there is not an ounce of fat on him.

His impish responses have me overjoyed but I cannot let him know so I am evasive and mysterious. It feels great. My nether region has finally come alive and is weeping with joy just from the flirting. I want to feel more. He is definitely persistent in trying to get me to attend his party. My face starts to flush as I imagine him doing the things he is declaring. The images being placed in my head has caused my panties to become wet. When I move my legs a certain way the friction causes an even deeper arousal. He must see my discomfort but says nothing.

Maybe I should tell him my name, learn his and then we can really make friends. Just as my resolve starts to evaporate, my head goes back in the shell and I start to turn away. But I jog backwards so I can watch him and he watches me. There is a rope that connects us and it feels tangible. I really need to know who this guy is. Smiling at each other, I turn back around and jog off. *What the hell is happening to me?* First dancing with a total stranger and now this. It is the craziest feeling in the world. My resolve is firm; we are going to his party tonight.

--- --- --- ----

Tristan

Who was that woman? I don't like to play games but with her I am willing to play and do just about anything. She has me intrigued because I get the feeling she is not normally like this. She is familiar but unfamiliar. I cannot place her. When she turned around, jogging backwards, there was a connection. I saw it in her knowing smile.

As I climb the stairs two at a time to the house, re-energized, I remove my shirt and dive into the pool. It's refreshing and cools my raging hard on caused by this woman. Tyler comes out with two cups of coffee just as I finish my laps. Climbing out of the pool, I grab one from him.

"You got up early this morning. Everything okay?" He asks me hesitantly.

"Hmm… Everything's great!" I respond enthusiastically and sip the coffee. "What a beautiful morning. I can't wait for the party tonight. Everything is set. The caterer is working and the staff is preparing the house and grounds."

"Abigail should be here soon. She called from the car asking if we needed anything. I told her no we're good. I hope you don't mind."

"No, that's good. It's been awhile since I last saw her." My sister had been at boarding school and then at Oxford University for undergraduate studies. She starts NYU Medical School this fall. It will be nice having her on the same continent again. I don't like feeling like an only child because of her absence. Tyler is talking and I missed what he said because I was lost in my thoughts. "What did you say?"

"I said Lara and Sophia will be here later. Thanks again for last night. I appreciate you getting to know them. What time is Danny expected?"

"They arrived last night while you were walking the women home. They were drunk and exhausted."

He laughs. "It must be nice living the life of a rocker."

I'm saved from commenting on how the life of a rocker is not great because the life Danny leads is similar to the life I had at college when Abigail arrives.

"Hellllloooo! Where is everyone?" Abigail yells from the house. Her sing song voice is a telltale sign of her happiness.

"Back here, Ab." I answer.

"Tristan!" She excitedly runs to me dropping her bags near the back door. I have just enough time to put the cup of coffee down before she launches herself at me. I hug her laughingly. *God I missed her.*

"Hey sweetheart, I missed you." I look her in the eye, give her a great big bear hug and kiss the top of her head. "What's new?" She looks so much older yet is still the same little sister but with sophistication. Living abroad has changed her for the better, I think.

"Nothing new, except for finally being home." She sighs contentedly.

"I know." I agree. "Are you ready to party tonight?" I shake her shoulders in a faux dance.

"Not your type of partying, but yes I am."

"Hey Abigail." Tyler hugs her. "I missed you also."

She hugs him back. "Me too."

The house is buzzing with staff and construction people finishing the stage out back off of the pool deck as we head back in. Mom went to town with this party. Have I said what a great mom she is? After Abigail settles in and I have showered, we plan to go to town to get a late lunch.

CHAPTER FIVE

Kaitlyn

I have been plucked, made up and mistreated by my so called friends. In less than one month the woman in the mirror has been transformed from a girl to a woman I don't recognize. My hair now has beautiful silky waves. My lips are red and full meant for kissing. The dress and strappy heels reveal never ending legs. The woman in the mirror moves when I do. So guess what, it is me. Sophia and Lara love to play dress up with me and tonight, they played well. *Boy, they went all out.*

As I am waiting for the two for them to finish getting ready, I rehash the best part of my day so far- the run on the beach. Who was that guy? Talking naughty and throwing those looks my way turned me on to levels I did not know existed in me. I have never flirted nor had this sort of reaction to any guy before. I guess that is why I am still a member of the V card club but I would love to trade it in for a night with him. *Oh my God, was that me that just thought that?*

We cannot stay at Tristan's party too long tonight because going to beach guy's party is the only real option. I want to get to know this guy and explore every inch of him. The need to feel his lips on my lips, his mouth on my breasts and between my legs has become all-consuming. This need generates other more erotic fantasies of watching him as he enters me for the first time. They have caused a terrible itch between my legs that's ever growing, especially when I think of him. *Did I just think all that? Wow it's hot in here now.*

How to convince Lara and Sophia we need to leave Tristan's party sooner than they are willing without actually informing them why is an obstacle I have to overcome. Impossible I know. They both are going to be so consumed by their men I may not even have a chance. It would be much easier to go to beach guy's party by myself, however I am not stupid enough to do that. If I told the girls about him they would probably accompany me but then they may pressure me or I may act differently. I have made it this far with him on my own, no need to inform them yet.

The girls finally make their way downstairs looking stunning and out for blood. Lara is declaring, "Let's do a shot to get the night started right."

Sophia exclaims, "Great idea!"

I just nod and smile. One drink is a good start to help loosen me up. I won't get drunk on just one drink. But the fear of liking it too much is still there in the back of my mind.

They look at me like my body has been taken over by body snatchers because my new resolution is still a mystery to them. "What?!" I sigh and then giggle. "I'm taking your advice by loosening up and having fun." They have no clue what went down at the beach during my run. It's my secret and I want to keep it that way.

They shake their heads disbelievingly while Lara prepares the shots and hands one to each of us. "To a fun night!"

"To us." I chime in. We clink shot glasses. They throw them back, swallow, and slam them down on the counter top, like professionals. *When in Rome...* I follow suit and it burns slightly going down but tastes sweet. "What was that?" I ask amazed.

"Umm... Lara's Toasted Tasty Cocktail. You like?" She smiles as she just made up the name.

"Yeah, actually I did."

"One more." Sophia exclaims giddily. "To Kaitlyn, for learning to live and lighten up!" I push her with my shoulder, slightly embarrassed by her comment. "I'm proud of you honey."

"Here, here." Lara concurs and makes three more shots. This time we clink shot glasses, throw them back, swallow, and slam them down on the counter top together in unison. This one went down much easier and I think we may have just set a pattern for the night.

We leave the shot glasses on the counter and grab our purses. Lara yells, "Oh wait!" As we are about to close the door, she runs back into the house. Sophia and I look at each other dumbfounded.

She comes back out, out of breath. "Okay now we can go."

"What did you forget?" My inquiry is full of suspicion.

"These." She holds up a box of condoms giggling. "Here, you can have two apiece. I'm keeping the rest." She smiles while handing them out.

Sophia giggles and holds out her hand for them. "Thanks. Good thinking." I know the shots are starting to kick in by the way they are giggling. Sophia takes the ones intended for us and shoves some at me.

"I don't want them." Shaking my head no and backing away from them like they are hot coals, mortification seeping in to my bones.

"Kaitlyn, don't be stupid. Being prepared is smart and responsible." Lara replies.

"Nah uh. I'm not taking them. Let's go." I start to walk away when Sophia jerks my arm back grabbing my purse, almost ripping the purse and arm out of its socket. She unzips the purse and places the condoms in there. I look at them and then her and them again, speechless.

"There, now you're safe." She smiles sweetly, handing me the purse back gently. "Even if you don't ever use them, I know they're there and you're protected." I snatch it back, turn and stalk off.

"Crazy bitches." I grumble under my breath realizing a little too late I'm slightly dizzy from the quick turn, and falter in my step. *It's the damn high heels!* Refusing to even contemplate the effects of the shots are hitting me so rapidly.

I hear giggling behind me and flip them the bird causing more snorting to ensue. I make it to the bottom of the steps and turn towards the street but I hear Lara call out. "Wrong way."

I turn around and wait for them to catch up.

"We're going by way of the beach. It's faster and shorter." Sophia answers my questioning look prissily.

"In these heels?" I ask skeptically looking down at my shoes.

"No, we're going to take them off, silly. Then when we get to Tristan's house, we will put them back on." Even more cynical, I look down at my sandal clad feet, wondering how I'm going to get them off and on quickly without looking the imbecile.

"Welcome to the world of fashion, honey." Lara replies devilishly. "Come on, this way."

---   ---   ---   ----

Tristan

As the sun sets, I am leaning on the railing looking out at the ocean and watching the sun and its daily demise. It's quiet out here not too many beach goers left at this time. Only the distant waves crashing on the shore can be heard. The workers have all left. The wait staff is making final preparations in the kitchen. I hear my sister approach. "Penny for your thoughts," she inquires leaning next to me.

"Nothing, just thinking about life."

"Oh really this should be good. What have you seen oh Holy One?" She responds sarcastically.

"No seriously I was." I look at her chagrinned. "Mom and Dad have been acting very strange recently. Have you noticed?"

"Yeah, I noticed it especially when they would call me together towards the end of school. They never did that, not until recently. Dad never used to call me."

"There has to be something wrong. But with who? With dad, it can't be mom." I sigh. "You know dad has been praising me at work these past couple of weeks. He even had me present one of my ideas to the board. The really weird part that made me think something was wrong was when he told me to have fun this weekend, which he's never said to me. What do you think is up?"

"I don't actually know, but I definitely think something is wrong him. Maybe it's his health. They were adamant about me coming home for medical school. They said they didn't want me too far away."

"Mom has been less tolerant of my attitude towards him very recently. She keeps reminding me that one day he won't be here to help. She tries to tell me he loves me but in his own way and I have no reason to believe her. Not after years of him acting a certain way. What do you suppose that's all about?"

"I don't know but it must be serious for them to be acting this way. I'm sure we'll find out soon enough. So, tell me about the girl who is really causing you think out here now?" She flips the topic so quickly causing my head to spin.

"What? What girl?"

"Ahem. Okay, we'll play it that way." I smile at her answer because she sees right through me. She may be younger but she acts older than me.

"Thanks, I'll let you know about her when I know if there is something to tell. It may be nothing but it sure felt like something."

"Ah huh."

My phone rings in my pocket. I look at the caller ID and see it is mom. "Tristan, honey, did your sister make it there okay?" She worries about my sister like she is still a child. But what mom forgets is that Abigail has been living abroad for more than ten years and is not a child but a grown adult

"Yeah mom, she's right here. Do you want to talk to her?"

"Yes, please honey. Have fun tonight by the way. Is everything to your liking?"

"You went overboard as usual, but yes thank you, everything is perfect. It will be the party of the century."

"Before you put your sister on the phone, I'm sorry to do this last minute but I need you to come home tomorrow for an early dinner with the family. Could you do that?"

"Sure mom is everything okay?"

"Nothing for you to worry about. We'll talk tomorrow. Now put your sister on the phone please."

"Okay mom, I love you. Bye"

"Love you too, sweetheart." I hand the phone to Abigail and she walks away from me.

I wonder what's up. Why does she need me to come back tomorrow? Well I can't worry about it tonight, I need to focus on getting to know runner girl when she shows up because I refuse to think she won't.

Tyler comes out of the house all freshly dressed and ready. He stammers. "Dude, you aren't ready yet?"

"Yeah, I'm going. Mom just called."

"Everything okay?"

"No, something's up. She's speaking with Abigail now and needs me home tomorrow for a family dinner. So, I'm going to leave about lunch time. Do you want me to drop you off at home? Or you could stay don't get me wrong. I'm coming back Monday sometime."

"I don't know. I'll let you know?"

"Yeah, no problem. You know everything I have is yours and at your disposal, cars and all."

"Yeah, I know and thanks."

As I emerge from my room an hour later, the music is blaring through the speakers throughout the house. Tyler's got great taste in music, alternative rock. People are talking and laughing. The doorbell chimes and someone answers it. Danny comes out of his room as I am about to go down stairs.

"Man thanks for letting us crash here last night. Sorry if we made too much noise when we got in."

"No problem. We were just cleaning up from a little get together. So it's all good man."

"About what time do you want us to go on and how many sets?"

"Let's do two sets and maybe start at nine and then eleven? How does that sound?"

"It sounds okay with me but let me check with the rest of the guys. Steve may be the only one who gives me a problem."

"Does he know it was me who helped you, not the band but you, get the record deal? If he gives you a problem you need to seriously get rid of his ass or point him in my direction and I'll set him straight. You are the talent dude. Don't let him dictate your band."

"I know you keep telling me that but we're a band. I can't just leave them. We've been friends since the ninth grade when we started the band."

"I know, just be careful with them. Don't let them pull you down. You're good enough to make it to the big times. Now go downstairs and wow us man with your voice and moves."

"Right." He smiles.

The house is almost busting with people. I haven't seen Abigail since she spoke with mom and I want to know what they spoke about. Tyler and her are talking very closely out by the stairs leading to the beach. *Is she confiding in him and not me?*

As I attempt to make my way there, I am waylaid by a blonde, whose name escapes me right now, but she has shared my bed a few times. Not my type really. She had said she was a submissive and I tried to dominate her every time we were together but she does not take commands well and did not like the disciplining that followed. *So why is she trying now?*

She puts her arms around my neck trying to pull me towards her to kiss, but my resistance causes her reach up, her body rubbing against mine, as her tongue skims along my lower lip seeking permission to enter. Denying it entry, her tongue takes the opportunity to enter when I try to pull away and say hello trying to be polite. Kissing her is doing absolutely nothing for me and after a few moments she notices my lack of response and stops.

"What's wrong baby, aren't you happy to see me?" She says in a drunken way as her hand glides over the front of my jeans and pouts her disappointment. I take her hand and remove it.

"It's been awhile. The last time we were together was just that, the last time. You didn't like my style and I didn't like yours. So move along and find someone else because you are not sharing my bed ever again. So stop trying." I don't want any misinterpretations that she has any chance of scoring with me tonight. The only scoring tonight will hopefully be with runner girl.

As I walk away from the blonde, Tyler and Abigail have moved and I can't seem to find them. Searching the crowd for them, I'm waylaid again. This time by one of CI's youngest board members. He and I have become friends recently. He is only five years older than me and has made a name for himself at the company and in the industry, making his first million shortly after joining us.

"Hey Tristan. Great party."

"Thanks Cole. Are you having fun?"

"Yeah. You made a great presentation this week."

"Do you think the rest of the board liked it?"

"I know many did. We've already started to implement some changes as you know. The board knows the company needs to take this step in order to secure the future. It was great thinking on your part."

"Thanks, I needed to hear that."

"You will make one hell of a CEO. Your father is very proud of you."

I hide my surprise to the comments he's made. *What the hell is he talking about?* A short petite brunette walks up to him and puts her hands around his waist from behind. He looks lovingly back at her smiling.

"Tristan, do you know my fiancée, Marni?"

"No, I don't think we've had the pleasure." I kiss her hand. "I didn't know you were engaged."

"I'm not getting any younger you know."

"You're only five years older than me."

"I know but when you meet the one, you just know." Not believing him for a minute but then runner girl enters my thoughts and maybe it can. I have never had this type of reaction to a woman before. She is perfect for me. The only problem is that she does not know who I am. She could end up despising me for what she may have read in the papers. I never thought I would actually care what the papers have written about me. It never bothered me before until this moment.

"Nice to meet you Tristan." Marni says smiling. "Cole, are you ready to go?"

"Sure sweetheart." He kisses her forehead, like she is precious glass. "Tristan, again great job. I look forward to working more closely with you in the near future. Have fun tonight."

"Me too. Good night Cole. Marni it was a pleasure meeting you. I hope you both enjoyed yourselves."

"Thank you Tristan, it was a great party but now I would like some alone time with my fiancée." She winks at me and they depart holding hands.

--- --- --- ----

Kaitlyn

As we walk the beach, I realize what a beautiful night it is. There is no moon tonight which blackens the ocean and makes it difficult to see in front of us. The only lights are the ones coming from houses in the distance. The only sound, besides our breathing, is the ocean beating against the beach. The dunes hide the houses muffling the sounds emanating from them. It is so peaceful here.

We are near the house when the music can be heard in the near distance. When we arrive at the house, more like a mansion, we sit on the steps leading up to the landing to don our shoes again. *What must it be like to live in this type of splendor?*

The lights from the property illuminate the surrounding area. People are milling around down by the beach. Some are frolicking near the water, while others have taken seats in the chairs prearranged down here. I even notice some couples appear melded together in the shadows and if you listen closely, I am sure you would hear more telltale sounds of what may be going on.

Tyler is standing at the top of the steps talking to a blonde I have never seen before. She's beautiful. I immediately glance to Lara and see if she notices but she hasn't. When she stands up and straightens her dress, she does become aware of them and her eyes narrow in on the couple. Tyler makes no move to leave the blonde's side as he waves to us. He is either oblivious to Lara's anger or ignorant of the image he is displaying by standing in such close proximity to the blonde.

When we reach the landing, Tyler tries to hug Lara but she dodges him. She looks at him expecting an introduction, which when he finally comes to his senses he does. "Oh, Lara, Sophia and Kaitlyn, this is my cousin Abigail, Tristan's sister." Lara visibly relaxes at the mention of Abigail being his cousin.

"Nice to finally meet you." Lara embraces her.

"Finally, it's nice to meet you also. Tyler has said nothing but wonderful things about you. Sorry we have not met sooner but being abroad makes meeting people from home more difficult."

"Nice to meet you. I didn't know Tristan had a sister. The papers never mention you." Sophia seems so stuck on Tristan's image and the paparazzi.

Accepting Sophia's hand, Abigail responds. "Yes, my brother and I are completely different people. He loves the lime light and I love the quiet."

"Hi." I wave shyly at her and she waves back.

Tyler takes Lara's hand and leads us into the house. My senses are overwhelmed and words cannot even begin to describe what I am feeling. It feels as if we have stepped into a party you only see in a movie. If I was claustrophobic I would be running from this house screaming. There are wall to wall people. Most are grouped off. Everyone has a glass or bottle of some sort in their hands. The music coming from the speakers is definitely loud. Moving deeper into the house looking for the bar, waiters are passing by with elegant trays laden with food. The bar is three people deep but we don't have to wait long since the bartender recognizes Abigail and Tyler as the hosts.

"What can I get you guys?" He asks.

"Can I have a sex on the beach?" Sophia asks flirtatiously.

"Water." I respond casually.

"A beer." Lara replies.

"Diet Coke, no ice, lime." Abigail responds.

"Okay, you got it. Give me two minutes." The bartender replies and is back two minutes later with our order. While heading out to the pool deck, many drunken people jar us, offering no apologies. Most do not know they bumped us. We move to the front of the stage area and continue our conversation while the band prepares for their first set..

"So Abigail, if you're nothing like your brother, what do you do?" Sophia asks.

"I'm going to start my first year of medical school at NYU."

Surprised, I respond, "I'm starting at Hofstra."

"Tyler, you didn't say anything." She looks at Tyler questioningly.

"Sorry, I wasn't thinking. I didn't actually know if Kaitlyn was coming tonight."

"Why wouldn't you come?" Abigail questions, looking from Tyler to me.

"Oh, I was supposed to work tonight." Not wanting to mention the debacle with her brother's sexcapades the night of Tyler's party.

Tyler shakes his head at me. "She got an eyeful of Tristan at my party with two girls. She was embarrassed and is trying to spare your feelings and not shame you." Just reliving the memory has me turning crimson.

She bursts out laughing. "Oh, you walked in on them. That's too funny and one for the books. Did anyone get a picture of his face? Tell me, how did he respond?"

"I didn't stick around long enough to see his face or snap a picture. The papers, from what I understand, would have had a field day with pictures. I probably could have gotten good money for them now that I think about it." I jokingly respond to her good nature. "No really, I hightailed myself out of there as fast as my feet could take me." Feeling more comfortable with her, I ask, "Where is the stud anyway?" I smile widely at my choice of words describing her brother.

My friends choke on their drinks. *I seem to be shocking them tonight.* Sophia asks no one in particular, "Did she just say stud?" I laugh at their incredulous stares. They are trying to recover themselves when the band starts tuning their instruments.

Danny notices us and jumps down from the stage. "Hey man, good to see you again." He claps Tyler on the back and walks directly over to Sophia, briefly saying hello to the rest of us as he passes. Once in front of her he leans in and kisses her as a way of saying hello. Then he leans away. "Hola, mi amor."

"Hello," she responds demurely and embarrassed by his public display. *Sophia demure and embarrassed? What the hell?*

"Mi corazon, I have to go back up there," he nods in the direction of the stage, "You're staying right? Please, promise me you're staying?"

"I wouldn't dream of leaving." He smiles at her, nods and jumps back up on stage. I bump shoulders with her. She turns to me smiling brightly and mouths "OH MY GOD!"

I smile in response to her pleasure. He starts to sing and seems to be serenading her during the set. Sophia has eyes only for him. Abigail has excused herself from our group and gone off to locate her brother. Tyler and Lara are making eyes at each other while their hands roam each other's body. And here I am, alone.

--- --- --- ----

Tristan

The band is tuning their instruments on stage. I climb the stairs to get a better view and see Danny is in front of the stage talking to someone. Then I see Abigail, Tyler, Lara, and I'm assuming the other one is Kaitlyn but I can't really see because her back is towards me. There is something about her build that is familiar. Abigail says something to them and then departs. She approaches me and I turn around to talk with her.

"Can we talk?" She asks me, yelling over the crowd.

"Sure, let's go to the study where it's quieter." She has me alarmed by her somber tone and demeanor. We climb the stairs and enter the study where it is quieter but not much just as the band starts to play.

"What's up, Ab?" She hates my nickname for her.

"Well mom sort of alluded to what's been going on. Not exactly mentioning anything but just hinting."

"Okay?" I say warily.

"Well you're right, it's dad. He's sick. I don' know what but really sick."

"Oh fuck." My heart stops with fear of his loss. I grab my hair tugging it hard not wanting to feel this way. He has never shown me love but this all makes sense now. The way he has been acting towards me almost like he has been coaching. Then what Cole just mentioned about how I would be a great CEO. "He's handing over everything to me. He's been…. He's been grooming me… but…. I don't know if I'm ready. There are too many people who will be dependent on me. Abigail, what am I going to do?" I have to sit down. I'm feeling sick right now. My whole life is about to change drastically. Life as I know it no longer exists. I need a drink or two or three.

"Tristan, if anyone can do this it's you. You have been to hell and back and survived. You will make an excellent CEO, probably better than dad." She smiles reassuringly and my moment of panic is subsides. "You'll see everything will be fine. That's why mom wants to have a family dinner so they can tell us everything."

Thank God my other personality takes over, dismissing the scared little boy for good. The man, who demands submission from his peers as I have been brought up to be, is fully emerging. "Okay, there is nothing we can do tonight. This may be my last great party without any real responsibilities." Shit I think. The panic tries to resurface for a fleeting moment but I squelch it. "No wonder mom planned the party this way. She wants this to be my best party yet." Rising Abigail embraces me.

"You will be great a CEO. Don't worry about it. Have fun and party." She lets go and looks me in the eyes. "I'm going to stay up here for the remainder of the night. Do you mind?"

"No, I understand. Will you be driving back with me tomorrow?"

"Yes, I'll see you tomorrow. I love you big brother."

"I love you too sis."

--- --- --- ----

Kaitlyn

The guitarist is staring again and making me feel uncomfortable. When I try to move out of his line of sight he moves with me. He is so creepy I feel I have to escape. I make the excuse to my friends of having to use the bathroom. I tell them to watch my drink and leave it near them.

When I return, the band has finished their set. Danny and Sophia are talking. Tyler and Lara are only into each other and I am wondering briefly where Abigail has gone off to. The guitarist makes his way over to me. I pick up my drink, finish it and turn to walk off, when he stops me by placing his arm around my waist in a viselike grip. Turning me around, he locks me in an uncomfortable embrace. I try to wiggle lose and look at him then at my waist. His eyes are cold and calculating, scaring me. One thing I detest most in life is a man who thinks he can manhandle a woman.

"Excuse me." I say clearly aggravated by his hands on me and push away myself away. "Get your hands off me." No one notices my outburst or exchange with him.

"Hey beautiful, no harm no foul." He says placing his hands out in front of him in a placating gesture but his eyes say he is not sorry at all. I need to get away from him now. "What's your name beautiful?"

"Jane." I remark spitefully, really not liking this guy at all. I attempt to retreat again in hopes of escaping him. He stops me again but this time with a hand on my upper arm. He squeezes a bit too tight and I know there will be a bruise tomorrow.

"Well Jane, do you have a last name?"

"Doe." He has finally caught on and the air around us just dropped to freezing. Where there may have been a little humor in his eyes before, there is none now.

"Funny." He responds unpleasantly and tightens his grip

infinitesimally. "Well Jane," he tries again to flirt with me and waylays my escape. "I see my friend likes yours and yours likes my mine. Looks like we'll be spending some quality time together? Why don't we get to know each other better?" He leans in to make his point.

"I don't think so." Uncurling his grip from my arm, I storm off. Who does this guy think he is? The nerve of him to grab me like that. I should press charges for assault, the bruises will corroborate the charge. I have to tell Sophia to be careful of him but not in front of Danny. *Wow, my head doesn't feel right just now.* As I turn around again to find my friends, I see a pair of very familiar eyes. Wait could that be... him?

CHAPTER SIX

Kaitlyn

Holy cow, it is him. The guy from the beach is on the staircase. As I start to weave my way through the dense crowd towards him and away from my unwanted, overly aggressive suitor, I feel dizzy and drunk suddenly, rapidly followed by disorientation. Maybe I should not have had that last drink but it was water. The fresh air will clear my senses, so I try to walk outside for fresh air. I stumble, catching myself before I actually fall when the urgency to sit down before I pass out overcomes my better judgment to seek help.

I start to look for anything to sit on, anything, as my legs feel very sluggish and my mouth is dry. It becomes more difficult to concentrate. *What's happening? I have to find Sophia, Lara, someone I know.* This is one of my last thoughts when someone grabs my arm forcefully leading me away.

There are too many people around and no one takes notice of me as I am being dragged away. I try to see who is holding me, but I fail because they are standing slightly behind me, effectively hiding their face. In the distance I hear a man's voice question my abductor and my abductor answers the question, I think, laughing. My vision blurs as I try to look at the man asking the question and ask for his help. I try really hard to concentrate but my eyes and lips are not working properly.

Then what my abductor just said generates my foggy brain. *I only had two shots and water.* Someone says something but the mush in my brain acts like a time delay. We are moving again towards the stairs when some of what the stranger said registers. Stumbling, the hands gripping me tighten and I feebly try to fight them off. We make it up the stairs with no other incidents. I try to talk but what comes out is garbled and slurred.

Placing me on a chair in the hallway, my abductor fumbles with a key to open a door, leading somewhere I know I do not want to go.

What's going on? Then realization hits like a ton of bricks and I whimper. Someone must have slipped something into it. *Oh God Kaitlyn, you stupid cow. You know better than to leave your drink unattended.* I attempt to stand, but before I fall he picks me up and carries me into the room. He kicks the door shut with a bang and places me on a bed. I'm so scared, I'm whimpering again. The tears are streaming silently down my cheeks. I know I have to leave. Get out of here but I can't move. *Please, oh God, help me!* I think before I pass out.

--- --- --- ----

Tristan

Leaving Abigail alone just doesn't feel right but I have to escape. If it is even possible the party has grown since we departed. As I stand here on the staircase landing people watching and contemplating the new direction my life is about to take, Steve is approaching with a really drunk girl. He catches her as she stumbles. "Hey man, how much did she have to drink? She's totally wasted." I question him.

"Yeah man. She's a light weight. I'm taking her to my room to sleep it off."

She looks directly at me and I'm reeling, those eyes. The candy shop... the woman at the club.... swimmer... runner girl. All are looking back at me through Kaitlyn's eyes. Kaitlyn? There is no recognition of me in her eyes. Steve starts to climb the stairs with her tightly to his side. I am too shocked as they move by me heading for his room.

"Make sure she doesn't puke on my stuff." I yell after him still not able to move.

Is she with Steve? Kaitlyn didn't seem his type. In all our encounters, she never mentioned a boyfriend. Maybe that's why she was being so coy and mysterious today. But when I asked her to come to the party, she made no mention of knowing Steve or me for that fact. Never did she mention coming with Lara or Sophia, or knowing Tyler. Something is wrong.

We have never had a real conversation. At the candy store, that connection scared me so much I ran and I never got the chance to talk to her at Tyler's party. Then on the beach, we did not know who the other was, which was part of the fun. Every time we have been together in the same space, there has been a connection. But the connection was lost just now. She did not seem like the type to get so drunk much less leave with a guy during a party. She was embarrassed by what happened at Tyler's party but at the club she acted different. At the beach she was embarrassed then flirty. *I am so confused by her.* Maybe I should go check and make sure she is okay. I can use being the host as an excuse.

I knock on Steve's bedroom door and he yells, "Go away, we're busy." Busy? She was about to pass out. *What the fuck?*

I knock louder this time more urgently but he refuses to answer then I hear whimpering. I try the door knob but it is locked. Using my shoulder I try to break the door open. Damn door is made really fine. I kick the door in and nearly fall to my knees at the scene before me. *Oh God, I'm too late.*

Steve is lying on top of Kaitlyn with her breasts exposed. Her dress is up around her waist and her panties are gone. Steve is lying between her legs with his hand touching her pussy while the other hand is working his zipper down. When I look at Kaitlyn I notice she is passed out. *What a sick fuck!* He's yelling at me. "What the fuck? You're a cock blocker. Get out!"

I see red and there is no stopping me as I stalk towards the bed yelling. "Get off her you sick fuck!" But I stop dead as I hear his response.

"When I'm done with her you can have a go. She won't know the difference." The room is shaking until I realize it's me trembling with anger. *Calm down for Kaitlyn's sake.* She does not need to wake up to this nightmare. "Get the fuck out of here. NOW!" I roar, scaring myself with the intensity of my hatred towards this guy.

"I don't care what the fuck you want. Give us a couple more minutes to finish?"

"Don't fucking mess with me, shit head." He has no clue.

"Don't threaten me, asshole."

He must be high on something because he doesn't react when I rip him off of her, throwing him clear across the room. He crashes into the partially opened door causing it to crash into the wall. "Wait until the cops get here." I try to get at him but I notice Kaitlyn is awake. I lower my voice to a threatening whisper. "You're done. You will never touch another woman again."

"Fine man, but she came on to me." He stumbles out the door but I don't have time to chase him, tending to Kaitlyn is my priority so I slam the door shut.

--- --- --- ----

Kaitlyn

Upon wakening, I hear voices in the background. They're arguing and yelling. I catch snippets of the conversation as my mind is trying to work through the bouts of fuzziness. I become aware there is a heavy body on top of me and it is chilly. Someone close to me is yelling and there is a chillingly calm voice not far away. *Please don't leave me.* I beg the voice in my mind, still unable to voice my thoughts out loud. More arguing ensues and then the weight is lifted off me followed by a crash nearby and I whimper trying to move. *Please help me!* The last thing I hear before I pass out again is the door slam.

The next time I awaken I am floating in the clouds. The clouds embracing me are warm and carrying me somewhere. I have no idea where but I feel safe in them. I pass out again.

I awaken again with an odd sense of security as someone is murmuring in my ear. I should be scared but I'm not. Having no idea how much time has passed, I open my eyes and look in the direction of where a face should be but I still cannot focus. The energy it took to try to focus causes me to pass out again.

I am in a bedroom that is beautiful with fine rich details when I waken again. Strong arms are holding me whispering caring words in my ears which I better understand. The whispered words are telling me to rest, I'm safe and no one will ever hurt me again. I try to focus but I still cannot see straight.

Next time I awaken for a brief amount of time and I hear a door closing quietly submerging the room in complete darkness. Everything is quiet. *What time is it? Where are Sophia and Lara?* I pass out again wondering why they have not come looking for me.

--- --- --- ----

Tristan

After covering Kaitlyn up, I stop to think about her situation with Steve. But before I can make plans to protect her, I hear a light knock at the door and storm to it, ripping it open only to see a startled Abigail standing there. I close the door behind me, so she cannot see in there.

"Tristan is everything okay? I heard yelling."

"Yes, don't worry. Can you do me a favor and get Danny? Tell him I need to talk to him now."

"Sure, I will." She turns to leave but I stop her.

"Abigail, make sure he comes by himself, please."

"Tristan is something wrong."

"I said not to worry!" She blanches as I raise my voice. Calmly, I try again to reassure her. "I have everything under control. Kaitlyn just had a bit too much to drink, that's all." The words are like acid burning in my stomach because Kaitlyn is anything but fine. She has probably been drugged by Steve with a date rape drug most likely.

Danny knocks on the door minutes later. Opening the door, I allow him entry then quickly look out in the hallway to ensure no one was following him and close the door. "What's wrong? Abigail said you needed me." He looks me over then around the room. When his eyes fall on Kaitlyn, passed out in Steve's bed he questions me. "What's wrong with Kaitlyn? Why is she in Steve's bed? What happened Tristan? Where's Steve?" Danny voice is laced with concern.

Trying to control myself, I start to explain but decide to let him jump to the same conclusions I have. "Have you ever known Steve to drug a girl before?"

"NO! What happened?" He is adamant with his quick response, but when I don't answer his question he continues. "He's always lucky with the girls. For some reason he only picks up the really drunk ones. You know the ones who can barely walk or talk. The ones most guys stay away from. The ones who need help to…" he stops himself as realization occurs. "Oh fuck!" He says defeated.

"That's the way a girl will act when she has been slipped something in her drink."

"Yeah, I know. We ran into some guys a while ago who bragged about doing this sort of thing to girls. I felt sick that night after hearing that. Steve started to hang out with them shortly thereafter. When I found out he had befriended them, I gave him a choice between the band and his new friends. He chose us or so I thought."

"Well, he almost did it again tonight."

"To who?" He knows the answer but does not want to believe it.

"Kaitlyn. Now you know why I wanted you alone. Sophia can't know until I speak with Kaitlyn."

"Did he…?" He asks uncertainly. "Will she be okay?"

"She'll be fine because I'll take care of her. She and I have a connection and I believe we are meant to be together. We've been running into each other, never knowing who the other was until now. I had decided earlier today, after our last run in, to get to know her better tonight and learn her name. She's mine, now that I know who she is, make no mistake. But I don't want anyone to know just yet. I'll take care of her and everything else."

"Tristan, you need to call the cops. Let me get her friends." I know he's right but I need to care for her, no one else.

"No, I'll handle this. When she wakens if she wants to call the cops then we'll do it together. But until then I need you to make excuses for her. Tell her friends she and I went for a walk to get to know each other."

"Tristan, I still think you need to tell her friends." Shaking my head vehemently. "Fine, I'll do it but I don't agree with you. I've never seen you act like this before."

"I'll handle Steve as well. I threw him out and threatened him. He will never perform with you or anyone in the future ever again. If he knows what's good for him he will find the deepest hole and bury himself in it. I control your contract and I will destroy him. If I ever see him again he will rue the day. His career is done."

"That might be hard. He was never the type to give up. You told me to be careful around him and I should have listened sooner then maybe this wouldn't have happened to her." He looks to me apologetically. "Recently, part of me has been afraid of him that's why I never got rid of him. After that night with those scumbags, he changed. He became darker. I wouldn't put anything past him."

"Hey, you had no idea. If I thought you knew I wouldn't have asked you for your help now."

"Yeah, but I should have gotten rid of him like you said all those months ago. But I was too much of a pussy. I thought the band meant more to him. Do you need me to do anything else?"

"Just make sure Abigail says nothing. She knows something happened but doesn't have a clue as to what. I can't afford for her to say anything to Kaitlyn's friends."

"No problem, I will."

"Thanks, let me get back to her before she wakes up."

He quickly and quietly leaves the room. I notice tear stains on the sides of her face. Did she know what was happening? *Oh God, no, please don't let her remember.* Gently lifting her into my arms and grabbing her stuff, I walk with her cradled in my arms like a child, protecting her face from the spying eyes of curious people. Fucking people always want to know what's happening in my life. *My life is not some sort of television show, fuckers.*

My room is in a separate wing away from the party. I gently place her on my bed and close the door behind me after depositing her purse and shoes outside in the hallway. I climb into the bed behind her, spooning. I lift her into my embrace and start talking gently to her so she won't be afraid when she wakes up.

"Kaitlyn, you're safe. There's nothing for you to worry about. No one will ever touch you again." She opens her eyes and tries to move so she can see me so I turn her slightly affording her a better view of me but her eyes don't focus. She nestles in closer to me, whimpering.

"Shhh, sweetheart. No need to cry. You're safe. No one will ever touch you again. You're mine and I'll protect you." She is killing me slowly with the whimpering. My heart is breaking for her. I keep repeating these words and rocking her until she passes out again. She wakens once more and we repeat this process. Finally as she snuggles deeper into me she falls into a peaceful sleep.

This woman is now my life. How did this happen so quickly? The overpowering urge to protect her at all costs is overwhelming. Her eyes, her voice, her sassy attitude has bewitched me from the very beginning. I don't really know her but what I do has me believing in the possibility of love. I will never let her go.

There is a knock at the door irritating me because whoever is on the other side of this door is taking me away from her. Carefully, I disentangle myself from her not wanting to waken her. Looking back at her peaceful sleeping form, it is the most beautiful sight I have ever seen. She makes my bed complete and is all I will ever need. Opening the door to an angry Sophia was not what I was expecting. Kaitlyn is starting to stir, whether from nightmares or the noise, I am unsure. My first instinct is to go back to her and make her feel safe but I can't, I have to deal with Sophia.

"What can I do for you, Sophia? Are you enjoying the party?" I question calmly.

"Where is Kaitlyn?" She demands. "Danny said you and her went for a walk. I want to make sure she's okay. She has no experience when it comes to guys like you, Tristan." *No experience?*

"Sophia, don't worry I left her at Lara's house unscathed. Her time spent with me was uneventful and actually quite boring. Now if you don't mind, I would like to go back to my bed companion for the night."

I hated saying those words but if I told her the truth, she would never leave. Right now I cannot afford for Sophia to find out. I need to make sure Kaitlyn is okay first. If Sophia thinks Kaitlyn is at Lara's house then she will continue on with her night and won't go looking for her until tomorrow morning at the earliest. By that time she and I would have discussed how she wants to proceed. She and I would have grown better acquainted.

"You can be such an asshole at times, you know that Tristan. I know she's not in the same league as the other women you have had but you don't have to be so crass. Kaitlyn's special." *She is way out of my league, better than me and very special.* "She's not sexually experienced. But when she finds someone special, it will be special for her. That guy will be one lucky man."

The thought of Kaitlyn finding someone else sets my blood boiling. She will never need someone else to teach her anything. I will be all the teacher she needs. "Well if what you say is true, then Kaitlyn's virginity is still intact. I don't do amateurs remember?" I comment obnoxiously. If I knew at Tyler's party what I know now, I would have spoken to Kaitlyn and this night would not have happened. How could Sophia and Lara not have seen what went down with Kaitlyn and Steve?

As I silently fume at the two of them, I wonder how they will react when they find out what happened. They were supposed to be looking out for her.

"Asshole." She mutters.

"Now if you don't mind. Why don't you go back to Danny? I'm sure he's waiting."

"Fine, but she better be perfect when I see her tomorrow."

"Good night Sophia."

"Good night Tristan."

I wander around out here trying to release my excess frustration for this entire situation. Kaitlyn's shoes and purse are visible for anyone to see. Surprisingly Sophia did not see them. I only move them slightly making them less visible to the hallway and only seen when the bedroom door is open.

Noticing the party has just about ended, the few stragglers remaining are mainly women hoping I will come back downstairs and ask one of them to be my bed companion for the night. Unfortunately for all of them, I am unofficially off the market. My bed is currently occupied and will remain that way indefinitely. If Kaitlyn doesn't wish for this position, then I will work relentlessly in my pursuit of her until I change her mind.

Pursuing her will to have be carefully planned so as to not spook her. Dealing with the aftermath of tonight's events will take time and patience. Wooing her and providing her with a safe environment to heal are my priorities. If she feels she is broken I will help reassure and repair her if needed. To me she is perfect and conveying that feeling to her will be important to her healing process.

My mind is a million miles away when I hear someone calling my name. As I descend the stairs I see the blonde chick from earlier tonight. The clock by the front door chimes four in the morning. "Tristan, aren't you going to ask me up?"

"No, why would I do that? Didn't you understand me before?" Wow this chick is not the brightest colored crayon in the box. "It's getting late and I think it's time for you to leave. I already have a permanent bed companion. Now, thank you for coming and good night." I could not be more direct even if I tried harder. Some might even say I was downright rude. Holding the door open for her, the comment finally registers and she huffs departing.

Looking around the vacant house, I lock up and close down. Mounting the stairs two at a time, I ponder if I should lie down next to her again and spoon with her or find a guest room. My better judgment triumphs and I look for the guest room closest to mine, so I am not far away. I do not like the idea of being separated from her. My emotions are in turmoil having never experienced anything like this.

After taking a cold shower, I lie down in a cold barren bed. Knowing she is next door makes sleep difficult to find. Remembering how she looked like an angel sleeping in my bed and felt lying next to me, I wonder about her wants, wishes and desires. What makes her happy, sad, mad or angry?

My conversation with Cole is beginning to make sense when he said he knew Marni was the one when he first saw her. But how long before he knew for sure? Had he gotten to know her first or was it love at first sight? Love? It cannot be that so soon.

Love is something I have not felt before, besides my mother's unwavering love. There was a brief time I thought I was in love with Tara but this emotion trumps those feelings. The feelings I had with Tara, in retrospect, were more of a best friend with benefits type of feeling. We were close for so long it became evident we should date. I cannot afford to think about Tara now, knowing Kaitlyn is next door, possibly suffering. My thoughts roam back to Kaitlyn and I drift off to sleep thinking of her.

--- --- --- ----

Kaitlyn

Finally my eyes flutter open and I am afraid to think of what has happened. All I can hear is my heart pounding in my chest so I don't think anyone is in the room with me. I test the mobility of my arms and legs quietly and it has returned. I sit up cautiously and try to take notice of my surroundings. The room spins slightly but my equilibrium stabilizes however my head feels like it's been hit by a train and my tongue has grown hair on it overnight. My muscles are weak like a baby as I attempt to stand and falter causing me to sit back down. Next time I attempt it I succeed.

Looking down at myself, my clothes are on but I am missing my bra and panties. *Don't think about it now.* I can't find my shoes or purse. *Get out now!* I open the door as quietly as I can and peek down the hallway. No one is around but my shoes and purse are out here. I grab for them and stumble knocking into a side table making a small noise. I fix myself then listen for movement elsewhere- nothing.

Finding the stairs, I rush down them as quickly as I can without falling. I stumble slightly when I reach the base because I hear movement from above. The clock indicates its five thirty in the morning as I flee the house. The beach is my destination but I am not sure which direction to go. So I just run.

I stop about a mile away and sit in the dunes hiding, trying to catch my breath. Unsure if I am being followed, I listen intently but hear nothing except for the waves crashing against the beach. I start to plan my next steps. I observe my surroundings uncertain of where I am. Standing up hesitantly, I walk down to the beach and see a board walk in the short distance. I race towards it not looking back. I am focused on escape and each step brings it closer within my grasp. Rife with tension, my heart accelerates, I am afraid to look back and see someone following me.

Once on the boardwalk, I notice a taxi stand not far away. I climb in an unoccupied car scaring the driver awake. "The bus depot please." I demand. He looks at me disgruntled. As we drive off, I turn around to notice a man climbing the board walk from the direction I came from. *Don't think about him.*

CHAPTER SEVEN

Tristan

What was that? I jerk awake disoriented. Kaitlyn? I trip over my shoes getting out of bed, crashing into the armoire stubbing my toes and cursing- I think I may have broken a toe or two. Hobbling to the door, I notice the door to my bedroom is open. The bed is empty. Where is she? Where could she have gone? Her shoes and purse are gone. *Shit!* Despite the pain, I run back to my room and quickly put on a pair of pants, shirt and shoes. I rush down the stairs, careful not to trip and I glimpse the clock- five thirty eight in the morning.

Swinging the front door wide, I sprint down the steps. Looking right then left, I can't decide which way to go. She probably went back to Lara's, that direction it is. When I arrive there the house is still locked up tight. *Shit!* Realizing I made the wrong direction choice, I take off back toward my house and keep running pass it.

As I approach the board walk, I think there is no way she ran this far but where could she have gone. I race up to the board walk and see a taxi pulling away. Just as I am about to go back and look for her, the passenger in the taxi turns around and it is her. Looking out the rear window of the taxi are the eyes I have connected with.

Running after the taxi, unsuccessful in stopping it or getting the taxi driver's attention, I fall to my knees and plead with God for help. I just found her I cannot lose her. What do I do? *Think Tristan think!* Pulling on my hair frustrated and racking my brain for what my next step is, I am having a hard time thinking straight.

I have no idea where she lives or where she would go? Her friends are here. Who would she run to, to feel safe? *Fuck!* I scream in my head frustrated "where is she going?!" *Her friends.* I need to speak with Sophia and Lara. They may know where she would go. I grab my cell from my back pocket and realize I forgot it. *Shit!* I start to run back home and stop quickly in the house to retrieve it and my keys.

Out the back door and down the steps to the beach, I am running back to Lara's. When I reach the sliding glass door I pound on it, waking the entire house hold. Sophia and Danny are the first to come down and open the door, followed very quickly by Tyler and Lara. Sleep still evident in the eyes, everyone is confused by my arrival this early in the morning. The only one who knows what happened is Danny. He looks at me alarmed.

"Where would Kaitlyn go?" I yell frantically at Sophia and Lara.

"What do you mean where would Kaitlyn go?" Sophia asks confused.

"She left, where would she go?"

"What are you talking about?" Lara asks baffled. Sleep starting to depart from her eyes.

"Tristan, what's going on?" Tyler questions me.

"She's upstairs sleeping." Lara states

Sophia's quick to catch on that something is seriously wrong. "What the fuck is wrong with Kaitlyn, Tristan?"

"It's a long story, please where would she go if she felt scared?" This is not the right way to go about asking them for help but I am too panic-stricken to think straight. Sophia lunges for me but Danny grabs her before she makes contact.

"Sophia calm down, Tristan is worried about her? Where would she go sweetheart? Answer him." Danny tries to reason with her but it's not working. She is like a wild animal being caged trying to escape her restraints.

"Please someone answer me before it's too late." I look to them all and to no one in particular. They stare back as if I lost my mind. Lara approaches me warily like you would a deranged person.

"Tristan, you walked her home last night. She's upstairs. You told Sophia that nothing happened. Don't you remem-"

"I lied last night." I yell at her. "Okay, I lied. She was with me. She never came back here. She stayed in my bed last night." Now Lara comes charging at me but my cousin is faster and stronger. Sophia has redoubled her efforts to break free.

"You asshole! What did you do to her?" Her hatred towards me is tangible. "She's innocent you fucking asshole. If you hurt her so help you God, I will kill you." She is spiting mad, breathing heavy and trying to twist her way out of Danny's grip.

"I would never fucking hurt her." I quietly respond to her accusations. The quiet belies my current emotional turmoil.

"Tyler let go of me. If you love me you'll let go now." Lara tries talking to Tyler rationally but looks at me with pure hatred. I see his resolve softening, torn between his girlfriend's wants and my wellbeing. If he lets go, she is determined to hurt me, I have no doubt about that. If either of these two gets loose I am a dead man. But I deserve it, I failed Kaitlyn.

"Please, where would she go?" I plead trying one last time before I explain why I care so much.

Danny starts talking before I get the chance. "Sophia, it's not what you think. Tristan didn't do anything to her. Just tell him what he wants to know. I'm sure he'll explain everything, right Tristan?" He looks to me for verification.

"How do you know what he did or didn't do to her last night?" The accusatory words are thrown back at Danny and he winces.

"Because I knew she was there. Honey, listen to me," he forcefully sits her down on the couch. "She was drugged last night with a date rape drug."

The girl's faces pale. Tyler has to catch Lara before she falls from his arms. They both look to me and I see them blaming me. Why wouldn't they think that, I have always been the worst kind of guy to a woman? I use them and move on, not caring for their well-being afterwards. But I would never go that far. I have never had to beg for sex or drug a woman for it.

I quickly stammer to defend myself. "I found her before she was raped and stopped it. Please tell me where she would go to feel safe? Would she go home? I know nothing about her so please help me." I grovel.

Lara's crying into Tyler's shoulder. Sophia is on the verge of tears but she answers me stoically.

"She wouldn't go home. Her family wouldn't help her. They're useless. They offer her nothing but heartache." She stops to think. "She may go to my house, to my mom. Let me call home. How long ago did she leave?"

"What time is it?" I have no idea how much time has been wasted trying to find her.

"Six in the morning." Only twenty minutes or so since I last saw her. She could not have gotten too far.

"About twenty minutes ago. I saw her leave by taxi. I'm assuming the taxi driver wouldn't drive her back west." Sophia's dialing before I finish talking.

"Mom, it's me. Can you call me if Kaitlyn shows up there? She probably wouldn't be there for about another forty-five minutes to an hour."

"I don't know." She sounds scared and her mom has to hear this as well.

"No mom, I don't know if she is okay or not."

"I don't know mom." She repeats with frustration. "Mom all I know is that she was almost raped last night." She sobs to her mom. Danny envelopes her in his arms trying to soothe.

"No mom she wasn't actually raped. I don't know what happened. We were at a party."

"I don't know mom!" She is angry either at her mom for asking questions she does not have the answers to or at the situation in general, probably both. *Join the crowd of helpless.*

"Okay, please call me if she shows up. I will. Love you too."

She turns tears streaming down her face. "You need to tell us everything you know." She starts dialing another number before I can start. "Kaitlyn it's me please call me as soon as you get this. I need to know you're okay. Don't leave me thinking the worst. You know how my mind wanders. Right now my thoughts are incomplete because you're not here with us to finish them. Call me." She hangs up and looks at me with worry. "It went right to voice mail. She must've turned it off."

"Now tell us what happened, from the beginning." Lara says between blowing her nose and wiping her eyes.

"Let me first start by telling you about our encounters." I briefly tell them how we met at the candy store and we connected, then how I overheard them talking at Tyler's party, my decision to have the party, our dancing at the club, swimming and then our mishap on the beach yesterday morning. They stare speechless.

"She never said any of this to us." Sophia interjects disbelievingly. "Why wouldn't she tell us?"

"In her defense, we didn't or haven't exchanged any personal information. It was sort of like a game." They look incredulously at me. "What?"

"Are you sure it was Kaitlyn?" Lara questions me doubtfully. "She wouldn't do or say the things you're implying she did. That's not the Kaitlyn we know."

"I know. One minute she was shy and timid, like a scared rabbit but then when we danced and flirted she was totally different. I never would've made the connection they were both the same woman until I saw her in Steve's arms. The rest of the connections formed when she was being dragged up stairs." They whimper and the guys wrap them in their arms.

"When I realized she didn't recognize me I knew something was wrong but I started to doubt myself and our connection. At first I thought it may have been one-sided and she was playing with me at the beach. Then I thought Steve was her boyfriend. I wasted precious moments with those thoughts that I will never forgive myself for."

"How could you have known?" Tyler tries to reassure me but I brush it off. I feel just as guilty as if I had done it. *More guilt.*

"You didn't know. It's not your fault." Danny remarks.

"Whatever guys, when I finally realized my mistake I ran upstairs and tried to open the door. When I heard her whimpering I redoubled my efforts and kicked the damn door in. I almost lost my shit when I found him on her and saw red. I threw him off of her." Refraining from telling them the condition I found her in, I continue on.. "I transferred her to my room where I knew it was safe. She was in no condition to be moved from the house. In case she remembered anything, I didn't want her waking up in that room scared. She was in and out of consciousness most of the night. I stayed in the room next door and must have fallen asleep. It wasn't my intention to sleep. I'm so sorry." No one says anything so I finish. "I wanted her to know she was not alone, that she and I would get through this together." The shock of my statement is apparent in their facial expressions.

"I knew in my heart that once she found out it was me who stayed with her she would've been fine. We have a connection, I know it. When I realized she was awake and had flown my house, I searched for her and that's when I saw her in the cab. The rest you know." A pin could be heard hitting the marble tiles.

"Tristan, thank you for taking care of her. Hearing how you speak of her, I think you really do care for her well-being. I still don't know if I trust you completely with her but thank you." Sophia gets up from Danny, walks over to me and hugs me. Now to drop my bomb and surprise them further with my confession because I only now just appreciated that what I am about to say is the truth.

"Sophia, I will never, ever, let anything happen to her again. I will always protect her. I realized last night when you came to my bedroom looking for her, that I will never be parted from her again. Fate intervened. She and I belong together." Sophia, Danny and Tyler look at me skeptically. What can I say I don't blame them. Tyler and Danny know I have never felt this way about a girl before. "I need to find her and tell her how I feel. She needs to know it has always been me. I need to allay any fears she may have. It's my responsibility to make sure she is fine."

"I don't think she would take the train. She doesn't have the money. Her car is at the bus depot. Let's go to the bus depot and see if we can find her. Then you can tell her everything." Sophia says sounding more positive though I can still see the underlying worry etched on her face.

--- --- --- ----

Kaitlyn

On the bus leaning my head against the window, I try not to think about the events of last night. At this time of day on the Long Island Expressway there are very few cars heading in our direction. Most city people will leave tonight. If I focus on any of the events of last night or their implications I may just lose myself. The feeling of being violated makes me feel insecure and like I am being followed. It is probably just a reaction to the situation. These whirling emotions need to be tamped down until I can hash them out. But who can I talk this over with? Who will support me and not blame me? My mother will say I asked for it. My father probably would just look at me differently. My sisters and brother can never know. *My grandparents.* I know it's early but they will most likely be awake. Hesitantly, I dial their number.

"Hi Nanny."

"Kaitlyn, honey."

"I know it's early but I needed to talk to you."

"What's wrong? Is everything okay?" Her questions are laced with concern.

"Nanny, can I come for a visit? Please?" I beg and hear the hitch in my voice knowing I want to cry.

"Of course honey. Tell me what's wrong. You're starting to scare me." I hear my grandfather in the background asking for the phone.

"Kaity, honey," my grandfather gets on the phone and uses his nickname for me. He's the only one I allow to use it. He used to sing a silly song when I was much younger and either upset or angry- 'Kaity Baity ate a datey…' I have always felt safe with him. "You're scaring your grandmother. Is everything okay?" He doesn't like to see my grandmother scared because nothing ever shakes that woman; after all she is a retired detective's wife.

"I just need to come for a visit, please."

"Of course honey, when do you want to come?" Not pushing for more answers, he agrees.

"I'm on the bus now coming back from the Hamptons. I should be able to get to you by eleven this morning the absolute latest."

"We won't ask questions now because I can hear it in your voice that you can't talk, but when you get here you're going to explain what happened to put you in this state. We'll sit, have tea and talk this out." This is why I love my grandparents. No questions asked just support and concern. They know me so well. My parents are too self-absorbed to know me. "Are you sure you're okay to drive?"

"I'll be fine. Please don't call mommy."

"Does this have anything to do with her or your father?" He sounds angry. He knows the way they have always treated me but he has only been able to intervene a few times. My mother has long ago ignored what my grandparents have to say about her life style. They have tried to protect my siblings and I as much as they can but when they moved away there was no help and I know that has always bothered him.

"No, I'll tell you everything when I get there."

"Okay honey, drive safe and we'll see you when you get here."

With my plans set, again my mind wanders back to last night. What happened? My mind is still so fuzzy about the events. Who was he? What happened to my friends last night? Why didn't they come to find me? Were they so busy they didn't notice my disappearance? Did anyone notice? Did I dream someone whispering words in my ears?

Quietly the tears fall. I need time away to feel safe again. Feeling lost and alone right now all I want to do is fade into the shadows and become unnoticeable. It has a certain appeal at the moment.

Sophia and Lara are going to be vexed about my quick departure but I can't worry about them right now. They can speculate just like I am. I know it is selfish but if I tell them what I think happened, they will feel at fault or make me face it. I cannot do either of that just yet. Denial is my coping mechanism of choice. It is becoming my best friend very fast.

Pennsylvania is the only option for now. Home offers me no comfort with my parent's drunkenness and the lack warmth from them. Regaining my sense of safety and security are the priorities to salvaging my normal life. I know it is extreme but I have to. When I feel safer I will return.

Last night changed my fate. My future is no longer mapped out, but blurred by the events of last night. The only beacon in this storm of emotions is the soothing voice that haunts my waking dreams. The one who stayed with me telling me I was safe. *Was he real?* I may never know the answer.

Swiping at the tears and regaining my composure, reality sinks in. I am a strong woman and have overcome some horrible situations no child should be exposed to and triumphed. Yes, there were costs paid at my expense but I prevailed. The events of last night will not win but I need to retreat for a brief time to gather my strength to face the brewing storm. Determined not to let last night alter the current course my life is taking, I feel more comfortable with my decision for a short "vacation."

--- --- --- ----

Tristan

When we arrive at the bus depot, the bus heading west left almost thirty minutes ago. We were able to confirm with the desk clerk that a woman matching Kaitlyn's description boarded the bus. She paid for her ticket with cash. The clerk did inform us Kaitlyn seemed to be nervously looking over her shoulder. This made me angry and sad because she should not be looking over her shoulder.

"Okay so what's the plan now?" Danny asks looking between Sophia and me.

"I'm heading west. I'm going to the bus depot and then my mother is expecting me for dinner tonight. Hopefully, I will get to her in time."

"I'm going with you." Sophia tells me. "I want to knock some sense into her. Her car should be there but she was having problems with it on Thursday. Maybe we'll be lucky and it won't start again." Sophia asks Lara, "Can you drive my car back to your house?"

"No, I'm coming too." Lara stated. "But I'll drive your car."

"She was at work on Thursday? It figures. It's almost like fate is playing with us." I mention to no one in particular.

"What are you going on about?" Tyler questions me.

"Before I picked you up on Thursday, I drove past the store hoping she was working. If she was there I planned on finally talking to her. I know her car from when I tried talking to her the first night we met, but her car was not in the parking lot so I never ventured into the store. I should have gone in then maybe none of this would have happened." I explain upset with myself for not going in.

"You couldn't have known on Thursday or last night what would have happened. Kaitlyn has a firm belief that everything happens for a reason. That fate has plans for us all. You two having chance encounters and meeting like this is for a reason. Always believe that, Tristan." Sophia tries to reassure me. "You are not the person I thought you were originally and I trust you now. I am grateful you were there last night for her even though you lied to me. I will do everything I can to help the two of you. I believe you will make her happy."

I smile at her for her encouraging words. "Okay let's go. We're wasting time. I want to get there before the bus arrives. I'm not going home. Does anyone mind if we leave from here?" Everyone agrees. "I'm coming back on Monday. Tyler, do you want to come with me or Lara?"

We all start walking to the cars while continuing our conversation.

"I'm driving with Lara. Danny, are you coming with us?" Tyler asks.

"Sophia what are we doing here?" He asks her pointing between the two of them. "I have a gig on Wednesday but I can stay until Tuesday. I really want to get to know you better and spend time with you."

"I'm not happy about you lying to me last night but I think I understand why you did it. We just have to work on that." She informs him smiling bashfully. "We have something special starting here. So I want you with me please, if you don't mind." Sophia beams at him.

"Great, Tristan we're driving with you. We can talk further in the car." He grabs her hand.

Once we are settled and driving, we try to call Kaitlyn again. Tyler even attempts from his phone. I even texted her my number to call me back. Hopefully she will listen to my message before she sees the text.

--- --- --- ----

Kaitlyn

The bus arrived in the depot ten minutes early. My grandparents graciously embraced my request for a visit and they should be able to help me make sense of what happened. There are no bags for me to stop and retrieve because everything is still in the Hamptons. I left everything behind and just ran, scared. Hopefully, Sophia or Lara will return with them when they come home tomorrow.

I search for the keys in my purse as I walk to the car. Nervously I frequently look over my shoulder as if someone is watching me but no one is around just a few cars, a minivan or two and a white pick-up truck. Otherwise the parking lot is empty. Once in my car I lock the doors and double check they are all locked. As I wait for the car to warm up, I call Bethany's cell phone knowing she is still asleep and will not wake to answer it. On the fourth ring it goes to voicemail, as I thought, I leave a message.

"Hey Bethany, it's me. I spoke with Nanny and Poppy this morning and I'm going to go visit them this week. I'm leaving straight from the bus depot. I know it's a crazy request but don't tell anyone where I went. I'll call Ralph, Sophia and Lara. I just need time away before I start medical school. Too much has been going on at home. If you need me call Nanny's. Sorry to leave you like this. I love you sis."

Now to leave Ralph a message. This will be a bit harder because he knows me so well. He always picks up on the smallest hitch in my voice. Usually, he asks Sophia what is happening when he is concerned. Even though I do not want her know where I am, he still needs to know so he can plan the schedule accordingly. I'm not in work until tomorrow, so he can work out the schedule before then.

The answering machine picks up after the first ring. "Hey Ralph, it's me Kaitlyn." Sounding chirper, I continue. "I know this is last minute but I won't be able to come in this week. Something came up unexpectedly and I will be out of town. Crazy request though, please don't mention this to anyone. My grandparents and sister know where I am. Thanks, I'll call you during the week."

Okay, all the necessary phone calls have been taken care of and as I am about to turn off my phone to preserve the battery I see there are nine missed calls. Quickly, I look to see who they are from- Sophia, Mrs. Duncan, Lara, Tyler and an unknown caller. Curious, I listen to them.

Sunday July 16
6:00 am (Sophia's call)- "Kaitlyn, it's me please call me as soon as you get this. I need to know you're okay. Don't leave me thinking the worst. You know how my mind wanders. Right now my thoughts are incomplete because you're not here to finish them. Call me."
Typical Sophia pissed but worried- delete.

Sunday July 16
6:05 am (Mrs. Duncan)- "Kaitlyn honey, it's me Mrs. Duncan. I don't know what happened but you need to call me. I spoke with Sophia very briefly this morning and she is frantic about you. Please call me honey." *I feel bad not calling her back now but it will have to wait-* save.

Sunday July 16
6:18 am (Lara's call)- "Kaitlyn we're at the bus depot looking for you. Please call us." Delete.

Sunday July 16
6:31 am (Sophia's call)- "Kaitlyn you're pissing me off! Stop ignoring our calls. Whatever! Urghh just do it and call us." *Boy, she is really pissed now. Where were they last night when I needed them? I'm starting to get angry at her-* delete.

Sunday July 16
7:03 am (Lara's call)- "Kaitlyn we left the Hamptons. Sophia, Tyler, Danny, Tristan and me. We're driving to the bus depot now to find you. If you get there before we do please don't leave, just wait for us." *They all are heading there. Why? Tristan?? I need to get under way quickly.*

Sunday July 16
7:18 am (Tyler's call)- "Kaitlyn, it's me Tyler. Lara
asked that I call you seeing as how you're not
answering anyone's phone calls. It was a long shot.
We're a bit worried. Please call us. We're headed to
the bus depot to find you. Please call us." *They aren't
pulling any punches-* delete.

Sunday July 16
7:39 am (Sophia's call)- "Bitch it's me. I'm revoking my
best friend card if you don't call me. Tristan told us
everything that happened. You need to call us. We're
all worried." She sighs. "Honey, I need to know you're
okay. Please." *Tristan told them everything? How could he
know? I'm really confused now-* save.

Sunday July 16
7:48 am (Unknown caller)- "Hi Kaitlyn," *mystery man's
voice from the beach has caught my attention now and I look at my
phone like he is actually talking to me.* "It's me Tristan."
Tristan? "We've not been formally introduced but you
and I have been running into each other for a while now
but neither of us knew it. The last time we saw each
other, that you would remember, is on the beach
yesterday morning during our run. Please call me. I
need to hear my angel's voice. My number is 516-555-
5555. Please call me as soon as you get this. I'm not
sure you really know what happened last night but I do,
so please call. I can clarify everything for you. You
must have so many questions. Let me answer them all
please. I'm usually opposed to begging but for you I
would do more than beg. Call please." *Wow-* definitely
saving.

They may be here any minute. Having wasted too much time here
listening to messages I back out of the parking space quickly and make to
leave but the car stalls. I say a quick pray to the fates asking for help. The
car does not turn over. *Shit!* I look around me worried. *That white truck
wasn't this close was it?*

Eventually it starts and I am underway. As I merge onto the
parkway, I reflect on Tristan's phone call. Why would he call me? What

does he know about last night? *Angel's voice?* He is the mystery man from the beach? How could that be? He would do more than beg just to hear my voice? I have so many questions and no one to answer them. Maybe I should call him back.

How could I have not seen the similarities between the man on the beach and Tristan? I am so stupid. In retrospect the similarities are there but he was acting completely different than the personality the papers portray him to have. *Stupid, stupid girl.* I'm so consumed by my thoughts of Tristan I forgot to turn the phone off and it rings again- an unknown caller. Letting it go to voice mail, I go to turn off the phone when I notice there is a text from an unknown number. Pulling over to the side of the parkway, I am curious to see the message.

> Unknown caller: It's Tristan. In case you didn't get the
> voice mail. Call me 516-555-5555. We need to talk. :)

Now he's texting me and sending me smiley faces. *Do I or don't I respond?* Banging my head on the steering wheel, indecision rages through me. We had fun flirting yesterday and I want to know him in every way a man and woman are meant to know each other. We connected but then last night happened...

If he knows what happened last night, I owe it to myself to find out, right? But do I really want to know? Wouldn't ignorance be bliss? I am strong, I am strong. I repeat this mantra a few more times. My attacker from last night has already taken enough from me and I am determined to not allow him to take more. Resolved I text him back.

> Me: I got your VM. How do u know what happened
> last night?

Waiting for his reply, I merge back on to the parkway then my phone beeps indicating I have a message. Knowing I cannot stop to look at it now, it sits there like a neon flashing light. As soon as I stop for gas I will read it. *God what does he have to say?* Right before the bridge, I get off the parkway and head to the nearest gas station. While they fill the gas tank, I check the text message, it's burning a hole in my front seat.

> Unknown caller: Where r u?

There is some urgency to respond. A sort of pull between us I cannot ignore. So I text him back, unable to stop myself.

> Me: on my way out of town.

Almost immediately he responds.

Unknown Caller: What? No wait. Where?

Me: I have 2 get out of town. Tell Sophia and Lara 2 stop calling. I'll call when I get where I'm headed

My phone rings. It's him. I let it go to voice mail. I am too scared to actually talk to him. Texting is easier.

Unknown caller: NO!! Pick up the damn phone! Angel PICK UP!

The demanding angry tone comes through in his message.

Me: I'm turning off my phone now to get back on the road. Talk 2 you later.

I feel bad for not answering his call but I cannot afford to have a conversation with him right now. Since I met him, he has a way of making me act differently. *Maybe I need that right now.*

--- --- --- ----

Tristan

The drive back home seemed longer than it should. My thoughts are consumed by Kaitlyn. Right now the goal is to get to the bus hopefully before it arrives but deep down I know we probably will not make it. She is most likely confused as to why I called and texted. Sophia and Danny are talking and getting to know each other more.

I interrupt them with a question. "Danny, have you heard anything from Steve yet?"

"Are you fucking kidding me?" He looks to Sophia sheepishly. "I'm sorry about the language babe, but he'd be crazy to contact me."

"Nothing at all?" I cannot believe he would just disappear like this. He knows the band is about to make a lot of money. The private investigator we use at CI can search for him. "I don't like not knowing where he is. He doesn't get to do something like this to someone I care about and get away with it. I want to know where he is so I can personally watch his destruction." Sophia looks stunned by the volatile reaction.

"I called the other guys and asked if they heard from him. No one has seen or spoken to him since last night's set. They didn't even see him leave."

"What rock is he hiding under? He'll never be able to play the guitar again professionally without me knowing. I'll make sure about that. He may be able to hide his identity and location, but come Monday morning he will wish he never knew me."

"I wish I knew." He looks to Sophia and me apologetically. "I want him just as bad. He betrayed my trust. You know how many girls I have seen in that condition with him? I feel like I could have stopped it if only I realized sooner." Sophia puts her hand in his and hugs him with her other.

"You couldn't have known." She and I say at once.

"But I was there when he befriended those assholes." He sighs like he's telling a big secret. "I should have seen his fascination with them."

"Danny, there's really no way you could've known. Stop beating yourself up for this." I take a deep breath and continue because I know in my heart I am the one at fault. I could have stopped him sooner. "I'm the one who saw her go upstairs with him. I thought she was playing me and I was about to say fuck it and leave her be." Sophia shoots me a look of worry and shivers at the thought when she realizes what could have happened if I did.

"Tristan, stop! You both have to stop beating yourselves up. How do you think Lara and I feel? We didn't even see her leave or better yet according to your account be dragged away." Fresh tears are glistening in her eyes. The guilt eating away at her. After all Kaitlyn is her best friend and she let her down. "You saved her because you knew on some level what was happening was wrong. You and she also, as you say, connected. That connection doesn't always happen." She is looking at me with such admiration. "You stopped him, that's what counts and what you have to focus on. Not the what ifs or I should haves."

I have to change the topic. Nothing anyone is going to say will make me feel any better about myself. "Where would she go?"

"I don't know for sure. She really doesn't have anyone here."

I look at Sophia in the rearview mirror questioningly. "What do you mean she really doesn't have anyone? She has a family right?"

"Yes, she has a family for what good that gets her. They are very dysfunctional." She looks at me and sighs. "It's not my story to tell but let's just say she is the parent there. She has to be the one to tell you more, if she trusts you. She won't go home trust me."

I think about what she is not saying. But I don't question her further. I don't want to betray any confidences and anyway Kaitlyn will tell me eventually. If Kaitlyn's family is dysfunctional then she won't go home. "Does she have any other family nearby?"

"Most of her family is in Florida but her grandparents are in

Pennsylvania. She wouldn't want to go to them because she would feel like she is bothering them. I don't know where she would go." Kaitlyn should never feel like a bother to anyone.

Pennsylvania is probably where she will go. Thinking about this, I text the tech guys at the office and have them perform a search on her grandparents. The information file will be emailed to me along with her grandparent's address. Pulling into the bus depot, we see the bus has already arrived.

The car is barely in park when I rush out over to the bus, while Sophia and Danny search the parking lot. "Have you seen a girl about five feet ten inches with long brown hair, grey eyes, and high cheek bones? Beautiful? She was wearing a dress." I ask the bus driver who looks half asleep and probably would not have noticed anything this early in the morning. He shakes his head no and I feel deflated. As I start to turn around my phone chimes and Kaitlyn has texted me. She's answering me. *Thank fuck, make your texts count.* She can turn off her phone at any minute.

As I wait for her reply, which takes a while to receive, I call the tech guys and ask them to trace her cell phone signal. I want to know where she is. *I hope she's not texting and driving.*. The tech guys call me back quickly informing me she has stopped right before the bridge. She is heading out of state towards her grandparents after all. Sophia cannot know just yet. Kaitlyn responds so I immediately respond. We text back and forth for a while. I even try to call her to stop her from leaving but it goes straight to voice mail no ring just straight to voice mail. I am angry with her for not answering. *Shit!!!* I text back hoping she sees it before she turns off her phone.

Nothing. No response, no call, no nothing. I want to throw my cell phone in frustration. *Think Tristan think.* Will she call me later, like she said she would? Okay if I go storming to Pennsylvania now, I might scare her further despite my good intentions. I will bide my time until she contacts me again. The thought of calling one of CI's security personnel to keep watch over her is very enticing but after the description the clerk in the bus depot gave, it would just add to her insecurities. Waiting has never been a strong attribute of mine.

It is getting late and I have to get to my parent's house soon. The events of the last couple of hours have really tired me out and I could use some sleep in order to deal with the upcoming important conversation with my parents. Sophia and Danny are running back to the car.

"Sophia, any luck? Did you find her car?"

"No, there are only a few cars and two minivans. It's basically deserted here. She must've left. What did the bus driver say?"

"He wouldn't have remembered her either way. He was probably in a sleep daze the whole way back."

"Man, sorry Tristan. What now?" Danny eyes me suspiciously because he knows I'm hiding something so I pretend to check my phone.

"She texted me."

"What did it say?" Sophia asks hopefully trying to get closer to see.

"That she doesn't want you or Lara to keep calling and she needs some time." I see the hurt briefly flash across her face.

"That's okay she can have her time but does it say where she's going?" She recovers herself quickly.

"No just that." I don't like lying to her but Kaitlyn asked this of me. "I think I'm going to head home and hope she calls me or you. My family is having a dinner tonight and I'm expected." Danny's surprised look has me laughing. "I know, I was shocked too."

"Okay, maybe mom heard from her. I'll call you if I hear anything and you do the same. Can you drive us to my house please?"

"Yeah, sure, no problem. Text Lara so she knows where you're going." She texts Lara and receives an answer back that they will meet her there. After dropping them off I drive home, wondering what tonight will bring. How is Kaitlyn? What are my parents expecting from Abigail and me? My thoughts are all over the place.

CHAPTER EIGHT

Kaitlyn

The ride was long, so when I pull in to my grandparent's driveway I am happy to have arrived. The sense of safety this home represents overcomes the choking fear of being followed I could not lose during the drive. The love they offer me is always what I need, especially now. They are on the porch waiting for me when I arrive. Taking a deep breath, I get out of the car and start walking towards them, crying by the time I reach them. My grandmother engulfs me in a hug while my grandfather pats my head lovingly. They usher me into the house and my grandfather starts the tea kettle without asking questions.

We are quiet and I know they are giving me time to collect myself. I excuse myself to the bathroom in hopes to wash away the memories and filth of last night. I need to delay the upcoming conversation. My grandmother hands me one of my grandfather's old t-shirts and sweatpants. The clothes are swimming on me but it feels good and smells like him giving me an added sense of security. She and I know I have clothing here but still she offers his clothing. The shower is very long and hot. I rub aggressively at my skin making it raw, but I still feel dirty. After a while my grandmother comes to check on me.

"Kaitlyn, you're going to turn into a prune if you don't come out of there soon. Your skin will wrinkle permanently before your time."

"I'll be right out. It just feels so good." I turn off the shower and start to vigorously dry myself off.

When I return to the kitchen, I hear them murmuring amongst themselves and I know they are talking about me because when I entered and sat down between them they quieted down. They wait patiently for me to begin and do not force an explanation but I made a promise to them. I take a sip of my tea and bite of the lemon cookies they always lay out when serving tea. *Okay here it goes.*

"I was drugged last night." *Wow, that was blunt.*

Almost in unison, they exclaim

"What!?" My grandmother questions me clearly upset.

"What do you mean drugged?" My grandfather questions while trying to remain calm to get the facts. Being a retired cop has always allowed him to look at the evidence then make rational decisions. "Sweetheart, start at the beginning. Give me all the facts." He looks to my grandmother and pats her hand. "Let's let her explain. Then we'll question her if we need to."

"Last night Sophia, Lara and I were at a party in the Hamptons. We had two shots before we left Lara's house. Lara and Sophia were a little giddy when we left the house but the walk to the party helped to sober them. Tyler, Lara's boyfriend, met us there along with his cousin, Abigail. Abigail's brother was the one who was throwing the party. We all started talking and hanging out. When we went to the bar to get drinks, I ordered water, Abigail a diet coke and the other three ordered cocktails. Then we went to watch the band. By this time Abigail left to search for her brother. I felt uncomfortable being a fifth wheel so I went to the bathroom leaving my water with them to watch." I stop here to take a sip of my tea and steady myself for what I'm about to say. Having had to admit to my idiocy for leaving my drink was difficult.

"When I returned from the bathroom, the band was finished playing. I noticed the guitarist was leering at me and made me feel uncomfortable. He had made me feel uncomfortable once before but I didn't think anything of it at the time. At the end of the set, Danny joined Sophia and the guitarist tried to join me. I brushed him off but he wasn't taking my brush off kindly. He grabbed me twice and he didn't like my response but tried to hide it. When I walked away from him and went a few feet, I started to feel really dizzy. I tried to make it outside to get fresh air but my legs started to feel very sluggish. Next thing I know I'm being dragged along to a bedroom upstairs." My grandmother gasps and places her hand over her mouth to hold back her cry. The spoon my grandfather is holding starts to bend.

"I kept trying to flee and talk but it made me look and sound like a drunken mess. I looked like a girl who could not hold her liquor. When my attacker was asked a question by another guest on the way up the stairs, he responded that I had too much to drink and he was taking me to lie down. It was then that I realized I had been drugged but I couldn't speak at this point. Once we were up stairs he carried me into the bedroom and placed me on the bed. I could barely move now. When I knew what he intended to do I started to cry and passed out then."

"Fuck." My grandfather quietly cursed scaring me. I have never heard him use such profanity in my presence before.

"Oh, sweet Jesus, Mary and Joseph." My grandmother says while crossing herself and then wrapping her arms around herself rocking back and forth. She tried to get up to come to me but I won't be able to finish if she does, so I put out my hands up to hold her back.

"Let me finish Nanny. No matter how much I need your hug right now, if you do I won't be able to finish." She sits back down nodding, tears spilling and allows me to continue. My grandfather isn't looking at me, which is upsetting and hurtful. I thought he would help me but I can see the disgust by his demeanor. I know he is disappointed in me and is thinking he has seen this too many times throughout his career. When I was getting ready for college, he would drill it into me to never ever accept a drink from anyone or to leave my drink unattended. How many times Sophia, Lara and I were lectured about this? But in the end I didn't listen. I failed him and became another statistic.

Taking a huge breath, I continue on with my story. "When I came to the first time, someone was on top of me. There was arguing going on and then I heard a crash. I passed out again shortly after that. When I woke again, it felt like I was floating in the clouds but I think I was being carried somewhere by I think someone else. My mind was so fuzzy I'm unsure the sequence of the events or if they did actually happen." My grandfather's head snaps up. "I passed out again, when I came to someone was whispering in my ear that I was safe. The final time I passed out, I felt safe but I thought maybe I was trying to make myself believe I was or was dreaming it. I couldn't really distinguish between fact and fiction. When I woke up this morning, I had no bra or panties on." The tears start falling freely now. "I know something bad happened but I can't remember. I can't remember it." I'm sobbing and repeating over and over again, "I can't remember." My grandmother is at my side holding and rocking me while my grandfather holds the both of us.

A little while later, we move to the couch. My grandfather starts asking his questions gently. "Katie, were you able to see the perp?"

"No, he was slightly behind me when he was dragging me up the stairs. I tried, I really did."

"I know you did, you did nothing wrong." He tries to reassure me.

"Where were your friends? Did they come looking for you at all?"

"I don't know. They may have. But according to their voice mails, I don't think they even noticed I was gone."

"Katie, please forgive me for asking this but I have to, are you sore down there?" He asks looking to my groin.

My embarrassment is clearly visible but I understand his line of questioning. "No, I don't think so." I whisper.

"Why didn't you call the police? Or go to the hospital?"

"I was too ashamed and embarrassed."

"Now that is right plain crazy talk. You have nothing to be ashamed or embarrassed of. You were attacked."

"But I left my drink unattended. I knew better. I'm so sorry poppy."

"Shhh, you have nothing to be sorry about, you did nothing wrong."

"But I didn't listen to you. I've disappointed you." I cry into his shoulder as he pulls me to him.

"Katie, Katie, what am I going to do with you?" He's rocking me and shaking his bald head. "You could never disappoint me. You are an amazing young woman with the world at her feet. You will become an incredible doctor. You have triumphed over some tough times. This will only strengthen you more." His blue eyes are blurred and red with unshed tears.

"Can we finish this later? I would like to go lie down and nap. It's been a long day so far and it is only lunch time." I laugh humorlessly.

"I have a few more questions, please." He is so persistent I nod. "You said the perp talked to someone. Someone must have seen you with him. Do you know who?"

"No, my vision was very fuzzy. And I don't think I could trust my memories anyway."

"Okay, that's plausible. What about the argument and then the crash you heard? Did you see or hear anything after that?"

"Yes, he was lifted forcefully off of me. Poppy, please no more." I plead, recalling the memory is very painful and upsetting. I try to change the subject. "I need to call Mrs. Duncan, Sophia's mom. Sophia called her and she is worried about me also."

"Katie, just one more important thing. Hear me out. Honey, I don't think you were raped, as in intercourse. It sounds like the perp was stopped prior to actually having intercourse with you." I look at him dumbfounded and lost. I stare at him speechless.

"You go call Mrs. Duncan honey, we're right here. That's enough for now John." My grandmother cuts him off from saying anything else. I know he wants more information but I do not remember much. The battery on my cell phone has died long ago. Borrowing my grandparent's charger, I plug my phone in and power it up. After a few moments, my phone starts to beep with missed calls and messages. Instead of answering them, I ignore them all and call Mrs. Duncan.

"Hello?" Mrs. Duncan answers.

"Hi, it's me Kaitlyn." I answer quietly.

"Oh honey are you okay. You've had me in such a state of worry."

"I'm fine. I'm out of state visiting with my grandparents. Something came up last minute so I had to leave." I know she knows something happened but I cannot face it yet.

"I understand but I am here for you to talk to, always. You don't have to run because you feel you have no one. I am always here for you. You know if I could have adopted you years ago I would have."

She used to tell me this when we were younger and she felt helpless about my situation. I know she is trying to make me feel better now. "Sophia's been trying to get in touch with you all morning. She and Lara are worried sick. Have you spoken to them?"

"No, I'm upset with them. They were so engrossed with what was going on with them they didn't notice I was gone or what had happened. I don't blame them but I'm hurt. I need time to get over this before I talk to either of them."

"Honey, don't you think they're upset with themselves?" She pauses before continuing. "But I understand. You have been through a lot in the last couple of hours. I'll tell them you're okay, that you need time away before you face everything. How's that?"

"Thank you that'd be perfect. I'm sorry to put you in this position."

"Don't worry about me. Just come back here soon so this can be straightened out. I love you Kaitlyn like you were my own daughter."

"I love you too. I'll call you when I'm coming home." We hang up and I'm exhausted. I fall asleep on top of the covers in the bedroom designated as mine from when I was younger.

--- --- --- ----

Tristan

Opening the gates to the driveway of my parent's house can usually bring feelings of anxiousness, but tonight I settle for numb and exhaustion. The days and nights events have really put a strain on me. Never have I felt like this before not even four years ago. When I was younger I always had drivers and now I wish I had one. They would take me wherever I wanted to go not asking any questions. But my parents always found out and then my father would start in on me. The guys were not just paid to be drivers but body guards or babysitters as well. I learned fast they were not my friends like I thought.

Parking the car in front of the house, the doors open and I see Clarke, our head steward. "Good afternoon sir."

"Hi Clarke. Are my parents here?" I shake his hand.

"Yes sir, they are in their quarters. They weren't expecting you and

Miss Abigail until much later."

"I know. Something came up and I headed back early. Abigail probably won't be here until our originally planned time."

"Very good, sir."

"If anyone is looking for me I'll be in my room."

"Right, sir."

I veer off towards the kitchen, famished. Cook is in there preparing tonight's meal and the smells coming from the kitchen are heavenly. "Hi Mable." I kiss her cheek and she smiles.

"Hi Tristan. How are you today?" We have always had a very informal relationship. She used to make sure I received extra treats after school. I am sure mom knew but she never said anything. Mom knew everything.

"I've had better mornings."

"Can I make you a sandwich before dinner?" She knows my habits of looking through the cabinets but the kitchen is her domain and she hates it when I snoop. I should not be in here according to her, but she loves my visits.

"That would be great but I can get it."

"Pfft, like I would let you make something in my kitchen." She pushes me away from the refrigerator and directs me towards the prep bar as she gathers the necessary ingredients for one of her special sub sandwiches she usually whips up for me. The sandwich became my favorite before games in high school. When her back is turned I grab a soda from the refrigerator, earning myself a look from her when I return to my seat. She hands me the sandwich when she is done preparing it.

"Made with love, Tristan." She makes this comment about all the food she prepares.

"Thank you Mable. What's for dinner tonight?"

"Crown rib roast, new potatoes in my special sauce, asparagus and lemon sorbet."

"Hmm... sounds delicious. I can't wait." I kiss her other cheek as I leave the kitchen with my tray in hand. "See you later."

I climb the stairs two at a time to my room. When I get there, I switch on my computer and eat my sandwich. My room has not really changed since I was in high school. The king sized bed centers the room with the desk to the right. The closet is on the other side. Sitting at my desk, I finish my sandwich and review the report the IT guys sent about Kaitlyn's grandparents. I email the private investigator to start investigating Kaitlyn because I want to know everything there is to know about her. On Monday I will talk to him in person about Steve's investigation. Once finished, I decide to nap until dinner and climb into bed fully clothed. Sleeps arrives quickly as I think of only Kaitlyn.

--- --- --- ----

We just finished dinner and my parents still have not said anything to either of Abigail or me. The tension is thick in the room and the conversation during dinner was almost nonexistent. The staff has started to remove the table settings while Clarke asks if dessert can be served. Mom answers, "Not yet. Please inform the staff they may take their meal now while we talk."

"Very well Madame. I will inform them of such immediately." He turns to leave and eyes me solemnly. He knows what is going on. Why didn't I think to ask him earlier about it? He knows everything in this house. No one has a secret in this house from him. *You were too occupied with Kaitlyn's problem.*

The tension in the air has just increased dramatically. My parents look to each other probably deciding how to start this conversation. I feel like Abigail and I are ten and thirteen again, when we would get into trouble so I decide to start.

"Mom, Dad. Abigail and I know something serious is going on so please just tell us. We're adults and will be able to handle what you're about to tell us."

Mom looks at us and smiles sadly first to Abigail and then me. Her eyes linger on me and I know the shit is about to hit the fan. "You're right Tristan, something serious is happening. Your father is dying." That's it no explanation, no nothing.

Abigail and I look at each other, then mom and finally dad. He's dying. Wow I did not see this coming. Abigail is the first to respond. "How long? And from what?" Always the doctor.

My father answers her. "Not long sweetheart." *Sweetheart?* He never uses terms of endearment. "Probably one to two years at most. It's a rare form of leukemia. We're going to try chemotherapy starting next Thursday." Dad turns to look at me. "Your mother and I have discussed this and Tristan it is time. You will be the next CEO effective next Monday."

Wow did you hear that explosion! My world as I knew it was just blown to smithereens. "Why next Monday? I'm not ready for this responsibility. You have on numerous occasions told me this."

"Nonsense! Son, I have grievously misled you. You have been ready for this for a while now. But being the old man I am, I never wanted to give it up. I have always wanted you to go the extra step and finishing your graduate program was part of that." There is astonishment on my face at his confession. I need to physically lift my jaw off the floor. "You have risen to every challenge I have placed in front of you. You make me so proud."

There are unshed tears forming in his eyes. *For me?* He knows how difficult he has been on me and what it has cost our relationship. It feels like an alternate universe. "Dad, I don't understand?"

"Tristan, there's a lot I need to atone for. I have always been proud of you and your accomplishments. Would you mind following me? I need to show you something." He sees my hesitancy. "Please, I just want to take you somewhere, just the two of us, to show you just how much I love you." I don't know how to respond but my head nods automatically. He rises from the table a bit too fast and has to sit back down.

"Are you okay Dad?" I raise and rush to his side. He looks fragile for just a minute, instead of the man whose presence is overwhelming, and all of a sudden I feel helpless. Where did this feeling of helplessness come from?

"I'm fine, just got up a bit too fast. No need to worry about me yet." He tries for humor but fails miserably. He attempts to rise again but I am there to help him. I cup his elbow assisting him and he looks at me proudly smiling. "Thank you, son." He places his hand on my cheek, lovingly and proudly. He seems so much older all of a sudden. When did he get this old? How have I not noticed this?

He looks to my mother and smiles at her fondly. Then to my sister he winks. He leads me to his private office in my parent's quarters. I haven't been in here since I was a kid when Abigail and I were playing hide and go seek. There are so many hidden rooms in this house that she and I have gotten lost on more than one occasion when we were younger. My mother only allowed us to play in a defined area of the house after the last time Abigail was lost for almost an entire day.

As he opens the door I notice the room has not changed in all this time. The only thing that has changed is the pictures. He has three on his desk, I notice. One of him and my mother on their wedding day. Another one of Abigail when she graduated high school. And the last is of me at one of my rowing races and we had just won. I remember this one. It was my first as Captain and I was so proud of my team mates. They gave me every ounce of everything they had to give that day when I asked for it. We celebrated big that night. I called mom after to let her know of our win. She said she knew and that she and my father were proud. I thought she was just being mom. I didn't know he was there. I look at him surprised and there are tears in both of our eyes again as it all clicks. He looks so proud now.

"That was one of the proudest and happiest moments of being your father." He informs me. I can't help but stare at him as if I have never met him before. "I have never missed an important time in your life. You never knew I was there for any of it because the worst thing I could have done was disappoint you again. If I told you I would show up to an event and then couldn't make in time because of work, like that one soccer game when you were five, the hurt and disappointment on your face I never wanted to see again."

"Why? I don't understand?" I look at him dumbfounded. "Instead I ended up hating you."

"Come with me and we can talk." We move to a hidden staircase that I never noticed before. When we emerge there are two doors. One door is painted a dark blue and has my name written on it and the other is a dark pink with Abigail's name on it. He takes a key from around his neck and unlocks the door. I always wondered where that key led to. Once I asked him about it and his response had been it led to one of the places where his heart lays. I never understood what he meant by that, but I must have been five or six at the time. As the door opens, I am flabbergasted at the depth of his answer from long ago as the room comes into view it strikes me right at the heart of my core. The tears have started to freely fall now. The magnitude of what he said has just hit home.

CHAPTER NINE

Tristan

This room is me. Everything has some sort of attachment to me. There are pictures that cover almost every inch on every wall. Pictures or tokens from events I did not even know he was aware of. There are old trophies, medals and ribbons, all mine. Tokens of my childhood are laid on display. The emotion this room represents is one of pure unconditional love. The love he never showed me.

"Why?" I look at him with wonder.

"Why what son? Why the room? Why my love?" He isn't sure what I'm asking because I guess I am not sure.

"Why did you never say anything? Why did you lead me to believe I was such a disappointment?" I pause as I look at him again in confusion as to what I want to try to convey. "Why were you always so cold?"

"Sit down son and let's start at the beginning." We turn to the only two seats in the room and there is coffee and sorbet. Clarke must have seen to it while we were talking downstairs. My father takes his time making his coffee and I follow suit.

"Hmm there's no coffee as good as Mable's. Just don't let her know I said that." I look at him in complete and utter confusion. Who is this man sitting next to me in this room all about me and my life? "If she knows she wouldn't keep trying to make it as good as she does." He takes another sip savoring it. "Tristan, the day I met your mother was the day my life changed. I started living and feeling."

He continues with his story. "We always kept running into each other, through friends, events, out at a dinner, different charity events. You name a way two people could run into each other and we did. The more these happenstances occurred the deeper our connection grew. We had a

95

true connection before we even started dating." He stops to take another sip of his coffee. I think to myself about my encounters with Kaitlyn. The similarities are uncanny.

"When I finally asked your mother out, she had the audacity to ask me what took me so long. She was very forward which is not how she portrayed herself to other chaps. She also felt it herself immediately. I know she's told you about our whirlwind romance and you nev-."

I cut him off, "Never believed any of it. I've never seen you show any emotion to her or any of us at all. So how could I believe her stories?" I finish. The hurt evident in my voice.

"I know son and for that I will be eternally sorry for. I'm afraid the way I've acted over the years has caused you unimaginable harm." He looks at me. "I will get to that shortly just hear me out while I explain."

I just nod because right now I am too choked up on emotion. The lump in my throat has wedged itself there permanently. "Within a short couple of months, I knew your mother was my soul mate and she would be my wife. One night at dinner after only dating a couple of months, I just asked her if she would do me the honor of becoming my wife. She did not hesitate to say yes. I was unprepared for her answer because it was the most unplanned thing I've ever done." He is staring off, most likely into the past like it was yesterday. The smile on his face is one of pure joy. A smile I am not used to seeing on his face.

"It was so unplanned that I hadn't purchased a ring or asked her parents for their blessing. But I was utterly astounded by her answer. We went the next day and purchased her ring, anything she wanted was hers. Then we went to her parent's house. At first they had concerns about our age difference but they were reassured eventually of our love for each other. My father had just passed away prior to us dating, so he never knew her and I had nothing to worry about from other distant relatives. As the sole survivor of my father I became head of CI, as you know. The position you are about to assume has only been held by your grandfather and myself." He stops so I can absorb the enormity of what he is saying. "There was no one to block my marriage to your mother. Your mother was my family then. Our wedding day was the second happiest day of my life. She and I could live on our love and our bed was a haven for me. Even when the business was having problems, I sought refuge in her arms in our bed. It was very easy for me to get lost in her." I do not want to hear this. It is just plain wrong.

"Dad, please can we skip this part. I still need to be able to look at the two of you and not get sick." He chuckles and apologizes. He tries some of his sorbet like it is something new. "Remind me to give Mable a well-deserved raise. This is delicious. That woman never ceases to amaze me with her culinary expertise." Again the man has baffled me.

"When we found out your mother was pregnant with you, this was the next happiest day of my life. The company was performing beyond anyone's expectations. We had made the list of companies to most watch. Your mother and I found this house shortly after the news of you. We made some adjustments prior to and after your birth like this one here. There are others you're not aware of. I look forward to showing you all the secrets of this house. It will be yours one day." The thought my parents may not be here one day is disconcerting.

"After your birth, your mother became obsessed about being a good mother that she forgot me sometimes. She forgot she was a wife as well. She explained how you needed her more than I did at that time and life would not always be like that. I'm ashamed to say I was jealous of my own son." I listen intently to what he's saying. *He was jealous of me?* He looks at me with sadness and shame. I allow him to continue. "A father should never be jealous of his son. I started working later and later. Eventually, I was missing dinners and important firsts for you. Your mother and I started to fight and that was unheard of in our relationship. I know I was the one who was wrong but I couldn't admit my failings as a father to her."

As he rises to his feet, I rise to see if he needs help. He shoos my help away. He paces around the room looking at the different items, deep in thought. "It was after one our fights that she realized what my problem was. Her solution was this room and a second honeymoon for her and me. You stayed with your grandparents while we were away recommitting our love to one another." It sounds so romantic. "When we came back, a short time later we found out your mom was pregnant with your sister. Again we were happy about the news. However once she was born, she required your mother's attention and then you. I wasn't a priority to her anymore. You were older and starting preschool and did not require her attention as much. Again I started working more and more. The company went international around this time. My time was consumed with work."

This is fascinating to hear but I am not sure what he is trying to explain. He must see my question because he starts again. "I need you to understand what happened and where I was coming from. You were about five and it was your first soccer game. It was a Sunday afternoon and I'd been called into work because an important deal was about to fall apart. We had planned to go as a family to your soccer game but I disappointed you because I went to work instead of your game. When I returned home that night for dinner, you would not talk to me or look at me. I had hurt you and couldn't bear the look in your eyes when you did look at me. So I started to distance myself. It was very selfish of me but it was self-preservation. If your mom saw how you looked at me I was afraid she would be angry with me. I couldn't afford that also." He stands near a picture of mom, him and me at my high school graduation. He seems sad.

"What's wrong dad?" I am curious to know the answer.

"I'm just upset with myself for wasting so many years with you and your sister. After the soccer game, I vowed to never miss anything of yours again. Eventually your mother found out what I was doing but she never said anything. She knew I was trying to be there in my own way but she didn't agree with my methods. When you started high school, your mother and I realized if I wasn't around you, you tended to work harder and were more successful. It was then I started to place demands on you. When you thought I was disappointed, you worked harder just to prove your worth to me. But son you never had to prove your worth to me." He grabs and pulls me close for a hug.

"I think I understand in a warped sort of way. But what of Tara? Why were you so adamantly against her?" I inquire slightly angry with him for all the years of perceived disappointment.

"That's a hard one to answer. I don't think you are really ready to talk about her yet. I see how you suffer despite your best intentions to hide it. You have never really faced that time of your life. We'll talk of her in more depth when you are ready but please believe when I say I was only looking out for your best interests. I have only ever had your best interests at heart."

"I believe you now. But I hated you so much and blamed you for so much."

"I know and I'm sorry. Every time we would be together in the same room I could see and feel your hatred." He is so saddened by that thought my heart completely thaws towards him.

"I forgive you father." And I hug him trying to convey my feelings. We lean slightly away from each other and notice we both have unshed tears shining in our eyes. Both of us laugh at ourselves and step away from each other.

"So tell me about Kaitlyn?" He keeps coming with the shocks but I guess after looking at this room he would know about her.

But still I choke out, "What?" And he laughs at me.

"Kaitlyn tell me about her."

"How do you know about her?"

He looks around the room and says, "The same way I know about everything in this room. Son, I know everything about you. I know about the two girls she walked in on you with or the woman who groped you at your party. It's the same way I know you're going to Pennsylvania tomorrow to speak with her and bring her home. I know you son." He says the last statement solemnly. "From what I have learned about her, she is a good woman. I'm glad you found someone like her. When you-"

I cut him off. "Dad, I just met her. I really don't know too much about her other than what her friends have told me. I don't even know where she lives. I know her home life sounds like it sucks but she is strong, dad. I'm looking forward to getting to know her."

"Good, so what are you going to do to rectify not really knowing her? How are you going to woo her?" *Woo her?* Who says woo nowadays?

"I'm not too sure. She's a mystery to me. One minute, dad, she's shy and innocent. Turning crimson at the slightest thing. But then she can switch and be flirty and forward."

"That's how your mother was with me. She surprised me and challenged me at every turn. Just when I thought I knew her she would surprise me yet again. Still to this day." He says dryly.

"Wow, really." He nods. "Well, I was going to play it by ear when I arrived there to see she how she reacts to me coming to her. She has no idea I'm coming." He looks thoughtfully at me and then startles me by yelling.

"I know! Do you still have the sailboat out east?"

"Yes, why?" Confused with where he is going with this.

"You have always been an excellent sailor. Take the next week to get to know her. Have the boat readied with a week's worth of supplies and just sail away with her. Just the two of you." He is a genius. Wow my father giving me advice on my love life. *Who would have thought?*

"Dad that's a great idea thanks." I hug him making him step back a bit.

"I never thought I would see this day. Son, I love you and am so proud of everything you have accomplished, overcome and will do. Please don't ever forget that even when I'm no longer here."

"Please dad, let's not think of that right now. I learned who you are and am not ready to lose you yet." Before tonight the thought would not have scared me as much as it does right now. God I can't lose him just yet I pray. "Dad, how bad is it really?"

"Pretty bad. The doctors aren't speculating on much. Some of them think the chemo is a waste of my energy. I don't know if it is or not. I know I want to live. I want to live for you, your mother and your sister. I have so much time to make up for."

"Okay then, let's not think anything bad. Only positive thoughts."

"Yes and let's go find your mother, I'm sure she's worried about us."

"Yeah let's go."

"I'm afraid you were the easier of the two confessions tonight. Your sister left the country because of me. I have lots of groveling and explaining to do." He muses lightly but there is no humor in his tone or facial expression.

"Dad, be honest with her. Show her the other room. That's what made it all sink in for me. I will be here to help if you need it."

"Thank you son but I have to face this on my own. I have to atone for my grievances. Any way you have some wooing to do in the next week. You better start at it. Your time will be limited starting next Monday." He pushes me towards the door while he grabs the serving tray. I quickly turn around and take the tray from him.

As we leave the hidden staircase, my mother and sister are patiently awaiting us in my parent's quarters talking amongst themselves. My mother's look is hesitant but after a quick look at my father her smile is one of pure happiness. Abigail on the other hand is full of hesitancy. I look to my sister encouragingly and say "Abs, listen to him. Hear him out before you pass judgment. Give him a chance."

"Thank you son but Abigail has to make her own decision. Hopefully she will heed your endorsement. Have fun with Kaitlyn and good luck. Call us if you need anything." I look at him lovingly and his look mirrors mine. Something I never thought I would say or feel about my father. I hug him and turn to leave. I hear him question Abigail as I close the door behind me. "Abigail what do you say, will you be brave and follow me?"

My father and I still have more things to discuss and it will take time and healing for a healthy relationship to evolve between us. However, we made a great start. As I start for my room, my mother calls after me. "Tristan, can we talk please?" I stop and turn towards her waiting for her to catch up.

"Mom, I really don't want to talk right now. I'm upset with you. I think you could have let on a little so my hatred towards dad wasn't as much as it was. You knew but yet you never said anything."

"Tristan, he is my husband and what happens between us is our business. What he went through so long ago influenced the way he interacted with you. I spoke with him, begged him to…" She halts because she is having a hard time speaking her thoughts. "… to let you know about it all. But he applied his logic and I understood it for what it was, I couldn't disagree with him. Everything he has ever done has always been in this family's best interest. Whether it was done on an individual basis or as a group, he did what he did for us."

"I know mom and I understand, I'm just hurt. I feel manipulated by him and yes by you." I see in her eyes the fear of losing me. "Mom, I just need some time to come to terms with everything. Dad had a great idea I'm going to take him up on. I love you always and nothing will ever change that. I'll always be there for you, never doubt that."

"Oh Tristan, I love you too." She is a blubbering mess of tears now. I hug her tightly to reinforce my statement.

"But mom, I really do need to go. It doesn't have anything to do with the family so don't worry." I turn to walk away but she stops me.

"Does it have to do with a certain woman by the name of Kaitlyn?"

"Holy cow is nothing a secret in this house?!" I sigh exasperated. "How did you find out? Dad?"

She does not answer but she smiles knowingly. My phone rings and Kaitlyn is the caller. "Please bring her by so we can meet her soon. From what I've heard she is just what you need. Good luck with whatever you're planning. When will you be back?"

"Mom, I have to take this it's her. I'm not sure. Definitely before Monday but I'll call you and let you know. Good bye mom." I leave the room as I pick up the call.

--- --- --- ----

Kaitlyn

When I wake up, it is with a clearer mind and I look at my cell which my grandmother must have brought in while I was sleeping. It is dark out. I must have been asleep for a while. My first conscious thought is the rape? One person says he knows what happened. So without thinking I scroll through my text messages to Tristan's with his number and save it. On impulse I call him.

I don't even think the phone rang before he's answering it. "Kaitlyn? Is that you?" Tristan asks. In the back ground I hear him talking to someone. "I have to take this."

"Yes, it's me."

"Where are you, I'm coming to you now?" I hear him closing a door.

"Tristan, am I interrupting something?"

"Nothing that can't wait a few minutes."

"Why are you trying to call me? I mean I don't mean to be rude but I don't even know you."

"I know Angel I can explain everything. Please let me come to you and explain?" *Angel?* Maybe the drugs are still affecting my hearing.

"I don't know you. I don't think it's right you coming here."

"Kaitlyn in the short time we have known each other, I think you are one of the few people who have actually seen the real me." He keeps making these nonsensical comments that baffle me.

"But Tristan that's just it, we don't know each other."

"Then let's fix that." He pleads. "Tell me where you are." Why is he so adamant about coming to me and seeing me?

"No I have to go it's getting late. I-"

"Don't hang up yet. Let's talk a little. Please?"

"What do you want to talk about?" What could we possibly have to talk about?

"Us"

"Us?" Is he on some sort of drugs? *There is no us.*

"Yes there is an us." He must have read my mind. "Do you remember a Saturday night a couple of weeks ago when you were at the candy store working? Your last customer asked for the milk chocolate covered marshmallows?" I am so confused right now you could tell me it is night but the sun is shining and I would believe you but I remember everything he's saying.

"Yes I worked and I remember him. But how did you know?"

"I had on my helmet and you were behind the counter. After you answered me and we made eye contact, I freaked the fuck out. I ran. Your voice was like an angel's." *Ah the nickname.* "Your eyes are so captivating that we connected. Did you feel it? Please tell me you did."

"I did." I answer shyly but I quickly counter it. "It was only a look. Don't get me wrong, I mean your eyes are beautiful and mesmerizing that I felt rooted to the spot and couldn't move. But then you left."

"I know. This connection or whatever it is scared me. I have never felt anything like it before." He admits.

"Me too." I whisper. I feel uncomfortably comfortable talking to him. I admit things I still haven't admitted to myself truthfully.

"Once I got over the fear and shock, I turned back because I needed to talk to you to know if you felt it as well. You were already getting into your car when I arrived back there. I was in the parking lot with you."

"I remember. I saw you there in my rear view mirror but didn't think you were there looking for me." I actually thought it was a little creepy but I don't tell him this. "Why me? I'm a plain Jane."

"You're anything but plain. You have captivated me the few times we've actually been together. At Tyler's party, your voice had me wanting to meet you. I had these plans to get to know you. Swimming and then when we danced together at the club, I knew you were mine." *That was him?*

"You did? How were you going to get to know me?" His confession has me flabbergasted and worried. *Could he have been my rapist?* No, I know it wasn't him in my heart.

"Yes, I did at the party yesterday. Then when we literally ran into each other on the beach and I knew it then too but I still didn't know you were the same woman. Fate has been working to push us together." He has fascinated me with his fate remark. Having always believed fate works in mysterious ways, it is funny he should mention her now. "Honey, you have snagged me, bewitched me, whatever you want to call it and we've only met a few times. I normally don't do this, ever."

"Oh." I whisper again in disbelief.

"Please let me come to you. We really need to talk in person. I need to see you, please."

"I need a couple of days to sort this out. How about I call you in a few days?"

"If you don't call me tomorrow morning, I will find you and come there." He sounds serious. Would he? I remember all the feelings he provokes in me. Never before have I had these feelings and right now just listening to him talking has me all hot and bothered.

"Fine, I'll call you tomorrow some time."

"Tomorrow morning! I'll find you and come whether you want me to or not. Don't doubt me on this, Angel." My pet name again. Weird but I like it.

"Fine, fine. I'll speak with you tomorrow morning." I try to sound annoyed but secretly I am delighted inside. "Good night Tristan."

"Good night Kaitlyn, my angel. Until we speak again in the morning." We hang up and I am on cloud nine. Tristan Chance likes me. *He likes me, he likes me.* My inner conscious is performing the happy dance. He thinks I'm beautiful. I fall back to sleep thinking of Tristan, green eyes, perfect body and his words, forgetting all my worries.

--- --- --- ----

Waking up feeling refreshed, I look at the clock and notice I have slept late today. It is one o'clock in the afternoon. *Well what do you expect, bad day yesterday and no responsibilities today.* My dreams return causing me to smile at them fondly. I quickly get up and head downstairs to spend time with my grandparents. When I get down to the kitchen, there is a note for me on the kitchen table.

> Kaitlyn,
> We went to the store to pick up groceries. We did not want to wake you knowing you could use the sleep. We should not be gone too long. You have our cell phone numbers if you need us. We love you.
> Nanny and Poppy

Looking in the refrigerator for something to eat, I see only rye bread. Deciding I am not hungry, I make myself a cup coffee. I was supposed to call Tristan this morning. *Shit!* Well before I call him I'm going for a run, to think on things.

I run upstairs and find a pair of my old running shoes in the closet, which must have been left here on one of our trips. I search the drawers for clothing I always have here. There is a pair of old worn shorts, not really running shorts but okay for today and a sports bra a bit too small. I wish I had my iPod. Out front I start to stretch and notice the street has changed since the last time I was here. There are more higher end cars here than there used to be. In the midst of all these cars is a white pick-up truck. *Huh, I didn't realize that model was so popular.*

Just as I am ready to start off, my grandparents pull into the driveway. They smile so I wait for them to get out of the car and help with the packages.

"Where are you off to this afternoon, Kaitey?" My grandfather inquires smiling.

"I'm going for a run. It usually helps me to think."

"Okay, we'll see you later. Don't overdo it." My grandmother hugs me.

"Be careful." My grandfather warns.

I start off slow and run towards the river. There is a trail from the river heading north for about five miles. That should be perfect for today. It has been about an hour and I decide to turn around. I feel as if someone is watching me but every time I look behind me no one is there. I am probably just reacting from last night. Just as I turn to run back, I hear a rustling in the bushes. Panicked I start to sprint home.

My thoughts are consumed by Tristan, making this run easier than it should be. From what I understand in his messages, he knows what happened two nights ago. Why didn't he mention it last night? Doesn't he think it is something I would want to hear immediately? Unless of course if it is bad. Then he would want to tell me in person. He probably wants to lessen the blow by being near should I lose it. Nearly two and half hours have elapsed since I left my grandparents.

--- --- --- ----

Tristan

Feelings of nervousness, anxiety, fear and elation are vying for control within me when I woke early this morning. Packing clothing for the week has me hoping clothes will be optional at times but only Kaitlyn will be able to decide that. I cannot push her after what happened and I feel like a shit for thinking these thoughts. But the thought of Kaitlyn naked for my eyes only has me adjusting my jeans.

By late mid-morning, I am on my way to her grandparent's house in Pennsylvania. She never called which just reinforced my resolve to see her. Trepidation about how she may react to my arrival has me second guessing myself at certain points during the drive.

When I arrive there, I knock on the door. Her grandfather answers the door. "Hello Sir, is Kaitlyn home?" He does not look happy to see me; in fact he looks down right belligerent.

"Who's asking?"

"I'm a friend of hers."

"She didn't tell us to expect anyone."

"Well, she didn't really know I was coming."

"Then goodbye." *What?* He closes the door. *What the hell man?* She must be out but then where is she? I venture back to the car to think and as I consider driving around and coming back a little later I look in my rearview mirror and see her approaching. *God does she look good.* She is like a salve to my soul.

--- --- --- ----

Kaitlyn

As I turn the corner of my grandparents block, there is a beautiful silver two door Mercedes parked in front of my grandparent's house. *Damn these cars are nice around here.* I come to a sudden stop when a male figure disembarks for the car. Leaning against the car with his long legs crossed at the ankles and his arms crossed in front of his chest, I would know that body anywhere. Tristan. *Oh my God! He's here.* He is wearing a pair of jeans, worn at the knee and a Caribbean blue colored tee shirt. His eyes are hidden behind a pair of aviators. I regain my composure and resume my run.

He notices me jogging towards the house and arches that one eye brow at me. His silent look is saying "I told you I would come." I try not to smile as I approach but I fail miserably. He returns my smile. I slow down to a walk and he pushes off the car to walk towards me meeting me halfway. We both start to talk at once.

"How did you find me?" I ask.

"I told you I would come." He says with mock annoyance. We both stop to let the other talk. When we realize the other is waiting, we start to talk at the same time again. We laugh.

Finally I say, "You go first."

"I told you if you didn't call me this morning I was coming. Well, you didn't call so I came."

"How did you find me? I was going to call but I over slept."

"Over slept?" He looks down my body leisurely and then back up to my eyes. My body tingles at his perusal. I cannot read his eyes because

105

of the sunglasses. He must read my thoughts because he takes them off and places them in the vee of his tee shirt. *Oh my God could he be any hotter?* "It looks like you decided to run instead of calling."

"How did you find me?" I ignore his statement and ask the question again.

"Don't worry about that. Let's just say you will never be able to hide from me, Angel. I will find you wherever you are. Don't ever doubt that." He answers the question, yes, but not to my liking.

I arch my eyebrow at him. "Oh, really?"

"We have some talking and getting acquainted to do first before I tell you my secrets." He leans into me whispering this. I flush at his proximity.

"Would you like to come in? It's my grandparent's house."

"Yes, I know whose house it is." I look at him questioningly. *He does?* "John and Emily Kipling. John is a retired detective and Emily is a home maker. Should I tell you more?" *Holy cow he isn't kidding me.*

"No, I get it."

When we approach the porch, my grandfather comes out in protective cop mode. He is clearly warning Tristan off. Instinctively I grab Tristan's hand and feel an electric current running up my arm from the point of contact throughout the rest of my body. I look up at Tristan to see if he is experiencing the same sensation and notice he is looking at our hands in amazement. He squeezes my hand gently. He's shocked as well but smiling brightly. It feels so natural holding his hand, almost like my hand was made for his. *This is right.* I give his hand a squeeze in return and introduce him to my grandfather.

"Poppy, this is Tristan Chance." I look at my grandfather silently asking him to behave but he will have none of it especially after the recent events. "Tristan this is my grandfather, John Kipling a retired detective." I knowingly smile.

Tristan extends his hand to my grandfather in a gentlemanly manner. My grandfather reluctantly shakes it. "Hello sir. It's nice to meet you."

My grandfather does not respond. "Poppy, we were just going to come inside and talk." He moves to the side to allow me to pass but tries to block Tristan. I'm stopped abruptly in the doorway because our hands are still clasped tightly together. My grandfather notices and grudgingly moves to the side.

When we finally get through the door way, my grandmother comes hustling over to us. I make the introductions again. "Nanny, this is Tristan Chance, a friend." Tristan frowns at me. I look at him questioningly. He slightly shakes his head no. "This is my grandmother, Emily Kipling." Still confused about his frown I brush it off.

"It's nice you meet, Tristan." She takes his offered hand. He releases my hand and I frown as I reluctantly allow him to let go. He chuckles slightly at my scowl.

"Likewise, Mrs. Kipling but I hope to be more than a friend to Kaitlyn." *Oh, I get it.* He didn't like the reference about him being a friend. He looks towards my grandfather and surprises me with his next statement. "Sir, I take full responsibility for everything Kaitlyn has been through in the last couple of days." Tristan stuns us all speechless with his confession.

It takes a couple of minutes before my grandfather responds but when he does, I know we are okay. "I'm assuming you are the one who rescued her?" Tristan looks to me questioningly and I just shrug my shoulder.

--- --- --- ----

Tristan

"Ah... yes sir." I stammer. "It was my party and I hired the band. However I did not know Steve, the guitarist, was a rapist. If I had known I would never have hired them. The lead singer, Danny, is one of my closest friends and he was also unaware, sir." I'm at a loss of what else to say. Kaitlyn shrugs when I glance at her for some sort of direction. So I just continue on.

"He never had the chance to," I look at Kaitlyn sympathetically and take her hand in mine giving it a gently squeeze showing her I support her. "Chance to rape her. I threw him off her and out of my house. Then I tended to her immediately. I stayed with her all night to make sure she was okay."

Again her grandfather surprises me by extending his hand to me standing. "Thank you son for protecting my granddaughter and clarifying what I was starting to piece together." He briefly looks at Kaitlyn and continues. "Can you fill in the rest of the blanks for us? Her mind is still a little fuzzy with the details."

I briefly review the events of the days prior to and up to that night. They do not need to know how I found her and what condition she was in, so I omit that part of the story. Kaitlyn and her grandmother are silently crying. When I finish, her grandmother hugs me.

"I've forgotten my manners. Can I get you something to drink?" She asks.

"No thank you Mrs. Kipling." Kaitlyn looks relieved. Eventually she will learn the condition I found her in, but not now.

"Please call me Emily. After everything you have done for Kaitlyn, it's the least I can do."

"I need a shower. Do you mind keeping him company, nanny?" Kaitlyn asks.

"Sure honey you go."

She looks at our hands and squeezes it questioningly. "Do you mind?"

"Yes, please go and shower you smell." I scrunch my nose in mock distaste. When she turns around I see I have embarrassed her so I gently pull her down and kiss her cheek causing them to flame further.

"Uh! I'll be quick, I promise." She's discombobulated and as affected as I am. *Great!*

Her grandparents and I sit down in the living room. Her grandfather starts to question me and my intentions. "Well sir I would like to get to know Kaitlyn more. I think we have a special connection." I explain to them what I mean and how we kept having those chance encounters.

"Well Tristan, that's all fine and good but she's going to have a rough time coming up when she does start to remember. I know you spared us the details of what happened but she may remember and what will you do then."

"Frankly sir, I hope she never knows what that fuck-" I stop abruptly and look to the both of them apologizing with my eyes for cursing. "I'm sorry. I just get so angry when I think what could've happened. But I'll be there for her. If she wants to press assault charges I will gladly take her." He looks at me with admiration. "I'll see Steve pays dearly for what he has done to her. Every resource I have is working to find him and then destroy him. He will regret the day he even looked in her direction."

He stands and offers me his hand again. "Thank you again for everything you have done for her. If I can be of assistance somehow, please let me know. I know a thing or two about investigations and finding someone from my time on the force. Please call me John."

"Thank you John, I'll let you know. I have an unlimited amount of resources at my fingertips, so hopefully he won't stay hidden too long." My tone rings with conviction. He will pay. Kaitlyn comes down stairs looking like an angel and my breath catches. I look to her grandparents and ask, "Do you mind if I take Kaitlyn out for a little while. I promise to feed her."

"Yes." They both say in unison.

"Tristan, I can't really go out for dinner. I left in such a hurry that I never grabbed my stuff." She appears embarrassed by her choice of clothing.

"Don't worry. We'll get take out if it would make you feel better. But honestly you look perfect. Would either of you like us to bring you back something?"

"No thank you we have dinner cooking now." Emily replies.

"Have fun. We'll probably be asleep when you get in. Will you be staying the night Tristan?"

I hadn't thought that far in advance. "I can stay in a hotel nearby."

"Nonsense! We will hear of no such thing. You can stay in the room across from ours. I will put out some towels for you should you want to shower."

"Thank you that is very generous of you."

"Please don't thank us. For what you have done for our granddaughter, this is the least we can do. We don't know how we'll ever repay you."

"No repayment is necessary. I would do it again in a heartbeat but this time I wouldn't let him out of my sight."

It appears Kaitlyn and I are astonished by her grandparent's invitation. However I would have liked to stay in a hotel so I could spend some quality time with her. But this is just as good.

CHAPTER TEN

Tristan

When we reach my car, I open the door for her, which seems to surprise her. Maybe she has never been treated like a lady. *Well Kaitlyn be prepared to be treated with the upmost respect.* I assist her into the car and attempt to secure her in the seat but the thought of restraining her in my bed while I explore her body with my mouth has me smiling and fumbling with the seatbelt. Finally getting it to click, I try, unsuccessfully, to control my lust for her. I look at her and lightly touch her thigh and press a kiss to her forehead. I walk around the back car to the driver's side adjusting my pants to allow my dick more room since it seems to have a mind of its own when in Kaitlyn's presence. The idea of restraining her is still fresh in my mind that I look to her seatbelt to ensure it is snug and smile at her.

I start the car and place it in drive but before releasing the brake I look towards her and take off. I feel the need for constant contact with her so I reach for her hand and intertwine our fingers. I bring our hands to my lips and kiss each of her fingers. I feel her shiver.

Stopping by the river, I get out and open her door. Offering her my hand, she takes it and I lead her to the front of the car. I pat the hood next to me hoping she will climb up and sit down, which she does.

Sitting beside me with our thighs touching, I glance at her out of the corner of my eye. This woman has captured me so completely and I feel like an inexperience kid about to get laid. I don't know what to do next. I look toward her and we start to drift towards each other feeling the connection so strongly. We should stop. It is too much too fast and too soon for her. As I inhale to speak, I catch her scent and she smells so good, clean and floral. *God how I want this woman.* She interrupts my thoughts.

--- --- --- ----

Kaitlyn

He won the trust of my grandfather which is usually hard but I
thought that especially after the events of the other night it would have
been more difficult. For some reason, when I should be scared of men, this
man makes me feel safe. Safer than I have felt in my whole life. "A penny
for your thoughts."

"I'm wondering who you are? I mean I know who you are, but
why am I having this reaction to you? I know I'm not explaining this in a
way for you to understand." He's right, he is not making sense but I
understand what he's trying to say because I feel the same way.

"I know what you're trying to say. I've been thinking the same
thing since I first met you."

"I would like to try an experiment. Would you mind? I mean, I
don't know…"

"What did you have in mind?"

"It's not right for me to ask especially after the other night."

"Tristan, what do you want to try? Ask me."

"I need to know what it's like to kiss and taste you." He looks at
me apologetically as if his comment will disgust me or scare me off. What
he doesn't realize is that since he told me I was not raped I feel almost
normal again especially around him. He makes me forget things in a
positive way, I think. "I need to know if it's different." He says wishfully.
"I can't get you out of my head. You're always in my thoughts now. So
much has happened in the last day and a half. But before I make any
necessary decisions, I need to know what this is."

He has me intrigued by his confession. I wanted to kiss him before
but now… "Kiss me Tristan." Shocking him doesn't stop the first real kiss
I have ever had.

He leans in from the side to gently cup my cheek and softly kisses
me. Pulling back hesitantly to gauge my reaction, he hears my sigh and
takes that as encouragement. He kisses me again, not letting go of my face.
His lips apply a bit more pressure enhancing the kiss. My heart rate
skyrockets. The butterflies in my stomach have resumed their flight,
fluttering all over the place. My breathing halts when I feel his tongue skim
over my lower lip, seeking permission to enter. I grant him permission and
open for him.

My tongue automatically seeks out his. Our tongues are
performing a seductive dance with each other. My arms of their own
accord have moved around his neck as he sucks my bottom lip into his
mouth and it is like he has hard wired my libido. He lets go of my face and

pulls my body closer to his, deepening the kiss further. Feeling bold, a feeling foreign to me, I climb over his lap to straddle him. We are lost to the feelings this kiss has evoked in us. I have never felt this sensation before. The feelings he conjures in me are a jumbled mess, but he makes me soar.

--- --- --- ----

Tristan

When she told me to kiss her, she was the picture of pure innocence. She did not know what she was asking of me. I can tell this is the first real kiss she has ever had and my spirits are soaring at the thought. When our tongues finally touch, I have made my peace and can die a happy man. She can be my salvation. Her arms wrap themselves around my neck pulling me closer and I support her by placing my hands at her waist lifting her slightly. She takes it as encouragement and climbs onto my lap straddling me. My arms tighten around her waist effectively pulling her closer. I feel how her breasts form to my body.

Feeling her against me has just shot all the blood circulating in my body straight to my dick. I think somewhere in the back of my mind, we have to slow this down, but then her tongue starts to tangle with mine and I am lost in her again. She moans and grinds her hips on to the hardness that is my dick. I redouble my efforts to pull back. Lowering my forehead to hers I whisper reverently. "Wow." My heart is pounding in my chest and my breathing erratic.

She tries to push away but I tighten my hold on her. "I'm sorry. I don't know what came over me. I've never acted this way before." Her cheeks redden slightly by her confession. Again she tries to move away. She is going nowhere right now. I want to kiss her again but instead I place a gentle kiss on her nose and then pullback to look her in the face.

"Kaitlyn, we need to talk. This kiss has clarified things for me. As I alluded to before so much has happened in the last day and a half, which will now affect us." She tries to interrupt but I stop her. "Hear me out. You can't deny there is something here between us. I want to explore and nurture it to its full potential. I think we may be it, the real thing. You know the ones they write about."

"I want that and feel it too but how are you so sure? We hardly know each other. There are things about me you don't know. You may not even want to be with me when you hear them." Her frighten expression has me concerned.

"There is nothing that could make me walk away right now."

"But Tristan you-"

"Stop and listen, please. I had a girlfriend once and we knew everything about each other." I feel Tara's loss again as my friend. I owed her so much more. "We had known each other for a while before we started dating. It was nothing like this. Nowhere near as close. This feeling is consuming. You are different, special." I kiss her hands again.

"Tristan, I want to explore this as well but I'm afraid. I'm starting medical school and that will require a great deal of my time. When I study, I become lost in it. I have never had a boyfriend before because, well mainly because, I never found the right person or time to look. But now I don't know if I will know how to balance the two."

She has just been honest with me and I am so happy. I kiss her out of pure joy but the kiss quickly turns passionate again. I halt again. "Kaitlyn, I am in a similar situation. I have only done the girlfriend thing once and vowed never to do it again." I let my words sink in. "Yesterday, my father made me CEO of Chance Industries as of next week. I have one week to get my personal affairs in order before taking on the full responsibility. This changes everything I currently know. You and I are just starting out and I hope the newness of us will be enough. My father was really never around because of work. I have to try to find a balance as well because I won't be like my father."

--- --- --- ----

Kaitlyn

A bucket of cold water being dumped on me could not have surprised me more than this new revelation. I am struck speechless. He starts to withdraw probably because I have not been able to respond to him yet. I rouse out of my stupor.

"Wow, th-th-that's great." I try to sound happy for him but am failing miserably. "That's great. We will work it out. Anything this good is worth working out, right?" I think I sound more positive with each passing moment. "I'm up to the challenge. You've returned to me a sense of myself. I didn't know what happened with Steve, and you filled in the blanks. You saved me. We owe it to ourselves to figure this out. If that's what you want?" Now that sounds excited and hopeful.

He jumps off the car, picks me up, elated and twirls me around. "Yes that's what I want. You make me so happy." His hands wrap around me holding me in a tight embrace below my butt. Tilting my head back I laugh that I have been able to make him this happy. He slides me down his front and I feel every contour of his body. *God what a body.* With one hand he cups my cheek while the other grips the back of my nape pulling me in for another soul searching kiss. This kiss holds promises of what is to come and fates being sealed. I feel as if I am being marked as his. Funny enough, my stomach decides at this point to make it known it has been neglected. Pulling back he laughs lightly.

"I believe I promised to feed you, Miss Daniels."

"Yes, you did. Already Mr. Chance you are breaking your promise to your girlfri…" I stop mid-sentence realizing I'm making assumptions.

"Yes, finish that thought. You are my girlfriend, so please enlighten me as to how I have failed you so far Miss Daniels." He jests with me.

"Breaking your promise to your girlfriend is usually frowned upon Mr. Chance. However you can regain my favor by making sure we have the best carpet picnic around."

"Carpet picnic?" He questions.

"Tell me you have never had a carpet picnic with your friends?" He shakes his head no. "Oh my God what you have been missing." There is a twinkle in my eye. "Let's get a pizza and I'll show you what a carper picnic is all about." I smile flirtatiously at him. We climb into the car and he asks for directions on where to find the best pizza in Pennsylvania.

We stop at Joe's Pizzeria, known for the best grandma's pizza around. The girl behind the counter is catching flies with her mouth when she glimpses my boyfriend. Yes, that's right you heard me my boyfriend. I want to scream it from the rooftops. I know it's immature but look at him. I mean really? My inner consciousness is doing her happy dance again. It is only now I realize all the women in the pizzeria are staring. That's right ladies take all the time you want to look because watch this everyone. I lean up to kiss him and responds back by bending me backwards and kissing me breathless. *Yes, he's marked now too.*

When I look back at the girl who took our order, she is scowling at me. I smile politely back. We go next door to the market to grab some drinks. When we reach the alcoholic beverages aisle, I tug him on, skipping that aisle. He looks at me questioningly. "No alcohol tonight please?" He nods.

When we get back to my grandparent's house, pizza and drinks in hand, the front porch light is on but it's dark inside. Tristan is right behind me when we enter because when I stop he bumps into me and grabs my waist. Smoothing his move he takes his arms and wraps them around my waist. Since the kiss at the river, he has not stopped touching me. Then at the pizzeria while we were waiting he either had his hands on my waist, intertwined with mine, around my shoulders or at the small of my back. We have had constant physical contact at all times.

I turn around and kiss him hesitantly at first but he encourages me further. The kiss promises so much more so we pull away slightly knowing if we start something now we may not be able to stop it. Hopefully my grandparents are asleep upstairs and will not hear us. I place the palms of my hands on his chest as I slightly push him away. But he does not allow this distance and he kisses me again. I moan, he groans and my stomach cries, thereby ending the kiss.

"So how does this carpet picnic work?" He whispers in my ear with his hands still on my waist. Not allowing any distance between us just yet. When he does let go, I glance down and see he a bulge in his pants. I moisten my lips involuntarily and he catches it. "If you look at me like that again, I will have no control and our first time will be here on this floor and not somewhere special like it should be. My control is usually iron clad but you are too tempting. My resolve starts to crumble around you. It's very dangerous this power you wield." He admits stoically.

"I guess there was no permanent damage done by my knee. And you weren't kidding when you said you weren't lacking." I say trying to lighten the mood and succeeding when he barks out a laugh at the mention of our encounter and I bat my eyelashes at him coquettishly. Sending goose bumps up my arm, I continue. "Well, let me get a blanket while you set the food out there on that table." He turns around to eye the coffee table and reluctantly disengages from me to start his chore. After retrieving a blanket from the hall closet, I move some furniture around with his help to allow the blanket to open fully. Once settled, I turn to grab the food and place it in front of us but he has me in his arms again and he dips me for another kiss. "You have to stop doing that. You are making my mind turn to mush. I have no control here either as you experienced by my moment near the river."

He chuckles and says, "No, I don't want to stop. I like kissing you and making you come undone. It will be fun to watch you learn control at my hands and my hands alone. Angel, knowing you have never been with another guy just brings out the Neanderthal in me."

I chidingly respond ignoring his last comment. "Okay caveman, now usually these types of picnics are best in bedrooms, more romantic that way. It could be turned into a bed picnic." I smile seductively at him.

"Our next picnic will be on the bed," he assures me. "And I get to pick the food. A buffet if you will, so I can sample a bit of everything. I'll have a nibble here," he nibbles at my neck. "A taste here," he sucks on my ear. "A bit here," he gently bites my nipple through my shirt and bra causing me to gasp. "And for dessert something very sweet." He places his hand between my legs. *Wow that's some buffet.*

Breathlessly I respond. "I'd like that picnic but only if I get to choose my food." I look him over seeing what I would like to eat first and lick my lips in anticipation. His eyes dilate and darken. I am having so much fun that when my stomach interrupts our moment again I pout. *Damn stomach and its demands.* "We should eat before my stomach ruins the moment again."

"Okay fine, let's eat." We finally settle on the floor comfortably and eat our pizza. Our conversation is minimal because we are too occupied with staring at the other. The air around us is charged with energy, sexual or nervous, hard to say which one. My grandparents are upstairs definitely sleeping by now. He asks me with a knowing smile when he has finished with his food. "So what do you suppose we do now?"

"I know what you're thinking but we have to go upstairs for that after you help me clean up." Completely pulling his leg and falsely leading him on.

"Upstairs?" He questions me skeptically with raised brow. That brow will get me in to trouble it is so hot.

"Yes upstairs." I smile flirtatiously at him then I burst his bubble. "That's where the board games are. Isn't that what you were thinking?" He looks at me dumbfounded. I make no move to correct the misunderstanding, knowing I did this on purpose until his expression changes. Then I jokingly push him laughing at his reaction and run towards the kitchen.

"Oh you think you're funny." He follows me into the kitchen. He tries to grab me but I quickly escape his grasp. The center island is between us now and I can see him calculating his best move. I fake right only to realize my mistake when he grabs me and starts to tickle me. Relentless in his tickling, I call mercy numerous times prior to him actually stopping. "Huh, that will teach you to mess with me."

While I am washing the dishes he stands directly behind touching my back with his front. He grabs my hips and grinds his hips into me. Instinctually I press back into him. I hear him inhale sharply. When the dishes are washed and drying on the counter, I turn around in his embrace and kiss him. I take his hand shyly and look him in the eyes before guiding him upstairs. He looks at me reflectively but I tug on his arm to follow me.

The air has become very heavy with desire. We are very quiet when we reach the landing because on the other side is my grandparent's bedroom door. Bypassing the room my grandparents have designated as his for the night, I lead him towards my room. It feels like we are teenagers sneaking around.

"Okay you have me here, now what are we going to do?" He inquires salaciously while closing the door quietly.

I push him gently towards my bed and he sits down on it looking up at me. The full size bed is dwarfed by his size. This very forward side of me is unfamiliar to me. It shocks and pleases me at the same time. He brings this out in me. He pushes himself further back on the bed so his legs are against the bed. Seeing him like this turns me on and I climb on to his lap straddling his thighs. My arms extend to rest on his shoulders while he wraps his arms around my waist pulling me closer.

"I need to tell you something and you may not want to hear it." I know his experienced reputation. "I have no experience what so ever when it comes to this." I point between us. "I mean I haven't even been kissed before tonight."

He looks at me thoughtfully and I am staring back into the most beautiful green eyes, lost. "Really, no one has ever kissed you? Are you sure because I thought the way you kissed me you had at least done it once." Swallowing, I feel uncomfortable. "I would never have guessed. Everyone is innocent once. You have nothing to worry about, especially with me. We'll only go as far as you want to. If you tell me to stop then we'll stop." He looks at me sincerely.

"However, if you think you're getting lucky tonight Miss Daniels, sorry I have a headache." He playfully teases and feigns a headache, lightening the mood. "But I'll still bring you a pleasure you have never felt before." He still wants me which emboldens me. I push him back and fall on top of him.

He takes this opportunity to kiss me. The kiss is so hot and deep it causes my heart rate to rise dramatically. His tongue is caressing and plunging. His hands start to roam over my body while mine are becoming acquainted with his body. Instinct seems to be taking over, my body on autopilot following the feelings he elicits. My body is aflame because of his touch.

Tugging his shirt out of his shorts and placing my hands under it, I feel the contours of his sculpted hard muscles. He leans up slightly allowing me to remove the shirt completely. I look down at him with awe. "It's only fair if I get to look as well. You once asked me if you were lacking and I said no, but that was before. I want to make sure I didn't lie to you. We can't start this relationship off with a lie now can we?" He teases as he reaches for my shirt.

"Uh, uh, uh," I playfully bat his hands away and lift my shirt over my head, leaving only my nearly see through lacey bra. One of my splurges when I have money is to buy expensive and beautiful undergarments. This has been an addiction since high school when Sophia took me shopping with her once. I'm glad I had at least some nice sets still here when I took my shower.

His gaze as it meanders across my body is one of pure lust. He lets go of my waist and I feel the cold loss of him however it is soon replaced with a scorching heat as he places them over my breast. His thumbs are gently grazing my nipples through the rough lace causing them to harden under his touch. My breathing has become very shallow. He has hard wired my libido again. I lean down to kiss him and he rolls me over so he is slightly on top of me. My mind briefly flashes back to the other night when

I awoke with a heavy body on me. I physically cringe at the thought and Tristan immediately pulls away and looks down at me.

"What's wrong Angel? Did I do something you didn't like?" I can't look at him because I'm ashamed by where my thoughts have gone and they have no place here in this moment with us.

"No, it's nothing." I lie. But he can see it and calls me on it.

"Don't lie, tell me. There is nothing you can say to make me change the way I feel about you. Lying to me just doesn't bode well for us if you start now." He gently chastises me.

"I'm sorry. I just had a flash back that's all." It registers in his mind as he starts to roll off of me. "Please don't move." I grab him to stop his withdrawal. "That's why I didn't tell you at first. It was a fleeting memory. I don't want to stop, please. Don't let him take more. He doesn't belong here with us."

I can see the indecision and uncertainty in his eyes. Without thinking, I lean up on my elbows and kiss him. He starts to pull away but I wrap my arms around his neck pulling him back down with me. This time I win, he doesn't try to pull away. He deepens the kiss by sucking my lower lip into his mouth. I swear the flood gates to my panties just opened.

He must sense my need because his hand finds its way under my bra and his thumb skims over my bare nipple and I moan. *What a feeling.* Hearing my reaction he unclasps the bra with his other hand and bares both breasts. He looks at them with awe and barely whispers, "Beautiful." His mouth descends onto one breast while his hand gently palms the other. It is suddenly very difficult to breathe. It's as if I'm breathing very thin air at a higher altitude. His teeth graze my nipple and it hardens further. He pulls away slightly blowing across it causing a pebble like reaction and repeats this with the other one.

I feel at a loss because I don't know what to do with my hands. Gently, I rub them up and down his spine. He moans ever so slightly. His eyes devour me and his kisses follow where his eyes landed sucking gently. My body is trembling with need. With him lying slightly on me he uses his knee to part my legs as his hand slowly glides over my body to rest between my legs. He gently starts to rub back and forth. As I start to move with his hand, he withdraws his hand and slides it into my shorts under my panties. My breathing changes as he touches me as no one has ever touched me before. The sensation is beyond words. I hear him mutter in my ear in surprise, "So wet." I groan as his fingers slide between the folds and apply gentle pressure to my opening. He withdraws his hand again causing me to open my eyes and look at him.

"Baby, I need these off." He gestures to my shorts. "Help me take them off?" *He doesn't have to ask me twice!* I unzip the shorts and shimmy out. He inhales deeply as he sees the panties. They are completely see through, matching the bra. "Baby, I don't want to take this much farther tonight, because what I want to do to you will require your full surrender to me and you will be screaming my name by the end of the night. We can't afford that with your grandparents down the hall." He chortles at my pout.

He starts to kiss me and slips my panties down my legs. As the panties reach my calves, I kick them the rest of the way off. With his free hand he lifts my leg from behind the knee and places it off to the side, opening me for his viewing. This intimate gesture has me flushing crimson with embarrassment. He notices my embarrassment and comments.

"Don't ever be embarrassed with me there is nothing to be embarrassed about. I want to know if you like what I'm doing." His kiss overwhelms me while his hand slides down the outside of my leg to my foot and glides up the inside. His fingers slide in among the folds between my legs. As he glides his fingers back and forth, he gently inserts a finger into my folds. "So tight. Hmmm." I writhe under him at this new incredible feeling. He starts to withdraw his finger then startles me when he pushes it back in. He repeats this movement multiple times and I feel myself building. Building to what, I have no idea but I want to know. Instinctively, I start to move against his hand.

His palm applies pressure to my bud and I groan into his kiss. "That's it baby. Feel it. God you are even more beautiful aroused." His kisses and touches are causing me to come apart at the seams. His finger hits a spot inside me that intensifies this building feeling. This must be what Sophia and Lara are always talking about. His finger is moving faster and repeatedly bumping that spot. I feel like I am about to explode. He is relentless, my hips are moving with his fingers. Finally, I am soaring, feeling like I jumped off a cliff. He stifles my cries with his kisses. My insides are clenching around his finger. After what seems like hours, I return to earth while he withdraws his finger and kisses me so deeply and reverently I am lost.

I look at him with wonder. "Did I just…?" I can't seem to say the word. But he knows what I want to say so he says.

"Come? Yes baby you did. And you're amazing when you do. God I can't wait until I feel you tightening around my dick." I blush at the thoughts his erotic crass statement has caused.

"Then why don't you." I say coyly but his answer is to growl at me.

"Grrr…. Don't tempt me. I am barely holding on to my control here. You have me wound so tightly right now. I want you to myself. To own you. I want to experience your uninhibited side. Here and now is not the time." His groan is deep and seductive causing me to melt at his feet.

"Oh." I sulk disappointed.

"Would you come away with me somewhere?"

119

"I don't know. Why?"

"To get to know each other. Experience each other. I have this whole week before I have to attend to business next week. I want to spend this time with you."

How can I say no? The time off from work has been taken care of, so I am free. Figuring out where this will go is what we both agreed to. Sophia and Lara are always telling me to take risks and Tristan has proven himself. I trust him and recognize I would go with him anywhere. "Yes."

"Great!" He says excitedly. "Tomorrow you and I are going back to New York. From there it's a surprise."

"We have to stop off at my house so I can get some clothing. I don-"

"No need. I've arranged for everything. You'll want for nothing. Tomorrow you'll tell your grandparents we're going away for a short time." He just takes control and expects me to follow. A part of me wants to let him make all the decisions and this part is bigger than the part that balks at the idea. Settling in to this new revelation, I turn on my side with my back towards him yawning while he talks about our trip. I snuggle into him. He kisses my head and says, "Sleep Angel, this may be your last good night's sleep for the week."

I hum a response that sounds like okay. As I drift off to sleep, I feel him maneuvering himself out of bed to remove his clothing, keeping his underwear and tee shirt on. Wrapping me in his steely arms, he places his hand between my legs very possessively and leaves it there. *Wow!*

CHAPTER ELEVEN

Kaitlyn

The drive back to New York was entertaining. Tristan would not allow me to drive my car because he felt it was not suitable enough to drive. We argued and eventually we compromised. I allowed him to have someone pick it up and drive it to New York where it would be repaired to like new status which led to another argument over the affordability of said repairs and my lack of money. If looks could kill, well let's just say he would have been paying for a funeral instead of car repairs.

His taste in music is eclectic like mine. Talking about music and our similar tastes has been a distraction. Entering the city limits has me wondering where exactly we're going. He said we are spending the week together but it was a surprise.

"Where are we going?"

"To my loft."

"Why?"

"Because I have something there I need to bring with us. Do you mind making the quick pit stop?" He looks at me apologetically. "I should have asked first I'm sorry. Time sensitive papers were dropped off for my signature."

"No problem. I just wanted to know where we're going. You never said where so I was curious that's all."

"This isn't our final destination. We still have about another two hours depending on traffic. I promise it will be quick. I'll grab the papers, you can use the bathroom if you need to and maybe we can get something quick to eat. I want to be at our destination before night fall, preferably before the sun sets. It's beautiful to watch the sunset from there." He is so vague about where we are going I can't help but feel anxious.

"Where?"

"Nah uh, it's a surprise. You don't like surprises do you?"

"Well actually I don't think I've ever had any good surprises. So, no, I'm not good at them I suppose." That sucks I just realized. Who doesn't like surprises? People who have had really bad surprises such as birthday parties where you are told you ruined a parent's life or you plan a trip with friends only to find out your savings account has been drained to pay the bills for the month. That's only a few surprises. There are more, plenty more in fact.

"Then it's my goal to make surprises fun for you again."

"That's a big goal. Maybe you should start with something smaller such as telling me where we're going?" He chuckles.

Heading towards SoHo, he turns left into a gated underground garage. After parking in a spot closest to the elevator labeled "Reserved PH," he opens my car door. This takes some getting used to. We walk to the bank of elevators holding hands. He slips a card from his wallet into the key slot. A lone elevator on the other side dings informing us the elevator has arrived. Once in, the doors close, he inserts his card again. *Secure.* We are lifted swiftly up to the penthouse with no stops.

"Wow, no stops?" I look to him questioningly.

"One of the perks of this building is the loft has its own elevator which only myself and my father have the keys." The elevator is lined with mirrors and a security camera which is barely noticeable except for the red light through the vent, which I don't think I would have noticed if I wasn't looking up at Tristan.

"Well if you and your father are the only ones who have the keys, why then the security camera?" As I point to the camera the door opens swiftly to a foyer. He shrugs evading my question.

Tristan slips his card into the door and I am immersed in sunlight. The open floor plan is stunning with a spectacular view of the city. There are two floors, I notice. The main living space is mainly open and consists of the kitchen, living and dining areas. I notice a few other doors off a short wide hallway and staircase leading up.

"Tristan this is beautiful." I comment as I walk to the bank of windows. Off the windows is an amazing deck outfitted with lounge chairs, fireplace, large screen television, arbor, and more. It is a small slice of heaven. Secluded and unbelievably quiet. This space is luxurious. "The view is breathtaking, Tristan. I don't think I would ever tire of this."

When he said loft, I was expecting a remodeled industrial looking space with average size rooms. This loft is vast with oversized rooms on the main level and large floor to ceiling windows. The furniture is modern but comfortable looking. The décor is warm with its earth tones. The small fortune it must have cost to furnish this space is staggering. I have never been exposed to such wealth before now. *What it must have been like to grow up in this type of splendor?*

"Thank you, my mother found it originally for when she visited my dad at work. She never wanted my sister or I out of her sight for than a couple of hours at a time when we were younger. So she needed a place for us to stay on those late nights. Up until recently it would remain vacant for most of the year."

"So you have always lived like this?" I incorporate the surroundings using my hands.

"Yes, I have been very fortunate. Though at times I think I may have been spoiled. But mom would always bring me back to reality. She would ground me for the slightest transgression." *What type of transgressions?* Even if I were a very successful doctor I could never reach this type of wealth. "She had no problems humbling us. We always knew all this could disappear one day. We also knew that with this type of wealth we had certain responsibilities to people that most people would never have. At a very young age my sister and I learned the hard way that people usually liked us for what we had, not necessarily for who we were."

"How sad, what you were like growing up?" Turning from the view, I walk over to him and embrace him.

"Angel, all in due time because that is a loaded question. I want to know what you were like as well. That's what this week is for." He kisses my forehead.

"There really isn't too much for me to tell. I'm afraid you'll be bored."

"I could never be bored listening to you." He kisses me on the nose. "Do you have to use the bathroom?"

"Yes, please. I would like to freshen up before we leave. Where is it?"

Pointing down the hallway, he seems slightly distracted by something. "Is something wrong?" I inquire.

"No, I just wasn't expecting this much paperwork. You may be getting more sleep than I suggested last night." He grins wolfishly. Talking about last night makes me redden with embarrassment. I really need to stop blushing, though it seems to make him chuckle when I do. "I love making you blush. It reminds me of how innocent you truly are and how lucky I am."

"But it's so immature."

"There is nothing immature about you only innocence and I look forward to corrupting you." The wolfish smile appears again.

"Well then, I'll strive to blush more." *Holy cow did I just say that?* I sneak a peek at him through my eyelashes. His eyes have glazed over with lust. I lean on my tiptoes to kiss him and he ravages my mouth. This is not like the kisses of last night. Those were sweet, gentle and lustful but this one is filled with lust and something else. There is no gentleness here. This is marking ownership. Now it's my turn to say. "Wow."

"Your sassiness is going to get you in trouble. You better use the bathroom before I punish you for that sassiness." Turning around, I head to the bathroom but not before he swats my backside to prove his point. But the only point he has proven is I may just like that. I stick my tongue out at him mockingly. *What has come over me?*

"Oh Angel, you're poking a caged animal. Be careful before you bite off more than you can chew." Before I enter I catch his look and it is one of carnal passion. "Baby steps sweetheart, baby steps."

I pucker my lips at him to throw a kiss and he laughs out right. And with that I close the door, astonished by the bathroom. Is there no end to the magnificence of this loft? I feel like a queen in here on her throne and I laugh at the pun.

Tristan is reading some papers when I finally emerge. He notices my arrival and places them to the side. "Sorry, I made us some sandwiches to go, do you mind if we leave now? We'll come back eventually."

"Sure, let's go."

He places the stack of folders in a large messenger bag and grabs my hand. Once in the car, the street signs indicate Eastern Long Island. I search his iPod and find Jessie Ware's Devotion. *God I love this song.*

"Do you mind if I close my eyes?"

"No, if you want to take a nap please do." *Nap?* I am too excited about this trip to take a nap. What is he expecting from me? I have so many questions for him. I feel so comfortable with him it scares me. I should be afraid especially after what almost happened. But with him, I'm not. I haven't had the feelings of insecurity since I have been with him. I get it now why Sophia and Lara are always going on about their boyfriends.

"No, I just want to close my eyes for a bit." Not meaning to but a little while later with the hum of the car, the soft music and Tristan's hand gently rubbing mine, I fall asleep.

--- --- --- ----

Tristan

Kaitlyn fell asleep shortly after we started our drive. So much for conversation, instead I find myself rehashing the events of the past day and a half. CEO of CI, an innocent new girlfriend and a relationship with my father. The man I thought I was constantly disappointing when in actuality it was the opposite.

124

The papers the lawyers drew up at my father's request were numerous. Since the board of directors was made aware of my succession as CEO, they decided to send along proposals, contracts and other information for my review as well. The accountability of thousands of employees is a responsibility not to be taken lightly. The power which comes along with employing such a large amount of people can be overwhelming not to mention the types of contracts we hold. The directors of individual departments usually undertake the growth and development of employees but the teams I create will answer to me and I believe in nourishing their development. Any changes made within the company I want to be directly involved with. CI's employees need to feel confident in my leadership. The one sure way to encourage that confidence is to be hands on as much as possible.

We have become stagnant recently and our profits have remained steady but we should be growing in this economy. Our competitors, few as they may be, have benefited from our inactivity. Different management decisions, new blood and growth will help to bring this company into the new era of this industry. Decisions, easy and difficult, will need to be made. Meetings need to be arranged with each and every department head as well as some of the key stakeholders. Failure is not an option. Too many people are relying upon me to always perform at the top of my game. This job will take up much of my time in the next year or so. Traveling, meetings, luncheons, dinners, and parties are some of events which will need to be attended.

Where the beginning of most relationships are supposed to be fun and light hearted, Kaitlyn and my relationship will be filled with stress at least part of the time. Hopefully, some of these planned events will allow us to have fun and enjoy being a couple. Our time together will be limited by her schooling and my position. I hope to take her with me on as many of the trips as I can but scheduling conflicts will most likely arise.

Last night was a new experience for me. I have been with my fair share of women but none have ever responded to me the way Kaitlyn did. Abstaining last night was near impossible. I was wound tighter than a coil. She was so tight around my finger and blossomed under my touch she nearly had me coming with her. Watching her come undone for the first time was a stunning sight. There is a minx buried deep in her and I look forward to bringing it out to play. The thought of actually getting spanked thrilled her despite her inexperience.

My hope for this week is to lay the ground work for our budding relationship. We both carry baggage and will need to broach that in due time. Steve is an unknown wild card whose whereabouts still evade me. The need to protect her has the Neanderthal in me hitting his club looking for a fight. Tim, the private investigator, has performed some side investigations for me in the past so finding Steve should be no problem. I have to start that ball rolling so I might as well call him now.

"Tim Scathy Private Investigations, Chance Industries. How can I help you?"

"Tim, Tristan here."

"Oh hi Tristan what can I do for you today?"

"I need you to find someone for me."

"Okay who?"

"Steve Brandt, lead guitarist from-"

"Sexual Encounter. Yeah I know of him."

"Good then. I need you to find him but I don't want him to know we're looking."

"Oh… okay." He hesitates briefly. "Do you mind if I ask why?"

"He is in breach of his contract amongst other things."

"Okay."

"This is not to be repeated. I recently found out he's been sexually assaulting women using a date rape drug. He attacked a friend of mine. He left my house in a rush after the attack was stopped but before we were able to call the cops. We will involve the cops eventually but not until I know where he is. I want to find him first."

"Sure no problem, Tristan. I'll find him. How's your friend?"

"She's remarkably well and strong." The statement could not be truer of anyone. With the type of life Sophia briefly explained, it has been a hard life. "Tim, I don't have to tell you to keep this on the down low. I want no one knowing about it just yet."

"I hear you, no problem."

"Great, I want weekly updates. If you need more information on him, we own Sexual Encounter's record contract. Check with Entertainment to find out more on him."

"Okay, I will. Anything else?"

"No, that's it. But keep me in formed of your progress. Have a good day."

"You too. Bye." The call is disconnected. I trust Tim to use discretion when dealing with the Steve situation. The work he has done in the past has been top notch. I have no doubt Tim will find the bastard..

The papers I picked up need to be signed immediately but I need to speak with my father about what the implications are. I want it clear that when I assume this position it is not just a title in name only but as functioning CEO. Hitting my father's number, Kaitlyn stirs slightly but does not wake.

"Hello son." My father answers his cell phone on the first ring. "How are things going?"

"Hi, dad. How are you feeling?"

"Mostly good, but don't worry about me. You need to worry about the contracts and Kaitlyn. You're undertaking an important position and starting a new relationship. Were you able to pick up the documents I had delivered to the loft?"

"Yes, we stopped there on our way out here. It seems other items were also sent along. There were contracts for me to review, projects to look at and more." He hears the sarcasm in my voice about the other papers.

He chuckles lightly. "I thought they might do that when I requested the documents be drawn and delivered. Just make sure you sign the documents I sent." He knew about the others but did not say anything. Is he testing me again? I hope this is not what I have to look forward to, the constant testing from my father. "Those need to be signed and returned before you start on Monday. The rest you could either review so you get ahead or you could wait until you start."

"Thanks. I want to make sure the new position is as a functioning CEO and not just a title or lackey for you or the board?" He laughs proudly.

"There's my son. You take right after your old man, son. There is no doubt in my mind you'll do well especially after what you just said." He sounds proud. "Basically, it states you are everything. It is your responsibility to run the company as you see fit. The board will help you make decisions and guide you but you have final say in all aspects. Once you sign it is your company."

"It means a lot that you and mom have such faith in me. I'll sign them and have them delivered back to the offices."

"Son, can I make a suggestion though?"

"Sure what?"

"Read everything that was sent. You might be able to get ahead slightly." *As long as it does not interfere with my time with Kaitlyn.* This is supposed to be about romancing her and getting better acquainted before all the craziness begins. It's not much time but we need what we can get. "Don't misunderstand me. Enjoy your time with Kaitlyn but when she is otherwise occupied get some reading in." He seems to read my thoughts.

"I'll see what I can do. I've not been involved in the day to day business, but I have been keeping abreast of the goings on around there. But let me go we are nearly there."

"Have fun. I'll see you on Sunday. Will you think about bringing Kaitlyn by for dinner?"

"We'll see how things go, but I'll see you on Sunday."

"Goodbye son."

"Oh wait dad, when do you start chemotherapy again?"

"Thursday, so I'll have the weekend to recuperate."

"Great thanks dad, I'll check in during the week. Tell mom I said hi."

"Will do. Goodbye."

We disconnect just as I pull into the marina. Kaitlyn looks so peaceful that waking her seems shameful. I lightly caress her cheek with the back of my hand. She seems like such the Angel. How could anyone ever want to hurt her?

"Kaitlyn, honey we're here. Time to wake up." I lean in to nuzzle her neck.

"Hmmm." She stretches her arms over her head and her tee shirt rides up exposing her flat stomach. *Hmmm is right.* "Where are we?"

"We're here." I answer without really answering. She looks perplexed and I chuckle again. Before her, laughing did not seem important or necessary. Since we first met, I am laughing more now than I have in the last year.

Opening the car door for her, she climbs out and I guide her through the maze all sizes and types of boats. The sea air smells fresh and the sun is bright. We walk hand in hand down the docks to the end of the marina. She appears excited. Her eyes betray all her emotions.

"Sailing?" She asks.

"Yes, I hope you don't mind. I love to sail and wanted you to experience it with me." Her expression is off slightly. "Kaitlyn, what's wrong?"

"I... I... I've never been on a boat. It just doesn't seem safe."

Kissing her forehead, I respond. "You just have to look pretty." Climbing on board, I offer her my hand to help her. Electricity shoots through us as our hands clasp each other.

"It doesn't feel like its rocking." Amazement shines through her eyes.

I laugh because she truly is surprised. "The larger the boat the less it rocks. Do you like?"

"I always thought all boats rock and I would get sea sick. But I don't feel anything." She seems relieved. "It's huge. Are you going to drive it alone?"

Laughing I answer her cute question. "First of all, we don't drive it, we sail it and secondly, yes, we are going to sail it, you and I. You'll help me but before the week is out you'll be able to sail it yourself if you had to."

Looking dubiously at me she walks around the deck admiring it all. She mutters more to herself than to me. "I can do this."

"Yes, you can. Come below I want to show you our quarters."

"Our quarters?" She arches one brow in question.

"Yes, our quarters. We'll be spending every night together, Miss Daniels. I don't like being parted from you."

I take her hand and smiling she follows without question. "Here is the galley and living space." The wooden floors and sleek cabinetry make the kitchen modern. The living space is spacious and offers modern furniture and electronics. There is a large flat screen television. Next, we pass the twin bunks and the main bathroom. Finally, after showing her the office off the master cabin, we enter the master suite.

The focal point of the master suite is the oversized king bed. There are closets which hold our clothing and built in drawers for our undergarments and a few other necessary items. Placing my iPhone in the docking station on one of the night stands, I find one of my favorite play lists. Music is heard throughout the sailboat. She opens the door to the bathroom and I hear her gasp.

"This is beautiful. Did you know there is a Jacuzzi tub in here large enough for at least two people? Double sinks and a separate toilet closet. Never have I seen anything this amazing."

I think she forgot I own the boat, so I laugh. "Yes, I know about the tub and I'm glad you like. Later tonight we can try it together if you like."

"Yes, I think I would like that, Mr. Chance." She smiles coyly at me. Next she moves to the closets. Upon opening it, she gasps again this time at the clothing and shoes. "Tristan, what have you done?"

Coming up behind her and grabbing her by the waist. She leans into me and I nibble her neck. Moving her head slightly to the side, she offers me better access. Not being able to help myself, I kiss along on her throat to her collar bone where I suck gently. She moans and tries to turn around but I lock her in my arms. My hands come up to cup her breast and she arches forward allowing me better access. God this woman is breath taking in her responsiveness to my advances. I need to break this interlude before we miss the sunset. She pouts at me and I smile to myself.

"I've done nothing except provide you with clothing as promised. This is just the beginning. To be honest Sophia had to tell me your sizes and the shopper did the rest. However, she didn't know why I needed them." She turns around to read my expression and hers appears troubled by something. I am beginning to read her expressions and this one is about the distance she feels from her friends. "Don't you think maybe you should call her or Lara? They were very worried about you."

"I don't want to talk about it now. Can we save it for later?" She pulls away not wanting me to see her face.

"I'll let it go for now but we'll discuss this later." We leave the bedroom. The intimate moment between us is gone, for now. There is much to do to get under way. "Come above with me. We need to get going so we can watch the sunset." She starts to follow me but stops in the galley.

"Wait, what did you mean by the beginning?" The comment is only now registering in her thoughts.

"Well, as my girlfriend I get to spoil you and since I am new to this relationship thing, I think I may go overboard. So bear with me."

"Tristan, I don't feel comfortable with you spending your money on me. I don't want you buying me things it will make me feel bought. The only thing I want or need is you. Please don't buy me anything else without asking me first."

"Kaitlyn, it's my money and I'll spend it where and how I see fit. Don't ask me not to buy you things. What happens if we're out somewhere and I see something I think you might like? I can't buy it?"

"Okay, I see your point but it has to be within reason. Nothing crazy, please." She begs and pleads. *God how can I say no to her looking like that?* But I have to otherwise I tie my own hands. Her car has already been replaced without her knowing. If she did not have the scholarships I would have paid off her loans. Nothing will ever be enough for this woman.

"I'll keep it within reason, my reasoning. End of discussion."

"Fine." She huffs and changes the subject. "Can I get us something to drink and maybe a snack?"

"Angel, this sailboat is yours as well. Please help yourself to anything there is." Leaving her to throw a snack and some drinks together for us, I climb above to start this trip.

When she comes above later and looks for me, she has a tray of cheese, apple slices and crackers. She hands me a soda and keeps one for herself. While she was down there she must have gone back to the suite to freshen up because her hair has been tied back. I like it better loose. The wind is blowing as the boat glides along the water. I had just raised the sails prior to her coming up on deck. As she sits next to me, the wind is blowing through her hair and her cheeks are slightly flushed. Some of her hair has come undone from the tie and frames her face perfectly. *God she looks perfect.*

"Where are we going?" She asks.

"Nowhere in particular, just east, further out to sea. I figured we could see where the wind takes us. Are you up for that? We'll have to make a pit stop some place to drop off the documents after I have signed them."

"Yes, I am up for anything. You're in control." My nostrils flare at her simple innocent comment. If she only knew what she just relinquished to me.

We have been sailing for almost an hour and I'm starting to get hungry. The sun should be setting in about an hour. Dinner was prepared prior to our departure by the caretaker and is in the refrigerator. There is also champagne and strawberries in a light chocolate sauce for dessert.

"Dinner is in the refrigerator. Would you mind heating it up while I stay here and navigate?" I wink at her. "Or you could navigate?"

"Sure no problem, I'll heat dinner." Ignoring my comment, she continues. "Do I have to do anything special?"

"No, just think of it as a kitchen on land." She leans over to kiss me, grabs the dishes from our snack and then disappears below deck to get dinner ready.

--- --- --- ----

Kaitlyn

This kitchen is a cooks dream. It does not feel like a boat's galley. Heating dinner is easy, all I had to do is preheat the oven and put it in for about an hour. There is dessert and some champagne chilling in the refrigerator. After I put dinner in the oven, I go back to our cabin to freshen up again.

I cannot believe he bought me all these clothes. There is a brand new wardrobe here complete with matching shoes and bags. Where does he plan on taking me? Sophia will be surprised and delighted to know she contributed to my new digs in some way. She has been trying to get me to buy name brands since forever but I could never afford them. Well, Tristan has taken care of that and more. Part of me is delighted he did this for me but the other half feels cheap and bought. I don't know how to handle him buying me more things. He seems to go overboard.

The bathroom holds all the essentials a woman would need which costs a small fortune because everything is name brand again. The shampoo alone cost more than a month's supply of my normal shampoo. He has thought of everything. In such a short time this man has completely gotten under my skin and in my thoughts. Last night was amazing and I'm looking forward to what tonight might bring. The only problem with last night was when Steve appeared in my thoughts for that short period of time. I saw how much it hurt Tristan and I have to endeavor not to share those thoughts again. He feels so responsible. *But how do I stop the memories?*

Tristan is such a good man. I contemplate this while fixing my hair back into the pony tail. From what I remember of the few articles I ever read about him, the paparazzi have painted him as this cold hearted man slut. After the way he treated me last night, I cannot see how those articles could have even an ounce of truth to them. He has made some comments about his past but nothing too extreme. I mean the night at Tyler's party was enough to turn anyone off. Had he not came after me and been so persistent, I don't know if we would be here now. Who am I kidding? Before I knew his name I was attracted to him. We connected at the store, club, and beach and I was hooked then without even knowing him.

Looking at myself in the mirror I cannot help but wonder what does he see in me? I am so plain without an ounce of makeup on. My hair is pulled back in a ponytail, my favorite hairstyle. My clothing is seriously less than spectacular and offers no clue as to my shape underneath. I have never run in the same social circles as him, unless you include Sophia and Lara but even then it is limited. I'm so afraid I'll embarrass him or myself on some level.

The oven timer chimes. The smells wafting from there are divine. I could get use to this. Cooking at home is always a chore. Don't get me wrong, I am good at it and like to do it when I don't have to, but I have never experimented with it. Sophia and Lara have told me numerous times that if medicine does not work out then maybe I should become a chef. I know how to pay him back. Tomorrow I will cook him a gourmet breakfast with all the trimmings. The refrigerator is stocked with everything imaginable.

Putting the dishes on the tray along with the food, I venture back up on deck careful not to drop or spill anything. Once up here I look around for him and notice he is lowering the sails. We have stopped moving. The wind has died down. Tristan looks like the Greek God Poseidon. His muscles are flexing with his movements, accentuating the cut of them and he is my….. boyfriend. He is mine. How is it possible that a specimen as fine as him would want me? There has to be something I am missing. He assures me it is just me and only me. *Wow there is someone watching over me from above.*

CHAPTER TWELVE

Tristan

Dinner on the forward deck was romantic. The food was delicious, the company was even better and the conversation was easy. We learned each other's likes and dislikes. What our goals and dreams were prior to meeting each other. It seems they may have changed slightly since we met.

"So we said we would speak of them later and now is later."

"Them?" I have caught her unawares.

"Sophia and Lara."

"I know I have to talk about it and to them eventually, but I really don't want to right now." She sighs petulantly. The look I give her has no room for discussion or debate. "Fine, they hurt me and I'm upset with them. If they would have noticed what happened or if they paid some attention to me then this would not have happened."

"Right, and then you and I would not be here now."

"We were already on our way to meeting each other. Fate was seeing to that all on her own. Don't get me wrong I'm happy for them but I always watch out for them and question them when they want to leave with some guy. I always know where they are." She pauses then sighs. "Not that it has happened but if I was talking to a guy like they were, I would still have paid attention to them. I know it sounds like I'm jealous but really I'm not." She smiles up at me.

"Kaitlyn, they feel awful about everything that happened. But you have t-"

"They never even came to look for me. Why didn't they ask around? That hurts the most." She turns away from me and starts to clear the dishes but I hear her sniffle.

"Sophia came to my room after you were already in there passed out. I told her I left you back at Lara's. I was pretty rude to her so she wouldn't question me further. She did however tell me if I hurt you she would do bodily harm to me." She snickers and sniffles at that. When she turns back around I can see she is trying to suppress her tears.

"You know she would, right?"

"Yeah, she can be scary when she's angry or upset. When I went to Lara's yesterday to find out where you would go, she and Lara nearly attacked me. If Danny and Tyler weren't there to hold them back, I think I would've been hurt."

"Oh." She ponders this for a while then says, "I'll call them tomorrow. Tonight, it's just about us. It should have been just us Saturday night. You know, when I left you on the beach on Saturday morning, I knew I had to see you and I had every intention of coming to your party. Regardless of what Sophia or Lara had to say, we were going. I have never acted like that with anyone. You brought out a side of me that…"

"That what, Miss Daniels?"

"That I like, Mr. Chance." Her comment hangs in the air between us while we both mull it over.

The sun has almost finished its demise and I sit with one knee bent leaning back on one arm with Kaitlyn in the crook of my arms and legs. My arms wrap around her as I lean forward to inhale her intoxicating scent. She is shielded from the sudden gust of wind by my body. Watching the sunset has mesmerized us both by its beauty into a state of tranquility. She leans her head back and kisses me under the chin. I turn her head so I can kiss her lips.

Exploring her mouth has become one of my favorite past times. Withdrawing slightly, she turns around and lifts her legs so her thighs are resting on mine. Taking the opportunity she has given me, I cup her cheeks with both my hands and pull her towards me. I cover her lips with mine, parting them and sliding my tongue in, she groans. Her hands are roaming over my body causing my muscles to tighten like bowstrings. She lifts the shirt over my head to gain better access to my chest and she initiates kissing my neck and shoulders.

Imitating my moves from last night, she places feather light kisses along my neck and chest, slightly sucking as she ventures. *She is a quick learner.* I lift her shirt over her head leaving her in her bra only. The cool ocean air causes her nipples to harden. We are in the middle of the ocean with no one around. I kiss along her neckline to her shoulder. Her touch arouses me more than words can say and she shivers under my touch. "Are you cold?" Her only answer is to nod no. My other hand cups her breast and fondles it gently. As she moans and pulls herself closer to me, I realize we need to take this inside before I can't stop. I don't want her first time being on the hard deck.

I pull away slightly and start to rise. She looks confused not understanding what I'm doing. Her lips are red and swollen from my kisses. I offer her my hand to help her rise. She takes it and I lead her down to our quarters. Upon opening the door, I turn around to pull her sharply against me so our bodies are in complete alignment. I can feel every curve of her body and it ignites my body further and I ravage her mouth. Playing with her tongue, my tongue wants more. Our shirts have long been forgotten. I reach behind her and unclasp her bra. She lowers her arms and lets it glide off. Her tits are bared to me. I can't help but stare at the perfect globes with pink nipples that have hardened by her aroused state.

As I drop to my knees, I bury my head in the valley between her tits. Next my hands find their way to the waist band of her shorts, unbuttoning and unzipping them, the shorts come easily off leaving her standing only in her underwear. Grabbing her ass, I pull her closer and inhale her scent. I don't think I will ever forget her scent. I hook my thumbs in the elastic band of her panties and lower them while looking her directly in the eyes.

She steps gracefully out them then walks around me towards the bed. Climbing on it on all fours, she looks back at me with a fierce desire, finally settling on her back with her knees slightly bent in the middle of the bed. I will never forget that look as long as I live; it has been permanently seared in my mind. I don't think I have ever seen any look, look as sexually seductive and innocent at the same time. Not knowing the view she is affording me I nearly come in my shorts watching her. She crooks her finger at me to join her. *When did she become the seductress?*

I swear if I did not know she was a virgin, I would think she has done this before. Looking down at her on the bed naked has me removing my shorts quickly, leaving only my boxer briefs. I climb on the bed similar to how she had done. Stopping between her legs, she surprises me by opening them further. Looking down at me watching my movements, she again crooks her finger at me to venture further up. So I follow her command, for now. With this being her first time, I let her take the lead.

Coming up to lie slightly on her, she whispers in my ear. "Make love to me Tristan, please." *God she has completely undone me.*

"Oh Angel, I plan to but first I want to savor every inch of you." Ravaging her lips, I slide my hand between her legs to find her wet and ready for me. *God she is so responsive.*

While kissing her, I insert a finger deep into her wet folds. *So tight.* As I work her, trying to open her wider, she begins to move against my hand. Sucking her bottom lip into my mouth I add a second finger hoping to loosen her opening a bit more so when I enter her for the first time it won't be as painful. She gasps and moans triggering my need to taste her.

Kissing my way down her delectable body, I stop at her tits and suck on both of them taking my time until they pucker in response. Next, I place open-mouthed kisses at her hips. She starts to try to wiggle away as she catches on to my final destination. I withdraw my fingers and she shivers at the loss. I lift her leg bending her knee to bring her foot better into view. I slide between her legs and kiss the top of her foot, then behind her knee and finally to the inside of her thigh. I repeat this to the other leg. After her thigh I move closer to her folds, where I place a kiss above her mound giving her time to become accustomed to the new sensations I am eliciting in her.

Before she can think too much on my final destination, I gently lick her outer lips. "Sweet as cream, Angel, as I knew it would taste." She gasps shocked and tries to move away. I secure her by wrapping my arms around her legs, pulling her closer to my mouth. I suck on her bud causing her to moan. Alternating between sucking and licking, she soon grabs my head by the hair and I chuckle lightly while gently inserting a finger back into her. Flicking my tongue over her sensitized bud, she starts to thrash so I insert another finger curving them slightly. She is close to the edge. She moans her release as I move my fingers in and out of her causing her to orgasm.

--- --- --- ----

Kaitlyn

God I cannot believe he just did that. My second orgasm and it was better than the first. The sensations he provokes are so hard to describe. Nothing has ever prepared me for them. As I slowly float back to earth from my orgasm, he opens the bedside table draw and withdraws something. Then I hear a ripping sound. He has removed his underwear and as I look at him with what I am sure are lust filled eyes he is rolling on a condom. *Oh my God that won't fit.* He climbs over me and kisses right below my ear while whispering in my ear. "Now Angel, you will be mine and only mine." Hearing those words causes a smile to appear evaporating my fears because I am so happy to be his. He eases himself into me very slowly allowing me time to adjust to this new invasion. It is an incredible feeling. I am starting to feel needy again. *Can I really want this again, so soon?*

He stops and whispers to me. "I'm sorry baby." And then he thrusts forward causing me to gasp at the surprise. There was a slight pinch followed by fullness. I am trying to adjust to this new invasive feeling. But by the time he asks me, "Are you okay?" I have adjusted and start to move against him. I want him to move but he stops me. When he does not move, I understand he's waiting for an answer. When I look at him, I can see the thin thread of control he is holding onto starting to disintegrate.

"Yes, is that it?" I try to move again. No luck. He holds my hips in a vise like grip

"No, that was just me pushing through your innocence. I want to make sure you are okay before I start to move."

"It was supposed to hurt but all I felt was a slight pinch. I need you to move please." I beg him.

"I'm happy to hear that baby but how does this feel?" He starts to move and almost slides all the way out then back in.

"Oh God, Tristan that's amazing." I groan out loudly breathing heavy. "Please more." Taking this as his cue, he moves slowly at first making me slowly build again. I glide my hands down his back and rake my nails back up. He sinks deeper into me during the next thrust when I open my legs wider for him. My feet are firmly planted on the mattress so I can lift my hips to meet his thrusts. I cup his backside to pull him in even deeper and hold him there while I grind my hips against his. Searching for just the right spot to push me over the edge, he grinds back. Moaning loudly, he pulls back and thrust back deeply. I barely hold on and start to crest the wave. My muscles are beginning to clench down on him. He moves faster, deeper and harder. Our thrusts are in unison. A light sheen of sweat has formed above my brow and my breathing is labored. Our bodies are slick with sweat and his breaths are coming in pants.

"Come now for me Angel." He demands, thrusting once, twice, three times, "Come now!" I come screaming his name over and over while clenching around him. This is better than the other two orgasms I have had. It seems to just keep going. Then I feel him coming inside me and he triggers another orgasm. *Is that even possible?* The things this man can do to me. I am somewhere in the upper atmosphere floating not wanting to come down.

--- --- --- ----

Tristan

Knowing she is screaming my name only spikes my pleasure further and pushes me over the edge. If this woman bewitched me before she totally owns me now. I think she may have ruined me for other women, not that I could even think about anyone else now or probably ever.

"Tristan... Oh God don't stop... Yes Tristan..." I'm coming so hard now with my own release I gasp for air. Never have I had an orgasm this fierce before. She has me anchored so deep in her by her hands that even if I wanted to, which I don't, I cannot move. Both of us are returning back to earth slowly. I lower my forehead to hers and feel her heart pounding in her chest.

"Are you okay?" She just nods her head unable to speak just yet. "Good, I don't think I can move yet." She just nods again and I chuckle. Eventually I slide off her and lie next to her with my arm across her waist. Hearing her sigh, I gently kiss her.

She rolls on to her side and snuggles closer to me. She wriggles her behind against me and my dick sparks to life again. "Thank you, that was amazing," she murmurs and then her breathing evens out and I know she has fallen asleep. I lay there listening to her breathing thinking this is perfect.

That was the most amazing sexual experience I have ever had. She is mine, never been touched by another man. Never have I experienced anything close to this. I knew when I first met her, she was different and things with her would be different but I never knew how different.

Our future is so unsure but the chemistry is palpable. We both are about to enter new phases in our lives triggering drastic unknown changes to occur which will affect our futures. The thought of her with anyone else is very unsettling. No one can have her, not now. This has to work, I will make it work. I have marked her as mine. As if she heard my thoughts, she moves her head to the side and there on her collar bone is a love mark I left unknowingly and I can't help but smile at it. *Marked indeed.*

Reluctantly, I disengage myself from her, kiss her lips, slip on my shorts and leave the room. Up on deck, everything is still secure and the anchor is holding tight. I double check the sails and ensure they are still tied down. I gather our dishes and bring them down below to the galley. I make myself a cup of coffee and grab the documents we picked up earlier. Normally, I would prefer a drink but I feel so intoxicated by what just took place I don't need the alcohol. Making my way back up deck, I start to review them while sipping my coffee. They appear to be just what my father said and my signature now appears on the ones sent by him.

Wow, it's all mine. My father will still receive a sum on a consulting basis but besides that he has officially retired. My parents want to "downsize" with the house. They asked that I take the house but I am not ready yet. What are they thinking? Abigail now lives at home with them. I hear Kaitlyn approach me from behind. When she comes into view, I swear she is a vision in one of my button down shirts that barely covers her mid-thigh. The shirt is only buttoned half way up. I can see the curve of her breast beneath it. "What are you doing out here?" She asks.

"I was reading some of the documents while you slept. Sorry I wasn't there. I didn't want to wake you. You sort of passed out after. How are you feeling?" I ask her concern ringing in my voice.

"Fine. I passed out?" She smiles shyly.

"Yes, shortly after. You should be proud; most women don't orgasm during their first time and you had two." She turns crimson.

"Don't be embarrassed. I'm proud to have been the reason for them."

"I want more." She starts to straddle my legs but I stop her because no matter how I would love to bury myself deep in her again, I won't hurt her.

"I want to give you more, so much more believe me, but I think we should wait until tomorrow. I don't want to hurt you." She looks down at her feet nervously. "What is it Kaitlyn?"

"Uh… was… uh… was… was I okay?" I can't help but chuckle inside at her innocence.

"Oh Angel, you were more than okay. I could not have asked for more." I open my arms for her to join me and when she does I kiss her lightly. "You were amazing. I want to do it again and more. But we really need to wait and allow you time to heal. Are sure you aren't sore?"

"I'm not even a little bit sore." She smiles up at me. "Do you mind if I stay here with you for a while?"

"No, of course not. Do you want to talk?"

"No, I just want to be here with you. Please, finish reading. You have much to read before the weekend." Looking out at the dark sea and feeling her in my arms have me put me in a state of pure bliss. I cannot live without this, without her. God this happened so fast. I find myself playing with her hair as I read. She has completely rattled my world but completed it as well.

After a while she drifts off to sleep and my eyes are feeling heavy. I lift her and the documents without waking her and go below deck. Dropping the documents on the table in the galley, I proceed to the cabin still carrying her. Pulling back the covers, I place her gently on the bed. She stirs only slightly when I gently unbutton my shirt and slip it off her. I always sleep naked and now I want nothing more than to feel her warm skin against my body as I sleep. I pull the covers up and unfortunately cover her delicious body. My dick springs to life just looking at her. She rolls onto her stomach reaching out for me in her sleep. Chuckling softly at her, I climb in next to her. I lift her arm and place it across my abdomen. She sighs and I drift off to sleep at some point.

--- --- --- ----

Kaitlyn

My dreams were so peaceful, I did not wake once. When my eyes flutter open, I am confused as to where I am. It only takes a few minutes to remember where I am and that I'm not alone. Tristan is moving up the back of my legs and the feelings he invoked in me last night come crashing back. I look over my shoulder to see him kissing the back of my knees. Groaning, he looks up at me and smiles.

"Good morning Angel, how are you feeling this morning?" He continues his slow and steady ascent up my legs.

"Hmm, good. I like waking up to this and I could definitely get used to it." He bites me gently just below my ass cheek. I yelp. "Hey, watch it." He kisses the area only to bite harder on the other cheek. When I yelp again he kisses the area and chuckles. "Hey, don't leave any bite marks. I don't want to have to get a tetanus or rabies shot because you got carried away."

"Smart ass. I think I may have to teach you a lesson or two." He does not stop his attack. He continues to kiss his way further up my back, nipping along the way. Feeling his weight press me into the mattress, causes my sex to light up. I arch my neck around so I can appreciate him better. He lightly nips the back of my shoulder and then finally makes it to my lips, but I pull away slightly. "Bathroom." I mutter not wanting him to get a whiff of my morning breath.

He laughs outright at me, causing all his weight to crush me as he lays on top of me, head buried between my shoulder blades. *Way to ruin the moment Kaitlyn.* He eventually rolls off me and calms his amusement to a snicker. "Go use the bathroom, Miss Daniels."

"Thanks." I wiggle out from underneath him making sure not to talk in his direction. As I brush my teeth, the Jacuzzi reminds me of his promise to take a bath last night. A hot bath sounds enticing and should soothe my sore muscles. With a mouth full of toothpaste, I see if I can tempt him to a bath. *Sexy Kaitlyn, real sexy.* "We forgot our bath last night."

I look at him from the doorway waiting for an answer and when he does not answer promptly I turn around to spit in the sink unsure if he heard me or not. While rinsing my mouth, he enters without making a sound, startling me when I look up and he is directly behind me.

He starts to run the bath while still naked and Tristan naked is a wonderful sight producing frissons of desire. His hard body is perfection with tight abdominal muscles, toned legs, perfect butt and strong arms. It is every woman's fantasy made real. We make eye contact in the mirror. I feel a blush creeping up my neck and cheeks as he catches me staring. He has added wonderfully scented bath salts that permeate the bathroom.

As he approaches me again, I turn around facing him. His beautiful green eyes have darkened to the color of emeralds. I place my hands behind me on the counter for support as he cups my cheeks and starts to kiss me. "A bath will help soothe your sore muscles today." *Wait I never mentioned being sore, did I?*

"Hmm. Sounds good to me. But I'm not sore." I hold to this lie. "Will you be joining me?" He looks at me curiously.

"Who is going to wash your back and massage your shoulders if I'm not in there with you?" *Sounds deliciously nice.* He takes my hand leading me into the tub and I settle myself in, relaxing. "Move forward, Angel."

Moving forward enough for him to climb in behind me, he settles his legs alongside mine and pulls me snug against his chest. *Wow!* "This feels heavenly." I sigh numb, until I feel his hands slide up my waist to settle under my breasts. When his hand dips below the water and starts to caress my bud, I shiver.

All of a sudden feeling shy, I shoot forward. Using the soap, I start to clean myself but he grabs it from my hand resuming where my task left off. "What's wrong? Did I do something wrong?"

"Noth… nothing. I really don't know what came over me all of a sudden."

"Kaitlyn, I have seen, felt, kissed and tasted almost every inch of you. There is no reason to be shy or embarrassed. Are you sore?" I blush scarlet at his comments.

"You're right, I was embarrassed. But I'm not sore." To prove my point, I swivel around to face him. His eyes are burning with an intense passion. His gaze drops to my breasts. Taking the soap from his hand, I begin to lather my hands and start my own exploration of his body. I start at his shoulders and work my way to his arms and back up to his chest. Next, my hands sensually start at his feet. My foot has started caressing his shaft as my hands continue working their way up towards his groin but stop just below it. He is hard. I pull myself real close to him, close enough he could enter me. I see the conflict and lust in his eyes as to whether or not he should but the moment passes. Leaning back slightly, I begin on his chest and abdomen. I am about to grip his shaft when he grabs my hand.

"I think I can handle that on my own. No need in starting something you can't finish."

"Can't finish? Says who?" I ask seductively. He raises that brow at me questioningly.

Oh he wants me for sure. His eyes are smoldering. The temperature in the room rises ten degrees. I start to wash my hair leaning my head back. This proves to be too much for him. He needs to touch me and rinses my hair of all shampoo, dragging this out. Then he pounces on me splashing water over the sides of the Jacuzzi and surprising me with his intense need for me.

"Minx." He mutters under his breath. "Doesn't know what's good for you."

I can't help but smile up at him. He kisses me breathless then climbs out of the tub just as quickly. He wraps a towel around his waist and offers me his hand. Taking his hand, I step out of the tub and he wraps me in a towel. He leans against the counter watching me and thinking. *This is my opportunity.*

In one fluid motion, I have opened his towel to reveal his already erect shaft and dropped to my knees in front of him. I take him into my mouth and start to suck him as he did last night to me. In the background I hear him inhale sharply with surprise and I smile to myself. Being a novice at this, my instinct, which helped me last night, is guiding me. I start to wonder if I am doing this correctly when he starts to moan. "Fuck Angel. That feels good."

He grabs a fist full of my hair and starts to move himself back and forth plunging like he did last night. We continue like this for a couple of minutes. Before I know it, he pulls out of my mouth leaving a slightly salty taste behind and lifts me off the ground. Placing me on the counter top, opening my legs wide, he buries himself deep in me. Every inch of him is plunged repeatedly into me and his deep groan is the most erotic sound my ears have heard. He pushes me forward and I gasp out loud. He looks at me sternly and questions me harshly, "Are you sore?"

"No, you took me by surprise that's all." I lie. He just stares at me trying to discern the truth.

Eventually we move in sync on the counter top and the soreness has all but subsided replaced by an aching building need. He is so close. I wrap my legs around his waist pulling him harder and deeper in me. He tries to pull back but I lock him in place while I move against him. Our eyes lock onto each other.

--- --- --- ----

Tristan

This woman has taken my control. She is so passionate and giving. I could have gone in her mouth but she is too innocent for that. My dominant side is itching to take control of her but she needs to feel secure before I take the reins. Hard as it may be to allow her this control, I know it is only temporary. Her eyes are heavy with passion. Just as she is cresting, I start to move again hurtling us over the edge towards orgasm.

"Oh God, Tristan, Yes! Tristan! Don't stop!" She screams my name and I start shuddering.

"Kaitlyn!" Her name is a growl from my lips. My head is buried in the crook of her neck as I raggedly breathe. After a while I question her. "Where did you learn to do that?" She shrugs not saying anything.

"Was I okay?" She asks insecurely.

"Kaitlyn, were you okay? With your experience, you should have at least gagged once or twice baby. I'm sorry about that. I lost control." Pulling out of her I realize I never put a condom on. "Shit! Fuck!"

"What's wrong?" She asks perplexed.

"Shit, how could I have been so stupid?" Fuck, what was I

thinking? *That's the problem dickhead you weren't thinking. Well, you weren't thinking with the right head.* I rake my hands through my hair and pull on it while walking in circles thinking it out. I feel caged and need to leave this room before I do something I may regret. While walking through the door I punch it in frustration. The door swings close in my wake from the force of the punch. She gasps behind me but I'm too upset.

Cautiously she emerges from the bathroom with a towel wrapped securely around and I cannot look at her yet. I am pacing like the caged animal I feel I am.

"Tristan, what's wrong? Did I do something wrong?" She asks warily. When I finally face her and see the fear in her eyes, I start to feel bad for acting this way. She has no idea what I am thinking.

"No Angel, you didn't do anything wrong. It was me."

"What did you do then? Please you're scaring me and now you're ignoring me." She has no idea I could have just impregnated her.

"Please tell me you're on some sort of birth control?" I ask wistfully but it is edged with anger.

"No, I have never… OH!" Realization shows on her expression.

"Yes, oh. I forgot to put on a condom. I never forget one. I am very diligent in using them. No one is going to try to trap me with a pregnancy." I slept with a girl once who tried to pawn off her pregnancy as my problem. I was with her once and she didn't even know my name at the time. When she saw an article on me, that's when her lawyers started. I vowed I would never be put in that situation again.

Kaitlyn stalks about the room angry. Doesn't she realize I did not mean for this to happen. She yanks some clothing on ignoring me. I start to curse at her movements and her disregard for the gravity of our current problem. She could be pregnant. *Would that be so bad, if it was her? Would this be fate's way of working for us?*

--- --- --- ----

Kaitlyn

He follows me around the room and up on deck trying to get my attention as I try to escape him. He has no idea how the tirade he pulled in the bathroom reminded me of my parents. This is a conversation I do not want to have with him, ever. Although it would greatly hurt me, maybe even destroy me, hopefully he will get tired of me before I have to talk about my parents.

I have reached my breaking point with everything that has happened in the last couple of weeks and unfortunately he is the only target present so I lace into him. "Firstly, if you think that I am just trying to trap you by getting pregnant, then we have a bigger problem. I don't want or need a baby right now. My future is mapped out, thank you very much. I will be a doctor before I get pregnant. I have, and as you were witness to, never been with anyone else. I'm not the type of person who goes around having sex thinking 'okay let's try to trap this guy.' Secondly, I don't even know you that well yet. I may not even like you. So why would I try to trap you by having a baby with you. I'm not like the other women you have had sex with. They may want you for your money but I don't care about any of that."

How dare he compare me to other women he has slept with. "What I have in my life I've gotten by hard work and dedication. Not by lying on my back with my legs open or cheating my way through. I know what an unwanted pregnancy can do to a child, physically, emotionally and mentally. I know what it's like to not be wanted and to be told you ruined a life by being born. I've witnessed the destruction that follows when you tell a child you were a mistake. I know what that feels like damn it. Then to watch as it reduces a relationship to violence. So don't go accusing me of trying to get pregnant. Why would I inflict any of that on a child?"

Somewhere along the way I started crying. The tears are flowing spontaneously and I turn to move away but realize there is no place to go. I am stuck out here in the middle of nowhere with a man who thinks I am trying to trap him with a pregnancy. He reaches for me but I shy away. I cannot afford his touch right now. I will cave if he touches me now. Stiffly with tears I ask him, "Please take me home. I don't want be where I am not trusted."

"Kaitlyn, Angel, I trust you." He pleads with me. "I don't think you are trying to trap me, you misunderstood me."

"Misunderstood? How can I misunderstand that?" I yell back.

"Please let me explain. I'm the one who was irresponsible. I knew what I was doing but I lost control. I never lose control like that. I'm sorry you thought I meant you were trying to trap me." He's beseeching me to listen and believe him now. "I know that's not like you. If you were like that we wouldn't be here now." He tries again to reach for me. I am still too angry to accept his touch.

"Please Angel, listen to me. I would never do anything to hurt you. You have to believe me."

"Tristan you said some nasty things and they were directed at me. Even though you did not mention me specifically how could I misunderstand them?"

"Kaitlyn you have become an integral part of my life in such a short period of time. The thought of hurting you is abhorrent to me. Please you have to believe me. I'm angry with myself, never you." He tries once more to touch me but withdraws his hand afraid to be rejected again.

144

Slowly I walk over into his arms when I see the pain in his eyes. He hugs me to him like his life depends on it. *How could I ever remain mad at this man?* "Let me explain my anger a different way. You're not like anyone I've ever had sex with. What we just did was so spontaneous, that I lost control. Kaitlyn honey, I pride myself on my control in the bedroom and you make me loose it. What are you doing to me?"

"You hurt me Tristan. You made me sound like some, some... I don't know what, but someone not nice."

"I know, I'm so sorry. Can you forgive me?"

"Yes, but-"

"No buts, you forgive me." His smile is dazzling but then it fades to darkness. "Seriously, this is a problem. By some sort of luck are you on birth control?" Calculating in my head where I am in my cycle, my answer is not as forthcoming as he would like. "Kaitlyn, it's an easy question."

"I know and the answer is no, I'm not. I'm trying to figure where in my cycle I am to see if we have a problem or not." *My period was the end of June around the twenty-fourth.* "What's today's date?"

"July twentieth."

"Phew, we should be good. I'm due in about four days." Dawning realization about the topic of conversation makes me blush. I'm talking about my period with my boyfriend. As an adult this would be a normal topic but I have never had a boyfriend or discussed this with a man before. As soon as we get back I have to make an appointment with the doctor to get a prescription for birth control pills.

"Are you sure? I mean are you usually regular?" *How does he know so much about a woman's period?*

"Yes, Tristan. Now can we please change the subject from my expected period date to something else? I am really uncomfortable talking about this with you."

"You shouldn't be it, it concerns me as well. When we get back I'm making you an appointment with a doctor to discuss birth control options." I fume that he would think he has the right make that sort of appointment for me.

"Neanderthal, you will do no such thing. I have my own doctor whom I will see and discuss it with him. It does not concern you."

"Then tell me when it is because I want to be there for the discussion. I have-"

"Absolutely not! This is not about you and your body, but mine. So it does not involve you but me and only me."

"Kaitlyn be reasonable. It does concern me. I want to know the risks afforded to you, how accurate the pills are, and when they become effective."

"No. Do you think I'm stupid? Don't you think I would ask all those questions? Dammit Tristan, I'm studying to be a doctor. I know what questions to ask. I am very responsible. The answer is no Tristan, you're not coming with me to the doctors. End. Of. Story."

"Fine, for now. Make sure to find out how long you need to be on it before it's considered effective." He looks me in the eyes seriously. "Listen now and listen good, I have no intention of using a condom again with you. This was one of the most amazing sexual experiences I have ever had next to yesterday and this morning. Because it's you, I don't think I could go back to using one even if I wanted to." My jaw is somewhere on the floor and needs to be lifted closed with a crane. Secretly I'm happy with him for saying this. "Now, since you say we are in the clear, I want to do it again. This time I want to try something different."

Okay, what a drastic switch of emotions from him. "Ah okay…. What do you have in mind?"

"Come with me."

CHAPTER THIRTEEN

Kaitlyn

He grabs my hand and pulls me to the suite. Gently he tosses me on the bed. As I lay there, he starts to search the drawers looking for something. My anxiety level is growing with each passing moment he does not touch me. When he enters the closet, I hear items being moved and shuffled around. I jump once as something crashes to the floor. "Fuck, that hurt."

"Hey, can I help look for whatever you're looking for?"

"No, just stay there and don't move." He demands from the closet.

"Okay, okay, I won't move. Touchy much." I mutter to myself. He peeks his head out from behind the closet door to glare at me clearly hearing my comment.

"Watch that sassy mouth of yours. It is going to get you in trouble sooner rather than later." I smile sassily back at him as he resumes his search. "Aha, I found it! Now close your eyes."

"Really? Come on. Fine!" I sigh exasperated when he glares again at me. "They're closed. Happy?"

"Very. Now keep them closed." I can hear him coming closer and feel the bed dip as he sits on it. He trails a soft silky cloth of some sort up my body from my groin to my neck. He leaves the cloth across my neck. "Don't open your eyes no matter what?"

Okay now he has me freaked slightly. What is he planning? "What are you doing?"

"Right now, I am taking your clothes off."

"Ohh."

He makes quick work of removing my shirt and shorts. The satin cloth is removed from around my neck and placed across my eyes. "Lift your head."

I obediently do as he asks. He ties the cloth snuggly behind my head. "You can't see can you?"

"No."

"Good. Now I want to test the senses without the sense of sight. The sense of touch, sound, smell and taste. Are you ready Angel?"

Kinky fucker isn't he. "Yes. Bring it on."

"So confident. Let's see. Hmmm… I'm forgetting something. Oh that's right you can't touch anything only feel it." The bed shifts as he rises. He strides to the closet again only to return quickly. He grabs my arm and ties it to the head board. My breathing starts to increase when he grabs the other arm. "Angel, are you okay?"

"I… I… I'm fine."

"I'm not going to hurt you. You know that right?"

"Yes. It's just freaky not being able to move or see."

"This is also about trust. Do you trust me?"

I revisit everything this man has done and said to me since I have met him. I remind myself how my grandparents trusted him with my safety. I am reminded of every small and big detail he has done. *Do I trust him?*

"Implicitly." And I relax almost immediately.

"Good answer." He kisses my forehead. His hands start to roam over my bra and down my legs. Next his teeth gently graze my nipple causing a shot of desire to spike through me. It was so unexpected I think my panties melted away. My bra is removed and he bites and sucks on each nipple. They are radiating heat from his ministrations.

"Ohhh!!! God that's cold. What the fuck?" He chuckles at my reaction to the ice cubes he rubbed over each nipple simultaneously.

"Language Kaitlyn." He chides me. "What was it?"

"Ice cubes." I force out. "You've made me all wet." *What a pun.*

"Oh no baby I haven't made you wet enough yet." I can hear the seductive smile in his words. My underwear is ripped from my body and I do mean ripped. The dainty lace tearing.

"What the hell, those were one of my favorites." What the hell has gotten into him?

"Don't worry Angel, I'll replace them. I'm glad your sense of hearing is working fine. Now it's time for taste." Hmm, what can he want me to taste? The bed shifts again as he rises, I am sure to get something for me to taste.

The bed dips again as he returns but it dips near my feet. "Oh God, don't stop." He starts sucking my bud and then licks.

"Mmmm… tastes heavenly Angel. Like sugar and cream."

"Hmm…. I'm not complaining but you said this was about my

senses."

"Well, I could stop and try something else if you like?" He stops his delicious attack just long enough for me to cry out in disappointment.

--- --- --- ----

Tristan

The trust she has placed in me after such a short time since her near rape undoes me. This woman is the end all for me. I will never find this feeling with another person. I keep recalling my father's and Cole's comments about finding the one.

This game started off as testing her senses and teaching her control but seeing her tied to my bed causes such an intense desire in me to claim her it forces me to speed things up. This game is not going to last long. I need to regain some of my control. I place an ice cube on her navel.

"Ohh, that's cold."

"I know but you can't move. The ice is going to melt quickly and pool in your navel. If you move we'll be sleeping on a wet bed."

"Are you crazy? How do I not move?"

"Learn to control it, Angel." I resume my previous task of bringing her to climax. As she falls over the cliff, I suck the water off her then I slide into her and feel her clenching around me. *God she is so tight.* It is amazing being bare inside her with no condom. This is all I want. She meets me thrust for thrust. As I start to really move in her she crests again and I fall with her. I quickly untie her arms from the head board and massage feeling back into them. She turns in my arms and faces me.

"That was different."

"I know. Did you like it?" She smiles knowingly at me. "Would you want to do that and other stuff?"

"With you, yes." There is never any hesitation in her responses to me.

"Good, when we get back, we'll go to the loft and spend some time there. Just you and me. We can have your stuff moved in and go from there."

"Wait, what?" She looks at me puzzled. "What do you mean move my stuff in?"

"Well, you're going to move in with me."

"I can't move in with you. It's too soon. You're rushing this."

"I'm not rushing anything. I know this is right, you and me."

"Tristan, I can't." She starts to get out of bed and searches for her clothing. Once dressed she heads into the bathroom and closes the door. Wait what just happened? We just had an amazing time and now we are

149

arguing? *What the hell?* I knock on the bathroom door and hear her crying.

"Kaitlyn, what's wrong Angel?"

Sniffling she answers. "Nothing."

"Then why are you crying."

"I don't know. Things are moving too fast and it scares me."

"Open the door, Angel." When she opens the door and emerges, she walks straight into my arms. "We can slow things down. But Kaitlyn, I know this is right and I think you know it also."

"I do and that's what makes it so scary. I've never felt like this before. You bring out a side in me I never knew existed. I feel stronger around you. What we just did, it was…. Well it was fun."

"So what's the problem? I don't understand the tears." I wipe them off her cheeks with my thumbs before I gently kiss her lips.

"You know what, let's just chalk this up to me being premenstrual. I hate to use that as an excuse but I think it might really fit here. I hate women that use it as a crutch but right now my moods are swinging all over the place. Just bear with me, please."

"Always." I hug her tighter to me. *PMS huh.* I never had to deal with it before. I never stuck around long enough to experience the dreaded "PMS attitude" my friends have told me about. Some of the stories they told me are downright scary as shit. Tara was on the pill so she never had any moods swings I could recall. But then again when we were together I was drunk most of the time.

--- --- --- ----

Kaitlyn

Eventually when we leave the suite, the sun is starting its descent. My emotions are in absolute disarray. The only real reason I can think is PMS. I can usually get snippy but I never get this way. The trauma of the last couple of days is wreaking havoc on my system. Only three more days and I will return to normal. Hopefully. My stomach has started to protest from all the calories we burned off today alone. The man is insatiable.

"What do you want to do today?"

"Well, we're heading towards Block Island. The documents need to be dropped off and there is the perfect place. The helicopter will come to pick them up in about two hours. We could go shopping?" He doesn't know I don't like to shop.

"Yeah, that sounds like a great idea. I need to pick up a few things." I need unmentionables.

"Certainly. Are you hungry? How about some breakfast before we start?"

"Sounds perfect. Why don't I cook and you get us under way. Then we can eat out there." The thought of making him breakfast brings me some sort of gratification, even though breakfast was almost six hours ago.

"Great, I can't wait." As I turn to leave he smacks my behind and I gasp shocked. He smiles widely and raises his eyebrow at me. As he saunters off, I take notice of how pleased he appears.

Breakfast was delicious if I don't say so myself. After the dishes have been cleared and put away, I climb back up top and settle myself next to him. Watching him steer, flexing his tattooed arms, I have a flashback to that Saturday night. Him whispering sweet words in my ear and soothing my tears. I felt so safe in his arms even after everything that happened. I am still unsure of what actually happened and Tristan has not spoken of it. All I do know for sure was he is my knight in shining armor.

"Tristan, thank you for finding and saving me. You're my knight." I lean up and kiss his lips.

He saddens at my comment. "I'm no knight. My armor is quite tarnished. But you're welcome. I'm sorry I wasn't quicker. You know we really haven't spoken about that night."

Tarnished armor? What happened that has caused this pained saddened look? He looks lost in his thoughts. I do not want to push him. "I know, but I don't think there is much left to say."

"You know you'll never have to worry about him again. I'm taking care of the situation. I don't ever want you to worry about anything ever again."

"I really haven't thought of much except you. You've basically consumed my thoughts." I smile up at him and kiss his cheek.

"Good, I'm glad I occupy most of your thoughts. But I'm obviously not working hard enough if I haven't consumed your every waking thought and sleeping dreams." We chuckle at his cockiness. But he quickly sobers as if he thought of something. "You know you made some comments before that were a little disturbing. Do you care to explain them?" How can I talk about that with him? He does not need to hear about my family saga.

"Not really if you don't mind." He sees me closing down but he persists in finding the answers.

"Actually I do mind. I want to know all of you." He raises his eyebrows up and down sarcastically. "Seriously, this time, this week is for us to get to know each other. My question qualifies as getting to know you. You opened the box so to speak."

"Yes, but you don't want to know what Pandora has hidden in there. Please let's talk about something else. Ask me a different question. I promise I will answer anything."

He thinks and then asks. "Okay, tell me about your family life."

"Oh come on, that's almost the exact same question but worded differently."

"You promised." He repeats my promise and smiles because he knows he's going to get the answers he is seeking.

"Don't say I didn't warn you. Okay here it goes. Both my parents are alcoholics. My mother never wanted me but had me because she thought she had to or it was the next thing to do. I don't know. Something to that affect. She told me this on my sixteenth birthday. I have basically helped raise my younger siblings. My father is never home and when he does come home, he and my mother fight like cats and dogs. I didn't go away for my undergraduate degree because I was afraid of what I would come home to if I did. I felt I couldn't leave my siblings with my parents." I stop and walk over to the railing and look out contemplating my life so far. What must it look like to him?

"I have always acted as the shield between my mother and father, physically." Out of the corner of my eye, he approaches but his step falters almost like he's in pain. "I have always been there to protect my siblings from my parents when they become violent which is quite often. I have put my mother to bed as if she were a child so many times I feel like I'm the parent most of the time. I don't want my siblings exposed to that. They are getting older so it's becoming more difficult." As he nears me, I step away not wanting his comfort. He wanted this so I have to finish.

"I have had to leave functions because I received a distress call from either Bethany, my mother or a neighbor. Tristan, I'm so tired. I don't know how much more of this I can take. When we met on the beach, I wasn't me. It felt like a different person was talking to you. I felt free. You make me feel special." Trying to calm my raging emotions, I take a deep breath and trudge on. "My parents have never told me they love me. Instead of celebrating my sixteenth birthday, my mother told me how I ruined her life because she couldn't go and party with her friends. She was stuck at home with a new baby. Bethany was told she was a mistake and the pregnancy before her was terminated. What child wants to know that? How fucked up is that?" The tears start streaming down my face. He gently wipes them away with his thumbs and replaces them with a soft kiss.

"You see you don't want to have anything to do with me. I see the pity in your eyes. I'm damaged. I look good to the outside observer but ask Sophia or even Lara what I'm like on the inside. I am very self-conscious and insecure. In my head I know all this is bullshit, but in my heart I can't help but feel this way. I'm sorry." Sinking to the floor of the deck crying silently now, I allow him to envelop me in his arms. He made me open Pandora's Box and unleashes feelings I never wanted to face or express out loud.

"Shhh, sweetheart." He rocks me back and forth rubbing my back and stroking my hair causing more tears to spill out. The comfort he offers is so different than any I have ever received. And so the confession of my life continues.

"I have no idea what a normal relationship is supposed to be like. My parents have cheated on each other so many times I lost count. My mother would tell me about her affairs. Do you know how those made me feel? I felt everyone knew and it was hard to hold my head up in school. What child needs that? I think if it weren't for Sophia, I would never have had friends or been as social as I was which isn't saying much. Her mother is the only one who has ever shown me a parent's love. I owe the Duncan's a lot." His eyes are gentle when I finally look at him again. "You really don't want to be involved with me, Tristan. I have too much baggage for you. Let me go now before we get too involved so it won't hurt as much." I feel a sudden loss at the mention of not seeing him anymore. I shouldn't be this attached.

"Angel, I'm here. I'm not going anywhere. It's too late. You have touched me so deeply I don't think I could leave now without being hurt."

"You don't mean that. You can't. I just dumped a whole load of crap on you that no guy in their right mind would want to entertain. Please let me just get off when we dock and I can find my way back home."

He takes me in his arms and tries to impress upon me his feelings with a kiss. I feel this kiss at the center of my core, my very being, my essence. *God I love him.* How could this have happened? It seems so elemental and easy.

"I can't do that. You felt that also. We are already in too deep."

"I know but it's not fair to you. You didn't sign on for this."

"Kaitlyn, it doesn't matter now. No one will ever hurt you again. You're mine." He whispers his comment.

"Tristan, you can't promise me that. We don't know what tomorrow will bring." I sniffle.

"I can and I know. Please let me help you. Let me show you the person everyone sees, the one who has saved me. The one who protects everyone else at her own expense. You are beautiful, bright, giving, and generous. Anyone who has ever met you knows this."

This man, who has only known me but a couple of days, is promising what my parents should have promised a long time ago. How did I save him? With his arms wrapped around me, I feel like he could keep these promises and more.

"I've never expressed these feelings out loud to anyone not even Sophia. I think she knows. Tristan, I'm so tired, I just want to live and not feel any obligations. My whole life has been spent taking care of my family. Do you know how many times I just wanted to end it all and escape?"

"What stopped you?"

"My sisters and brother. When my grandparents moved away, that's when things started to get really bad. Prior to that my mom would only drink every other night. But then it changed to every day at night and now it's basically when she wakes up."

"Kaitlyn, I'm glad you stuck it out, otherwise we would not have found each other. We would not be here now. Can I ask you another question?"

"Sure what's stopping you, the box is open." I answer sarcastically and blow my nose in a napkin left behind from breakfast.

He looks at me apologetically. "Has either of your parents ever beaten you?" I look away so he won't see my eyes. They may not have beaten me but I watched as they hit Bethany when we were younger. I could do nothing to stop it. He takes my chin to turn my face towards him. "Kaitlyn?" Fresh tears have started to fall.

"No, but I wish they would have. I could've handled it better. When Bethany and I were younger they used to hit her. I was too young to stop it." I look away feeling ashamed. I'm whispering now. "I vowed when I was old enough they would never lay a hand on her again. I have kept that silent promise to her and my other siblings. My parents are free to go after each other. I'll only step in when I feel they have taken it too far but otherwise I let them be."

"Kaitlyn, Angel, you have nothing to be ashamed of, you were young. It sounds like you have never been given the opportunity to act your age, ever. You're due for a change. From this moment forward, you're going to act your age and have fun. I know it's going to be difficult for us starting next week but I swear I'll try to do everything in my power to focus on us. Do you believe me?"

Do I believe him, he asks. The amazing feats he has accomplished so far are awe inspiring. He made me believe in knights, found me at my grandparents and most importantly allowed me to open up to him about everything. He hasn't judged me like I thought he may, but then again he is nothing like I thought he would be. Yes, I do believe him. If he had the power he would make everything right.

"Yes, I believe you."

CHAPTER FOURTEEN

Tristan

The retelling of her life story did more damage than if she would have torn out my heart. I now have little respect for her parents. Those children need to be out of that house. Kaitlyn needs to start living a normal life. This woman I hold is remarkably strong and her sacrifices have cost her. I now understand why everyone is so protective over her. The urge to protect her and destroy anything that harms her is overwhelming. The situation with her parents is futile except maybe getting them help.

"Kaitlyn, have your parents ever tried getting help?"

She barks out a laugh filled with animosity. "They don't have a problem." The statement drips with sarcasm. "In their eyes there is nothing wrong. You can't help someone who feels there is no problem. It's very disturbing actually."

"Have you ever sought any type of help?"

"When have I really had time? I know Al anon and what they teach. It's not for me. I'm not good in group meetings. I tried once but never went back."

Okay it seems I cannot help here but I have to figure something out. But until then I can take her mind off of home. I stand up, take her hand and lead her to the helm. I pull her in front of me and place her hands on the wheel. She looks back at me apprehensively. "You can do this." I nod forward and she turns back around.

I explain to her what she wants to feel and what to look for. We go over the basics of sailing. As we near the island, I let go without her noticing. I move away so I can handle the sails and I hear her panicked voice calling to me. "Tristan, come back here. I don't know what I'm doing."

"You're doing fine, just head for those buoys. Remember the red ones are always on the right."

"Tristan, please. Come back here." I love hearing her beg. As soon as we drop off these documents, I am going to make her beg more.

"Not yet, I have to finish up here. Then I'll maneuver it into the slip."

She looks at me suspiciously. "I promise okay." I chuckle to myself.

We make it to the dock without any problems and rent two bicycles, which is unexpected. Riding around the island was not on the agenda but after seeing how much fun she had just going to the helipad, how could I resist. After we dropped off the documents, we decided to window shop and stop at a local convenience store. While we are on the other side of the island, we to race back. Knowing we are both very competitive, we know it will be a close race. We are tire to tire most of the way but as we round the bend to the bicycle rental shop, I pull forward by a hair and win. We did not decide on the prize prior to the race so she has no idea what I am thinking.

Back at the dock, we push off after dinner. The red hazed sun is nearly set. Kaitlyn's silhouette is framed beautifully by the sunset. I grab my phone taking some pictures. She does not like to have her picture taken I find out. It's dark now and I feel adventurous.

"Want to go for a night swim."

"Sure."

"Great, but we're skinny dipping." I quickly strip my clothes off and jump off the back of the boat. She is taking her time getting in. "Come on Kaitlyn, what's taking so long."

Before I know it she comes running and jumping off the back nearly colliding with me in the water. If it was not for her scream, I would not have known she was coming. When she surfaces she is looking around for me but cannot see me. I sneak up behind her and grab her. She screams bloody murder. I bark out a laugh and cannot stop. She pushes on my shoulders dunking me completely. I come up sputtering.

"Oh is that how you want to play." I tease her and start to swim to her. She backs away yelling at me.

"Don't come any closer." But she starts to laugh as I catch her and throw her. "Mercy." She screams.

I swim to her and we kiss. It starts off simple and innocent but as usual with us it progresses fast. She screams again scaring me.

"There's something here. I felt it against my legs."

I laugh at her until I feel the same thing and get freaked out as well. Grabbing her hand, we swim for the ladder. I almost throw her up there and jump on to the ladder myself. Once we are safely back on deck, we look at each other and start rolling around laughing at our reactions. Finally when we calm down enough, we decide it is time for a shower. I offer her it first knowing I will claim my prize shortly. I set the iPod to my favorite selections and the music is playing throughout the boat.

She must be thinking the same thoughts because when I enter the bathroom, it is lit only by candles. Her body is silhouetted in the shower. Her hands are washing her hair with her back towards me. She must have felt me because she says without turning around. "Are you just going to watch or are you joining me?"

I step in behind her and wrap my arms around. She tilts her head back on my shoulder. "God, you are so sexy. How did I get so lucky?" I say to her. She takes her arm and wraps it around my head while turning her head for a kiss. I kiss her passionately. Lost in her kisses, she starts to wash the salt water from my body. She is almost done when she grips my member firmly and starts to work it. It does not need much help as seeing her wet in the shower made me hard before I even entered. Dropping to her knees, she brings it to her mouth and starts sucking. Her tongue is swirling around the tip before she takes most of me in. As she pulls back her tongue glides under the shaft. Moaning, I grab her head firmly and start to move in and out of her mouth. Just as I am about to release I pull out forcefully. Breathing heavily, I kiss her, ravaging her mouth.

Pushing her against the wall I lift her leg and wrap it around my waist. I plunge two fingers in her to test her readiness and she is ready. *I love how she is always ready for me.* I circle her bud a few times until she is begging me to enter her then with a force barely controlled I enter her. She is panting and moaning. "Oh God, Tristan. More please." Being in her with no condom is irresponsible but the feeling is so real. There is no restriction. She is positive of her cycle and I trust her absolutely. I withdraw slightly and slam back in. "Harder, Tristan."

I lift her and she wraps both legs around my waist and meets me thrust for thrust. She is begging me not to stop. When she cries out, I lift her almost completely off me. "Not yet. Don't come yet."

"Tristan please now. I need to...."

"Not yet, hold on. I'll tell you when." I pant out.

She is riding up and down. Every time she comes back down, she grinds down trying to pull me in further. I feel her starting to clench and know she has reached her limit. I reach between her legs and help her over the cliff.

"Come now, Angel." She screams my name over and over again. I thrust twice more and fall myself. As I come down, my head is buried in her neck. "You're amazing."

I gently lift her off of me and reach behind her to turn off the shower. Opening the doors, I retrieve the towel and wrap her in it. Then grab one for myself. I dry her off gently and dry her hair. I quickly dry myself and lead her into the bedroom. I comb her hair after she has climbed into bed. We both recline and she falls almost immediately asleep but not before she mutters, "I love you."

Hearing her say those words for the first time, knowing she has never said them to another man, have set my heart and soul at ease. I feel so completed by her, in her, or around her. Instead of reading the rest of the documents on the deck or in the living space, I quickly get them and climb back in bed because the thought of being too far away from her is chilling. When she said those words, I felt no fear like I had when Tara used to say it. We were just kids so saying the words never meant anything to me. *Tara deserved so much more than she got.* It feels so right being here with Kaitlyn.

As I flip through the proposals my mind keeps wandering back to her life thus far. She told me things she never said to another soul before. With what she has survived, it is amazing she is as well-adjusted as she is and not damaged. She believes she is damaged but what the world sees is a determined young woman. Never does she ask for help and will suffer in silence. I have to remember that for future reference, her suffering in silence I will not tolerate. She needs to feel comfortable around me enough to put me in my place if need be. I know I can be a jerk at times.

--- --- --- ----

Kaitlyn

Skinny dipping was fun even though embarrassing at first, but it was dark and he wouldn't be able to see made it easier to jump. When he grabbed me, I thought of the movie *Deep Blue Sea* with the genetically altered sharks. He scared the crap out of me. My first instinct was to dunk him and I did because he deserved it. He was so playful and completely took my mind off of life. As we were playing around something actually brushed against my leg causing me to scream out loud.

Laughingly he said, "There's nothing in here. The fish are afraid of us. You're-" Then the look that crossed his face prior to his scream was priceless. "What the fuck was that?! Hurry up get to the boat!" Oh he was manly about it…. NOT! He is so good for my soul.

When he made love to me, I knew he was trying to erase the past and offer me a wonderful future. That's why when I told him I loved him it was so easy. I did not second guess it. He is right this is how it is supposed to be. Some would say it was the afterglow of sex but with him everything is different. I know I have no frame of reference to compare it to but maybe this is why I never found anyone? Even if I had, I know this is different.

Dawn is upon us. The sky is starting to lighten.. The room is no longer submerged in total darkness. Now I just lay here watching him and listening to his breathing. His eyelids are moving quickly back and forth. He must be in the throes of a nightmare. As if he is answering my question he starts to scream. He is thrashing in the bed until he grabs me shaking me still asleep. I try waking him softly but he does not hear me. It isn't until I start to shove at his shoulder when he wakens.

"What's wrong, Angel?" His voice is groggy and hoarse with sleep.

"You were screaming in your sleep." The concern present in my voice and my eyes feel wide with fright triggers a painful look from him. "You were yelling, 'No, not her too. I didn't mean it to happen again.' Tristan, what were you dreaming about."

"I have no idea. I usually don't have dreams I can remember." Could he really not remember a dream of this intensity? Something in his eyes has me wondering if he is withholding something from me.

He pulls me down in his arms and snuggles me closely, nestling his nose in my neck. "I'm sorry I woke you. Try to go back to sleep."

"Tristan, you know you can talk to me about anything, right? I'll listen and not judge as you did for me. Someday I'd really like for you to trust me like I trust you."

He kisses my nose, a gesture I am really starting to enjoy. At first I thought it was him being patronizing but I learned it is an affectionate gesture. "Knowing you would not judge me, Angel, fills my heart but I really don't have anything to say. You know everything there is to know about me." He is hiding something and it hurts he won't tell me. I hope he trusts me to tell me before I find out what it is. "Just go back to sleep baby it's still early yet."

"Fine, I won't push it. But I'm here to listen. Good night Tristan."

"Good night, my Angel."

The rest of the trip is similar to the first two days, where we just spend time talking, exploring each other's bodies and reading to each other. A majority of the time is spent in bed believe it or not just talking. The sex was amazing up until my period started. He still wanted to when it came but I could not get past it yet.

One night I confessed to him I like it when he takes control. He said he would show me real control back home in the city. He made a similar comment when he tied me to the bed. Secretly, I am excited about trying something new. This new side he brought out is wild and daring. I remember thinking when I first laid eyes on him, someone like him would be dangerous for me and boy was I right.

Yesterday he asked me to move my stuff into the loft. When I told him I cannot leave my siblings, his response was we would figure it out and he dropped it. Our last night out at sea is romantic and perfect. He asks me to move in with him again. This time he tries to reason with me.

"Kaitlyn, don't you see we'd see each other every night. I would go to bed next to you and wake up next to you."

"Tristan, this is moving way too fast. We hardly know each other."

"I know it's crazy but that's how I know it's right. I've never asked another woman to move in with me. I want you near me always."

"Tristan really, come on."

"Seriously Kaitlyn, what's going to happen when you start school and I have meetings? What then? We don't see each other for days on end? That won't work. I won't be able to concentrate wondering where you are or what you're doing. I'll be constantly worrying."

"Tristan, we both knew what we were getting into when we decided to pursue this. We said we'd make the best of it which is what I thought we were going to do. You can't go changing the rules to suit your needs."

"I can and I will." His voice is full of determination.

"Really, Tristan." I arch one brow at him. He knows I have a point but he won't concede to it. "Anyway, Hofstra is on the island. I can't keep putting the miles on my car and I definitely cannot afford to take the train. The bus would take too long. We can see each other on the weekends."

"Kaitlyn, that's not enough. I know you'll be studying and have seminars to attend. Eventually you'll have to intern limiting our time even more. Why not move in with me? This way we can be together while you study and I can do whatever I have to."

"Tristan, I can't. My family needs me."

"Okay how about a compromise?" *He wants to compromise?*

"What do you have in mind?"

"Well, you spend the weekends with me and one or two nights a week. I think that's reasonable. This way you spend half your time at home and the other half with me."

"I don't know... I want to don't get me wrong but there may be weekends when Bethany wants to go out. I have to think about it. The traveling is going to be too much on my car."

"Oh speaking of which, I forgot to tell you I received a message about your car." He looks at me apologetically. "Your car was totaled while the driver was picking it up. I'm sorry Angel."

"Wait what?" Did I hear him correctly, my car is totaled? Oh shit what am I going to do without a car? That car is my lifeline, was my lifeline. It allowed me to leave home when I needed an escape.

"Your car was totaled. You need to get a new car." Being in shock makes me repeat what he says.

"I'm sorry did you just say my car is totaled?"

"Yes on Thursday on the way back from Pennsylvania. You know the sharp turn after the bridge, well it seems your car can go quite fast when it's on a decline. He said the brakes failed and he tried to avoid hitting another car."

"Oh God, I'm sorry is he okay?" I knew the car was having problems but the brakes were just replaced recently. I feel guilty about getting them on sale. Maybe they were on sale because they were defective.

"Yes, he's fine not a scratch on him. I paid him well since it was my idea. You owed nothing on the car so the insurance is fine. When we get back tomorrow we'll get you another car."

"Tristan, I can't afford another car. I could barely afford that one. I have a job that barely pays any money, which I'll have to quit because of medical school. I still live at home even though you want to change that. Realistically I can't afford a new car's insurance." I feel ashamed of being so poor. He has so much money and I have nothing. Anyone who does not know me will think I am a gold digger.

"How am I going to get to you now? Wait how am I going to get to school? Shit!" This really sucks. I cannot ask my parents for their car. They have never allowed me to use it before.

"Angel, don't worry about it. We'll worry about it when we get back."

"You're right there's nothing I can do about it now."

When we arrive back at the dock, I feel like the dream has ended. Never have I felt so free before and I don't want it to come to an end. Life the last couple of days was ideal. Sighing I gather our bags and help Tristan bring them to the dock.

"Are you okay?" He inquires with an even tone.

"Yeah, I'm just sad it had to come to an end. I had so much fun. Thank you for this time." It sounds like I am saying good bye.

"Well, we can come back anytime you like. All you have to do is say the words."

"It felt like it was just you and I. I know it wasn't reality but it was nice to spend so much time with you alone. I hate to go back but I know we have to."

"You don't have to Angel. Move in with me."

"I thought we settled this." I laugh at his determination. He will make such a great CEO with his take charge and don't mess with me attitude. As we disembark from the boat, he informs me that the caretaker will properly wash down and clean both the interior and exterior of the boat. We stroll down the dock while he continues our conversation but not before I turn back around to memorize this moment.

--- --- --- ----

Tristan

Talking about the car made her feel guilty. I cannot tell her the truth- I had the car totaled so she can drive a better safer car. Her new car was delivered to the marina this morning and my car was driven back home. The car salesman took care of the insurance which has been paid for the year. My accountant set up an account which the insurance payments will come directly out of and has made arrangements for the account to always have money in it. Everything is in her name only, the car, car insurance, bank account and money. Her parents will never have any access to the money. This new account also has extra money being set aside in there for her. It is her turn to be taken care of and I plan on being the one.

"We did settle it but now you don't have an excuse now." She looks at me confused.

"What do you mean I don't have an excuse not to move in with you?"

"See?" I move out of her line of vision. There in the exact spot where my car was is a sleek red BMW Z4. Her expression is priceless and she seems to have lost her voice.

"Wh... Wh... What is that?" She eyes me suspiciously, hands on her hips, breaths coming a bit faster as her anger visibly grows.

"It's a BMW Z4. Do you like?" Oh yeah she's angry, her eyes darken with anger. "Are you angry?" I ask stupidly.

"Am I angry? Am I angry? What do you think?"

"Umm... yes?"

"You're damn right I'm angry. What gave you the right to buy me a car? Tristan, I can't afford this. I already told you I don't have this kind of money. You have no right to spend this kind of money on me."

Oh, no she did not just tell me how to spend my money. Now I am angry with her. Time to set the rules. I advance on her and she can see how upset I am. She instinctively backs up slightly and that stops me in my tracks. I don't like seeing her step away from me in fear so I try to control my anger. She needs to know I would never lay a hand on her but I know this is all she has ever been exposed to.

"First of all, please don't ever step away from me when you think I'm upset or angry with you. I will never lay a hand on you. I'm not your parents. Secondly, and listen carefully, I'll spend my money as I see fit. And right now I see fit spending it on you. There are no strings attached just accept the car. It was my fault your car was totaled. Therefore it's my responsibility to provide you with a new car. Knowing the insurance would be an issue, the first year insurance has been paid for." I stop to match her glare with one of my own. She is livid. Her face lights up when this angry. *God she is beautiful.* There is no fear of me now. "Finally, you are my girlfriend so get used to me buying you things, expensive things. While we are together you will want for nothing. If I feel I want to buy you a house I will, damn it. If we go out to a social function and it requires you to wear a gown, I'll buy it. There will also be no going "Dutch" when we go out." Oh that's it! I have pushed her over the edge. She starts to advance on me and forces me to step back. This is great!

"So I'm to be your Julia Roberts? Well think again, Mr. Chance. This was a mistake." She points between us. So I grab her and kiss her passionately. She becomes limp in my arms and then with a sudden fierceness she kisses me back just as passionately.

In a calm tone, which I am certainly not feeling, "Tell me again how this is a mistake, Miss Daniels." She looks away from me knowing I am right. "This is the second time in as many days where you are trying to walk away or saying this is a mistake. Don't for a second think I'm letting you walk away. This," Now it's my turn to point between us, "is not going anywhere. You have to trust in us. Trust that this will work. What are you afraid of?"

She looks at the car but not really looking at it because she's in deep thought. I want to take her in my arms and wipe away all her insecurities. Her parents have no idea the jewel they have in her. Maybe when I take her away they will come to realize it, but I sincerely doubt it.

"I don't know." She barely whispers.

"I think you do know but are afraid to admit it." I push her to admit what she is afraid of. She seems so hesitant to answer honestly. Placing my hands on her shoulders and turning her to look at me, I say. "Kaitlyn nothing you can say will make me leave you. Just tell me what you're afraid of."

She is thinking whether or not to tell me. "I'm afraid to rely on anyone. I'm afraid if I rely on you, you'll let me down like everyone else who's supposedly loved me has, even my grandparents." She starts to cry because I know she feels like she betrayed them by saying this. I hug her to me. "I'm afraid if I love and trust you than you'll leave or hurt me. I can't afford that anymore."

"But at what expense Kaitlyn? You've isolated yourself from almost everyone except a select few."

"I've only relied on myself for so long in order to survive it's all I know. The ones I trust are the ones who have not let me down, until recently. I'm sorry, Tristan. I really want to but I don't know if I can or will ever be able to."

"I understand but you have to start somewhere. So you really aren't angry about the car but what it means or represents?"

"I'm upset you would just buy me a car without talking to me. But yes, I don't want to rely on you to provide me with stuff. I don't want people to think I'm dating you because of your money"

"I don't give a fuck what people think and neither should you."

"But it's not your reputation that will be dragged through the mud."

"I'll protect you as much as I can. You have to not believe anything anyone says to you."

"I'll try but it will be hard."

"If I asked you about buying a car what would you have said?"

"No."

"That's why I didn't tell you."

"Because it's too much."

"It's not when you have as much money as I do. I am only going to get richer. You seem to not realize how much you have completed me. I didn't know I was so unfinished before you."

"Oh Tristan, you're not unfinished." She places her hands against my cheeks. Her tone oozes sincerity. "You're a good guy despite what the papers say. Don't put yourself down." *Time to change the subject.*

"Oh, so you do read the papers. What do you think?"

"From what I've read, which is not much because I don't have money to waste on such nonsense, I think the papers have you pegged wrong."

"No actually they're not far from the truth but that was before I met you. I have always felt something was off or missing even though I had everything I could ask for. Women were playthings for me. They would use me for notoriety and I would use them back. But then you came along and everything changed. Fate has a funny way of working. Just when I needed you, you appeared from behind a candy counter sounding like the angel you are."

"You know it's funny you should say that. Prior to meeting you that first night, I had just been thinking I needed a change because I could not keep going the way I was. Between my family life, work and school, there was no time for a social life. I mean I'm almost twenty-two years old, never been on a date and was still a virgin prior to you. I mean come on, really? I know it's not healthy which is why I needed the change. I guess fate is working for us like you said."

"You see fate is on our side." I hug her to me and she embraces me back. "So does this mean we get to have make-up sex now. That was our first real non PMS fight right?" I say teasingly with a smirk. She barks out a laugh.

"Is that all you think about?"

"When it comes to you and only you Angel, it is on the top of my list." She leans up, wraps her arms around my neck and kisses me squarely on the lips. "Now let's go. You're driving us back. We're going to my parent's house for dinner. They invited us. They really want to meet you. You wondered how I found you well I have a freakier one for you. My father knew about you before I got home on Sunday after my party. Now that's scary."

She looks shocked and nervous. "Tristan, I can't meet your parents dress like this. Let me run back to the boat and change." She runs back towards the boat with her new suitcase filled with all her new clothes in tow. "Are you coming, you have to help me?" She yells back at me.

Laughing at her fleeing body, I respond. "I'll be right there, let me just put these in the trunk." I look around the parking lot feeling like we were being watched. Nothing seems out of the norm, all the cars fit. A red minivan, beat up old Ford Explorer, white pick-up truck, and silver sedan. All normal. Maybe I'm just being paranoid. Dad scared me with some of the security stories. After we get back I have to increase the security around me due to the potential threats.

Eventually, I follow her back and help her on board. Almost an hour later, we are on the road to my parents but not before we properly made up and Kaitlyn redressed in something she felt was more appropriate.

CHAPTER FIFTEEN

Kaitlyn

We ended up leaving the marina later than we had expected. I begged Tristan to drive my new car because I was too scared to drive it just yet. He agreed because he wanted to see what it could do. But secretly I know he also liked me begging, something I am coming to realize he really likes especially during sex. He will withhold from me until I beg him. Truthfully it turns me on more, if that's even possible.

I have learned a lot about Tristan this past week. The time on the boat was what I think we both needed as he initially predicted. He is right we do have something spectacular here. I fear however I will muddle it up somehow. He hit a nerve with me and not trusting people. Actually he hit a few nerves that I have to work on. There is no doubt in my mind that I do love him. I didn't know it was possible to fall in love with someone so fast. But if it is meant to be then so be it.

I am meeting his parents already. Actually they wanted to meet me and according to Tristan they have this uncanny ability to know who their children are involved with. However in our case, we were not involved yet. *Freaky family.* I guess they have to be cautious when it comes to their family. They are such public figures and hold extreme power. They cannot just trust anyone.

When we arrive back in his hometown, he turns down the street leading to his parent's house and I am in awe of my surroundings. These houses are gorgeous. They are all mostly center hall colonials, Victorians or Tudors. I feel like I'm in a different state because the properties are spread farther apart than my town. Each property is beautifully manicured. As we near the end of the street, the houses become grander and are set farther apart. My car fits in with the houses in this area but I am not too sure about its current owner fitting in. Someone like Sophia or Lara would fit in here better than me.

We stop in front of a gated property. Tristan enters a code in and the gates slides open. *Wow.* "I ordered you a remote for the gate." I looked astonished at him. Why would he do that? "I want you to always have a place you can go even if I'm not around." He is always thinking of me. The house is coming into view and to call it a house is a tragedy. It is a mansion. There appears to be at least three floors and two wings. The front drive is circular and the garages are off the right hand side. Tristan parks the car in the front and someone opens my door, surprising me.

"Hi Clarke. Thanks for getting Kaitlyn's door."

"Hello Sir. How was your trip?" Clarke offers me his assistance. "Hello Miss Kaitlyn. I hope your trip was enjoyable." Tristan takes my hand and guides me into the entryway or grand foyer, not sure what they call it in a house this size.

"Hello Clarke it's nice to meet you." As I offer him my hand. Embarrassment halts any response I may have had about the trip. Does everyone know we went away alone? *What must they think of me?*

"Our trip was very restful, thank you for asking." Tristan smirks at me and I can't help but smile hitting him in the shoulder.

"Where is everyone?"

"They are in the informal living room. I think Miss Abigail is down by the pool. Would you care for a cocktail sir or Miss Kaitlyn?"

"No thank you, Clarke." Feeling a bit overwhelmed. "Please just call me Kaitlyn."

"As you wish, Kaitlyn." He smiles back at me and I like him. I know we will get along just fine. "I will leave the two of you to your business." And he takes his leave.

Finally able to take in my surroundings, I am in wonderment at the grandness of this place. The foyer is a three story open circular room with a massive chandelier hanging in the center. The staircase before us is huge. It divides at the first landing to take the individual in either direction of the wings. It reminds me of Scarlett O'Hara's staircase at the end of Gone with the Wind when Rhett Butler just left her. I can't help but wonder how many rooms are in this house.

"Tristan, this is where you grew up? How many rooms are there in here?" I look all around when I ask him the questions.

"There are eight suites each equipped with a living space, bedroom, and full bathroom. Then there is the kitchen, formal and informal dining rooms, formal and informal living rooms, library, two offices, play room, and more. Needless to say we had more room then we knew what to do with. My parents have hosted some amazing events here. Come on let's find them." He pulls my hand but I hesitate. "What's wrong?"

"I'm nervous. Do you think they'll like me? I mean I'm not like them."

"What do you mean you are not like them?"

"You know." I don't want to come across as poor, even though by his standards I am, but we are from two different social classes.

"No, I don't. Please explain." Is he just being obtuse or does he not really see it? He saw the simplicity of my grandparent's house. I have told him about my financial status. How could he not know?

"Tristan, you and I are from two different classes. Although my family is not considered poor, we don't have the luxuries you and your family have or even Sophia or Lara's. Look at the way you were brought up and the schooling you've had. I just don't want to embarrass you or me."

He comes closer to hug me and looks at me sincerely. "Have I ever made you feel like that?"

"No, of course not, except with the car." I smile shyly at him.

"Then what makes you think they would treat you any differently? They raised me, or my mother did. Dad as you know wasn't around. You could never embarrass me. You are a beautiful person inside and out. My father likes you already without even meeting you. He told me you were a determined young woman. You have nothing to be worried about."

He has relieved me of my insecurities and anxieties again. "Okay lead on then." My heart is pounding in my chest and my breathing is becoming a bit erratic. I may be having an anxiety attack. I have never had one before. "Tristan, I can't do this. I can't." Now he is literally dragging me but stops abruptly, turns around and kisses me halting any argument I may have had making me melt. Tristan stops when he hears someone clear their voice.

"Ahem." Not being able to think straight I wonder who this is. "Son, when did you get back?" He turns briefly to me. "I'm assuming you must be Kaitlyn?" The man comes closer to hug Tristan and then with his hand outstretched to me comes towards me. *Son? Oh God! I am so embarrassed.* I shoot Tristan the death stare and look back at his father who has a hint of amusement in his eyes. I take the offered hand and shake it.

"Nice to meet you, Mr. Chance. Sorry about that."

"No problem. I understand completely. When I first starting dating Tristan's mother, I could not stop kissing her either. So there's no need to apologize." His response is pleasant but I still can't help but feel embarrassed. "Please call me Charles. How was your trip?"

"It was nice thank you." I feel my face flush again. "You have a beautiful sailboat and an even more beautiful house. Thank you for inviting me."

"Thank you but the sailboat has always been Tristan's. How long ago did you purchase that son?"

"A little over five years ago. It was a steal." He comes behind me wrapping his arms around my waist. I try to step away but he holds me firmly.

"You see, it is his. Are you ready for medical school?" *Wow he really does know me.*

"I'm as ready as I'm ever going to be."

"That's the spirit. How was the drive?" He asks with a gleam in his eye.

"It was good, not too much traffic. Tristan drives much faster than I do. So we made excellent time."

"Yes, he does like to speed. There have been a few speeding tickets in his past. How's the car son?"

"Well, we drove Kaitlyn's new car back. You see Kaitlyn's car had an unfortunate accident last week."

"Oh sorry to hear that is everyone okay?" He inquires but it is said in a way that has me wondering if he already knew or suspected.

"Yes, no one was hurt thankfully, except the car was totaled."

"Since it was my idea to hire a driver to drive it back from Pennsylvania, I felt it was my responsibility to replace it. So she now has a beautiful red BMW. It's out front. Would you care to see it?" Tristan tone is light and jokingly. "Needless to say Kaitlyn was not happy with me."

His dad actually chuckles. "I'm sure she wasn't happy at all." Again he says it as if I am missing something. Tristan joins his dad laughing conspiratorially.

"Am I missing something?" I question the both of them.

"No Angel, absolutely nothing. Let's go find mom and Abigail, shall we." Nudging me along from behind, his father in tow, he pushes me towards the back of the house. When we get close to the living room, I'm assuming it's the living room, I hear two women talking. One is Abigail the other must be Tristan's mom. Abigail notices us and ventures over to hug me hello.

"Kaitlyn, it's so nice to see you again. How have you been?"

Hugging her back I say, "Hi Abigail, it's great to see you to."

"Kaitlyn, this is my mother, Carolyn. Mom this is Kaitlyn." Tristan makes the introductions.

"It's so nice to finally meet you." His mother comes in for a hug which is unexpected. I thought she would be more formal but she welcomes me like family. She takes my hand and leads me to the couch as if we are the best of friends.

"It's nice you meet you as well. Tristan speaks very highly of you." She still has a hold on my hand and squeezes it. Abigail enters with a tray laden with drinks and Tristan follows with snacks. I rise to help but Tristan shakes his head no.

"So when are you starting medical school?" Carolyn inquires of me.

"I'm starting at the end of next month. I'm looking forward to it finally. It has been a long time coming."

"Do you know if you want to specialize?"

"Yes, I think I would like to specialize in cardiothoracic surgery. I know it will take extra work and years but the thought of performing magic like that intrigues me." Tristan is looking at me shocked.

"Why didn't you tell me?" He sounds peeved.

"You never asked."

"Well it would have been nice of you to mention it."

"Why? Does it really matter?"

He thinks about it for a couple of minutes and finally answers. "No, I guess it doesn't. It's just more time apart." Ignoring his comment, I turn my attention to Abigail.

"Abigail, do you know what you want to do yet?" I ask her. "Specialize or not?"

"I think I want to specialize but I only recently decided oncological surgery." *Wow that takes a strong heart.* Some of those patients are so sick. Tristan alluded to something being wrong with his father. I wonder if her father's illness has helped to make this decision for her.

"Do you know what hospital you will intern at yet? Do you have a choice?"

"Yes, New York University Medical Center. What about you?"

"North Shore- LIJ Health System." Charles comes in just at the end of my statement and settles himself behind his wife, his arm around her shoulders. Tristan is sitting in a Chesterfield chair across from me.

"That's not far away from here. But too far from the city." Tristan grumbles. "Can't you get something in the city so you can spend the nights with me there?"

"Tristan!" I smack his leg as I redden again and he laughs. "No it's great for me. I won't have to travel far. I'm looking forward to the rotations and helping people." Tristan appears awestruck. "Did I say something wrong Tristan?"

"No Angel. You just keep surprising me at every turn." I look at him questioning what he means and he just shakes his head no at me, telling me to forget it.

"That's the hospital where I'll be receiving my treatments." Charles states to no one in particular. So I asked a question.

"Treatment for what?" The room becomes strangely quiet like I said something wrong.

"I have a rare type of leukemia and I start an aggressive

chemotherapy regimen on Thursday."

"Oh, I'm sorry I didn't know. Tristan said you were sick but I didn't know." I feel awkward at being caught off guard. "Is there anything I can do?"

"Nothing unfortunately. But we will beat this." He grabs Carolyn's hand and squeezes it reassuringly. She returns his smile though their eyes are sad. They know their time together is limited. I look at Tristan and can't help but feel their loss. If I were to loose Tristan, I would be devastated. I don't know how or if I could survive that.

Not knowing what else to say and feeling the sadness in the air I change subjects. "Can I help set the table or help with dinner at all?"

"Thank you for offering but the staff will handle that." And just like that I feel the social status difference. Carolyn has no idea of my discomfort at her statement because to her having staff caterer to them is normal. It really is a different lifestyle. With that Clarke enters the living room and informs us dinner is ready. We all rise at once and start for the dining room. Tristan pulls on my arm slightly to delay our departure.

"We'll be right there mom and dad." He answers their questioning looks. Once they are out of sight Tristan asks me. "Are you okay? I know I didn't tell you about my dad but I didn't know what to say. I was afraid you'd see it as me looking for sympathy."

Appalled he would think that of me. "Tristan, do you really think that little of me? Your family is going through a lot right now and I just wish you would have told me so I wouldn't have brought it up. I was Debbie Downer just a couple minutes ago. Some warning just would have been nice." I kiss his cheek tenderly trying to relay to him my concern and understanding.

"Are you sure? You're not mad."

"I am absolutely positively not angry. Please stop worrying. Let's go eat because I need to get home and check on my family. I also promised you I would speak with Sophia and Lara. So let's go join your family." I grab his hand, squeeze it reassuringly, and his smile is full of confidence. This smile can drop women's panties and have them begging for pleasure. This smile should be illegal it is so intoxicating and addicting.

Dinner is pleasant and the conversation easy. Abigail and I discuss our plans about medical school while Tristan and his father talk business. His mother absorbs it all.

"Son, did you have a chance to review those files?"

"Yes, I did. There were some things that were concerning. I think someone maybe stealing from us. Not enough to really make it noticeable to you or anyone else. But I guess I'm a new set of eyes."

"Really, what department?"

"I have narrowed it down to five. When I go in tomorrow I'll better understand the situation. I want to visit each department tomorrow and introduce myself. I want them to know I'm going to be hands on. Maybe force the thief out."

"Great idea. I would like to accompany you."

"Sounds good." He has only reviewed papers and already he uncovered something serious. I am proud to be his girlfriend at this moment. His father emanates pride at his son's discovery.

The food was delicious. The seafood paella was cook perfectly. The lemon meringue pie was out of this world. It had the right amount of sweet and tangy. When coffee and tea arrived, I was handed a cup of tea without being asked- it was my favorite brand as well. I look towards Tristan questioningly and he just smiles shaking his head as if saying "I don't know how they do it?"

Towards the end of dessert, Carolyn leans into me and whispers. "Thank you for making this night very special for our family. I see the way Tristan watches you out of the corner of his eye. He cares for you deeply. You two seem to be drawn together. I noticed you have been touching all through dinner." She smiles knowingly at me. "Please take care of his heart. I never thought I would see him this happy since that awful night."

I have no idea what night she is talking about and am about to ask her when Tristan rises and starts to say his goodbyes to everyone. "Are you ready Angel?"

"Uh, yes." I turn to Carolyn. "Thank you for inviting me. I hope we can do this again. I'll take special care of the item you just spoke to me about and treasure the rest of your statement." She engulfs me in a tender hug thanking me again. Next I turn to Abigail. "I hope to see you again real soon before school starts. Maybe we can get together?"

"That would be great. Call me." After we finish our hug, I turn to Charles.

"Thank you for dinner it was delicious. If there is anything I can do please let me know." He comes towards me for a hug and I hug him back.

But before we separate he whispers in my ear. "Thank you for loving him. He can be very difficult at times but he loves you and he will never stop no matter what." I pull back surprised at his statement. *Is he telling me Tristan loves me?* I smile at him, turn towards Tristan and kiss his cheek.

"Good night." I say to everyone as we depart. Tristan entwines our fingers as he escorts me to the car. When we reach the front door, Clarke opens the door bidding us a good night.

"Please inform who ever cooked the meal it was delicious."

"I will inform cook of your compliments. Thank you and good night Kaitlyn." Tristan and I descend the front steps. He opens the passenger door for me and I climb in. He walks around to the driver's side and gets in. As I am about to the grab my seatbelt he does it for me. I think he wants to restrain me again. *Looking forward to it baby.* We both smile knowingly at each and laugh.

The ride back to my parent's house is very quiet because he is unhappy leaving me there, especially after my confessions on the boat. I know he wants me to move in with him but this relationship is moving too fast. Only knowing him a month has me questioning my actions. I have never had a boyfriend or had sex with a man ever. But since meeting Tristan I have changed so much especially this last week that I wonder if Sophia will notice me.

Tomorrow I have to explain everything to Sophia. She has a few surprises coming her way. She will be upset with me for not telling her sooner. The topic of my sexual status should be done in person and not over the phone. I would have told her sooner if Tristan was not in the vicinity.

Pulling in front of my parent's house has him furrowing his brow. I know he does not want to leave me and I don't want him to leave. He starts his new position tomorrow and needs a good night sleep. The first few days of our trip neither of us slept all that much. We were pretty active.

Both my parents are home and Tristan is uncomfortable with just leaving. The lights are on, which means they are both still awake probably drunk. Bethany would have called if there were any problems, which reminds me I never checked my phone when we returned to shore. I quickly check my phone for messages or missed calls and there are two missed calls and one text message from Bethany.

> Bethany: Dad home drunk. Mom drunk also.
> Tension high. Kids r downstairs with me when r u
> comin home?

Shit! I have get in there really quick without alarming Tristan. He is in deep thought. If he knew what could potentially turn into a horrible mess, he would never let me go in there without him. With my heart rate rapidly increasing, I lean into him over the center console and kiss him good night. With calmness I am not feeling I reach for the door.

"Good night Tristan. It will be weird not lying next to you tonight. Have pleasant dreams." Opening my door to get out, he grabs my arm to halt me for leaving.

"Wait, can't I come in?" He asks innocently.

"The kids are probably asleep and if you come in it may wake them or my parents. I'll speak to you later once I'm settled. You have an early important day tomorrow and need a good night's sleep. We didn't do too much sleeping this past week." I say shyly.

"Don't remind me what I'm giving up by allowing you to leave me. But just so you know, the best sleep I've had in almost forever has been next to you. How am I going to go to sleep tonight?" He questions me temptingly. Deep down, intrinsically I know there is more truth to that statement then he wants me to know.

"Tristan, we'll talk later. Let me go make sure everybody is fine. We'll make plans for when we next see each other. I promise. Just let me get inside. Please." I start to beg.

"Kaitlyn, what's wrong?" His concern forces me to lie. *Shit!*

"Nothing. I've been gone for so long I'm worried. That's all." I reach over to try to kiss him but he evades my lips.

"Why don't I believe you? You know you can tell me anything and don't have to lie." He says this while caressing my cheek in a very simple loving way. I want to tell him but he would never let me go then.

"Please just trust me. I'll be fine and speak with you later." Just as my feet hit the asphalt, I hear a crash inside. Panicked, I turn to see if he heard anything, thankfully he did not. Closing my door, he hands me the keys. He straddles the motorcycle and revs it. Before he places the helmet on his head, he kisses me soundly making me want more. When he pulls back he knows it too. Knowing how he affected me, he smirks and grasps my chin.

"Okay, I have to go."

"Yes, I know and according to you so do I." He kisses me again making it harder to leave.

"Okay, this is me leaving." He just shakes his head agreeing but takes the kiss further as his hands start to roam over my body. Not knowing what has come over me, I climb in front of him on the motorcycle, my house forgotten. As his hands snake under my blouse, I pull back enough to speak. He tastes divine and has soaked my panties with this last kiss. "Okay, this really is me leaving." I will never get used to his kisses. They steal every breath I take. I lean back looking at him and slide against the hardness in his pants which elicits an unexpected moan from me and groan from him. *God he looks smoking hot on this motorcycle.*

"You need to get inside before I take you right here right now."

Sassily I reply. "Promises, promises."

"Oh baby don't go there." I climb off weak kneed and panting.

"Why is the motorcycle here and not the car?"

"The car needed a tune up, so the driver left the motorcycle. Do you want to go for a ride?" *Yes, yes, yes. Please!!* Ever since Michelle Pfeiffer sang Cool Rider in *Grease 2*, I have always fantasized about riding a motorcycle with my boyfriend. Unfortunately, tonight is not the night. Can you tell my social life has been lived through movies up until now?

"Yes, I want to but not now. How about next time? Seeing you on it does something to me?" I smile seductively and yearningly at him.

"Continue to look at me like that and you won't make it inside." He teases but there is a threat there as well. I have no doubt he would carry it out. This man does something to my thought processes because I would let him. *Promises, promises.* We kiss long and passionately making me forget again why I need to get inside. I pull back confused.

"Good night Angel. I'll speak with you later." He puts the helmet on and waits for me to reach the house. He speeds away once I am inside.

CHAPTER SIXTEEN

Kaitlyn

There is another crash in the next room. I cautiously stick my head in to see what is happening. My mother is throwing dishes at my father, how typical. They are both, as Bethany said, intoxicated. Neither of them will remember this tomorrow, except us kids.

Tristan is right I am too old for this. They need to grow up and act like adults. Deep in thought, I miss the insults and barbs being volleyed backed and forth between them. But one of them has hit its mark because my father comes charging at my mother with his fist aimed at her. That's when I step in between them and he halts seeing me but not in time for his fist to miss me.

His fist hits me right in the ribs and I hear a crack. Whoosh goes my breath as it leaves my body in a rush and I immediately double over to protect myself from any further hits that may befall me. Both my parents stop, they look at me holding back the tears. The pain is excruciating but somehow I manage to talk calmly with as much force as I can muster without causing myself more pain. "I think the both of you are done now. Get away from me before I call the cops on both of you. You need to sleep this off."

They measure each other up and then look at me. Neither of them asks me if I'm okay or can they help but instead go off to their separate rooms. The final straw or nail in the coffin is not asking if I was okay. That hurts more than the pain. They really don't care about me one way or the other. The little girl in me just grew up. *Why do I bother?*

Tenderly I assess my ribs, knowing the ribs are broken by the crack I heard, but the lung is not punctured. How am I going to explain this to

Tristan? This will bruise and then what? How do I get around it with him? He will insist, better yet demand, that I move in with him immediately and right now I tend to agree with him but what about my sisters and brother. On nights like these, God forgive me, I wish something would happen to my parents.

Going downstairs to check on my siblings, selfishly I hope Bethany is awake but they are all asleep thankfully. Even in sleep Bethany looks tired. There are black circles under her eyes. *God I hope she is okay.* I dare not wake her. She deserves the rest.

Walking back upstairs, unhappily I check on my parents. My father is passed out cold, face down on his bed fully clothed. My mother when I enter her room is barley awake with a cigarette in her hand. How many times have I woken up from a dead sleep to check on her and seen her like this? There have been a few times when the cigarette burned the mattress. An angel has been watching and protecting us all these years. I do not know how she has not managed to burn the house down before. Taking the cigarette from her hands, I extinguish it and turn off her television.

Sophia is the only one I can call to help. I find my purse and speed dial her. She answers on the first ring.

"Kaitlyn, are you okay? Where the fuck have you been?" She's angry and worried.

"Look, I'm sorry and you can bitch me out when you see me but can you come over like right now." I whimper because I inhaled too deeply. "Fuck! Please don't yell or argue with me just come over now?" I can't hold back the tears as they fall.

"I'm already on my way. What's wrong? What happened?" She's no longer angry just concerned.

"Dad's fist met my rib. I heard it crack and no one is awake to help me. I won't waken Bethany. She looks too exhausted."

"You heard it crack?"

"Yes." I say simply.

"We're going to the hospital and having it x-rayed. Then you're pressing charges against the both of them."

"No. I can't afford to have that happen. Who will take care of the kids? I'm the next responsible adult. What then, I don't go to medical school because I have to take care of them." I know I exaggerated but she needs to see the police cannot get involved. "When you get here I'll explain everything, I promise. Just hurry please." We disconnect.

Without knocking, Sophia walks through the front door less than five minutes later. She bear hugs me forgetting where ribs actually are. "OUCH!!"

"Oh God, I'm so sorry." She steps back gingerly releasing me careful not to jar me further. We walk to my bedroom where she can see the area. She helps me out of my shirt and we both wince, me because of the pain and her because the injury has started to bruise. She also notices the fading love mark Tristan left and quirks her eyebrow at me. "I know I have much to tell you."

After I have taken some Tylenol and still not gotten relief, Sophia finally convinces me after much arguing to go to the urgicenter in town. While we are waiting she starts her interrogation but my phone rings interrupting her questions. I glance at the caller id, Tristan. I didn't get a chance to call him yet. He's probably worried. If I ignore it he will return to my parent's house but if I answer then I may be able to get through this night. I answer the phone and hope for the best.

"Hi Angel."

"Hey Tristan." Sophia heard me mention Tristan's name and is actively listening in on my conversation. In fact she is leaning too close causing me to move and gasp in pain. I try to cover it up but I know Tristan heard.

--- --- --- ----

Tristan

This night was wonderful. My family really likes her. Dad almost spilled the beans about my part in the demise of her car and mom almost broke down telling Kaitlyn about my past. There is so much mom does not know. I know Kaitlyn is intrigued by what my mother wanted to say. When we kissed goodbye before, those kisses ignited something in me. It was hard for us to separate. Hopefully, she is thinking about sleeping alone tonight. Maybe she will reconsider moving in. She seemed in a rush to get out of the car. I hope her parents aren't giving her a hard time. Maybe I should call her to make sure everything is okay because she hasn't called yet. It takes four rings before she picks up.

"Hi Angel."

"Hey Tristan." She gasps out loud as if in pain.

"What's wrong?" My voice is edged with concern.

"Nothing just Sophia stepping on my toe. I called her and she came over to bitch me out."

"Good, I'm glad you called her but why so late?" Why didn't they just talk on the phone?

"She came by because she didn't want to risk losing me again. Hey, can I call you tomorrow? She and I need to talk." In the background someone calls her name.

"Kaitlyn, who's that calling your name?" I ask suspiciously.

"No one. Can I speak to you tomorrow?" I hear her cry out in pain. What the hell is going on?

"Kaitlyn, what the fuck is wrong?" I'm suddenly angry and no longer feeling the calmness of before.

"Fine, you'll find out sooner or later. I'm at the urgicenter in town."

"Why? What happened?" I grab my keys and run to the garage. "The urgicenter on Main Street?" I slam the door shut and start the car.

"Yes why? Tristan what are you doing?"

"I'm coming to you." I need to know she is okay in person rather than risk her lying to me. It is not in her nature to lie but when she feels she has to protect someone she does it easily. This woman has become my life and if there is something wrong with her I want to fix it.

"Tristan, you have an early start tomorrow. You need to stay home. Why do you think I called Sophia and not you?"

"We'll discuss that issue later. That deserves a punishment. I should always be the person you call first." I am livid, feeling helpless. "How did it happen? I want to know everything. Don't leave anything out."

"It was an accident Tristan. An honest to goodness accident."

"Fine an accident. Go on." *Accident my ass.* Not answering fast enough I growl my frustration. She is trying to cover something up. She was home what could have happened? What did her parents do to her? "Who hit you?"

"I stepped between my parents like I always do and my father stopped but not before his fist made contact with my rib." I swear I just bent the steering wheel and almost hit an oncoming car. I am so angry I slam my foot on the gas pedal.

"Why do you insist on putting yourself between them?" My voice is calm but I am anything but calm.

"I told you why a couple of days ago. Was that conversation not important enough for you?" She's angry with me? *What the fuck?* I am going to chalk this attitude up to her current state of mind. I respond very calmly because I don't want to upset her further. She does not need any crap from me, even though I just want to help her. Right now, she will see me as the enemy if I start to berate her parents. But God help me, they do not deserve the right to be called parents.

"I remember everything you've ever said to me because it's all very important. I just don't understand why. Why do you put yourself in danger like that? Why do you allow them to do this? They don't deserve you." I made it to her in record time. My last question is asked in person as I wrap her in my arms gently. She sighs and starts to cry.

--- --- --- ----

Kaitlyn

As soon as I am in his arms, I feel safe and secure. It is okay for me to lose it now. He will take care of everything. I cry about everything-cry because I hate my parents; cry because I feel guilty for hating them; cry because they did not ask if I was okay; cry because I mean nothing to them; cry because I let them do this and finally cry because I am tired of it all.

The doctor finally enters with the x-rays results confirming what I already knew, a hairline rib fracture. The doctor only now notices Tristan and his previously flirty demeanor has changed to strictly professional. After disengaging one of his arms from around me, Tristan holds out his hand to the doctor.

"Hello, Tristan Chance. Thank you for taking care of my girlfriend." Tristan places a feather light kiss on the crown of my head. "So what is the treatment for the rib?" *Pain meds as needed.*

"Pain medication and we encourage patients to take deep breathes at least once an hour to prevent complications." The doctor responds coolly. "If you'll excuse me, I'll get her a script for some stronger pain medication and you can get out of here."

When he returns he tries to gives me the prescription but Tristan intercepts it. He will fill it because he knows I won't. As we prepare to leave Tristan asks the doctor if he and I can have a few moments alone in the exam room. The doctor looks perplexed but allows it. Once the door closes Tristan's demeanor changes and he advances on me. Instinctively I back away until I remember doing this once before and him reacting badly that time. I stop moving and he smiles at me knowingly.

"You are not going home until we fix the problem at your house." His voice is soft but the tone is hiding his anger.

"Tristan, I don't want to argue about this, please. I'm tired. It has been a very long night. I just want to go home and climb into bed."

"Fine. I'm not arguing I'm just stating fact. You're coming back home with me."

"Tristan both my parents were passed out when Sophia and I left. There won't be any more problems tonight. Please take me home and verify I'm telling you the truth. Please." I try reasoning with him. He is scared for me. The minute I was out of his sight something else happened.

"Kaitlyn, the idea of you going back to that house after this and knowing I have no control over it scares the shit out of me. Can you please rethink moving in with me?" I shake my head no. He roughly pulls on his hair frustrated. "It would give me peace of mind."

"I can't. If I move in with you, Bethany will be stuck by herself caring for my brother and sister. If that was Bethany who walked between my parents instead of me, my father would have thrown her out of the way and attacked my mother. I scare my father for some reason."

"What are you saying Kaitlyn?"

"My father is afraid of me. I'm not sure when it happened or why exactly but I think it was three years ago. He tried to come after me once but as he advanced on me I advanced on him. When we met in the middle, he tried to push me with his belly so I pushed him in the chest with my hands knocking him down. When he tried to get back at me, I stopped that as well. He is afraid of my strength and knowledge. He thinks I would have no problem calling the cops on him and having him arrested."

"But you told me your parents never hit you?"

"He didn't actually hit me; he tried to push me but failed."

"That's a fine line Kaitlyn. Are you in danger of being home? I need to know."

"No." She's adamant but how can I trust her after what just happened. Can't she see the danger they represent.

"Fine, I'm spending the night. We can discuss what we'll do about living arrangements tomorrow."

"Tristan you can't spend the night. What will my parents say? You'll just make things worse."

"I don't care what they think. Let them try something while I'm there."

"Tristan please I can handle this. I love it that you want to take care of me but I have to do this on my own. I have always handled it on my own."

"But you're not alone anymore. You have me and I'll take care of you."

"Please Tristan. Tomorrow, I promise we'll talk about different arrangements. But tonight let me just stay there." Begrudgingly I relent.

"Fine, I'll come in to make sure they're still asleep then leave. But this isn't over Kaitlyn. We'll discuss it further tomorrow."

"Thank you Tristan. I know this is hard for you but I promise I'll be fine."

He hugs and kisses me gently not wanting to cause any additional discomfort. As we leave the exam room, Sophia jumps up and meets us half way. "What did the doctor say?"

"Fracture rib as I suspected. Thanks for taking me. Tristan is going to drive me home. Is that okay with you?"

"Yeah, fine. Tomorrow we're going out for breakfast so we can talk."

"Breakfast isn't good but lunch should be fine."

"Fine lunch it is. I'll pick you up so we can have more time to talk." We don't hug because of my ribs so we blow each other kisses good bye. Tristan takes my elbow leading me to a black heavily tinted Land Rover. I look to him questioningly.

"It's one of my other cars. I couldn't drive you on the motorcycle and the car is still in the shop. This is the car used to drive the CEO around in. It has special tinting and glass. This is one of the most secure cars around. Starting tomorrow, I will be driven around in it."

"A driver? Why?"

"Once it becomes public knowledge tomorrow about me becoming CEO, I become an easier target. So the security around me increases. We have too many government contracts and knowledge that more or less paints a bull's eye on my back."

"Tristan you're scaring me."

"I'm sorry Angel but the knowledge the company has could be damaging if it fell into the wrong hands. Threats have been made against my father numerous times. The head of security at the time of the first threat recommended we start using body guards. So my dad instituted that policy for all CEOs and some other valuable board members."

"Why didn't you tell me this sooner?" I asked peeved slightly not knowing his safety would be an issue.

"Honestly?" My arched brow indicates my affirmative answer. "Well, I was afraid I'd scare you off."

There is absolutely no way for me to respond to this except to petulantly say, "Well you should've said something."

When we arrive at my house he helps me exit the car careful not to hurt me. The dish fragments are still dispersed all over the floor. As I bend to clean it I gasp at the pain. I feel his eyes searing a hole into my back. "Sorry habit."

"Well break the habit. You're not the maid. Your parents should clean this up." I bark out a laugh, wince, and he starts to clean it up.

"That's funny. They'll wake up tomorrow and think it was one of us who caused this damage."

"Where's the fucking broom?" He huffs.

When he is done, we check on my parents and he believes they will sleep the night through. We quietly descend the basement stairs to check on my siblings who are still asleep as well. Promising to lock my bedroom door and call him if my parents should waken again, we say good night at the front door. He is very hesitant about leaving but eventually gives in. I know it goes against his nature to leave me in what he perceives as a dangerous situation. The way he cares for me is sweet but I know I won't be calling him tonight regardless of my parents waking or not.

Something needs to be done about my parents I agree but I don't know what to do. Neither of them will seek help for their problems and we have no real family here to help with my siblings. Bethany will be going off to college next year leaving Thomas and Serena to fend for themselves. I'm not sure how much time I'll be home during medical school. Maybe I could finagle something with Mrs. Duncan.

It shouldn't be my responsibility to figure this out. I need to discuss options with my grandparents. The best place for Thomas and Serena would be with them. Maybe we could arrange it somehow, temporary guardianship until they are old enough. Maybe Tristan could help me figure this out. I could focus more on us, maybe move in like he suggested. Sleep evades me most of the night but when I do finally succumb, it is restless and filled with nightmares.

The next day comes quickly and I am very tired having only fallen asleep after four in the morning. Bethany comes into my room at eight with Thomas and Serena in tow. They all look tired but when they look at me their faces light up. They scramble on my bed to snuggle with me but when I wince and gasp in pain their faces turn to concern.

"What's wrong Kaitlyn?" Thomas asks innocently.

"Nothing I just hurt myself yesterday and I have to be careful with my ribs." I try to hug him gently.

"How did you hurt yourself?" Serena asks.

"I fell into a counter top while on the sailboat." Sounds plausible, but Bethany looks at me shrewdly.

"Okay guys why don't we get breakfast started and then Kaitlyn can tell us about her trip." She ushers them out but before she leaves she questions me. "What happened really and don't give me a shit story. You're a terrible liar."

I smile because she's right. "When I came home last night they were fighting. Mom said the wrong thing and pushed dad's last button. He started to advance on her when I stepped into the room. He stopped immediately when he saw me but not before his fist met my ribs. You were sound asleep so you didn't hear a thing."

"Why didn't you wake me? I could've helped." She asks incredulously.

"You looked so tired even in sleep. However, when I heard the crack I knew I needed help so I called Sophia. She convinced me to have an x-ray so we went to the urgicenter in town. Tristan drove me home and helped to clean up the mess."

"Who's Tristan?"

"Oh that's right there is so much I have to tell you. Tristan would be my boyfriend." I state simply. A smile, that could light up the house not just a room, lights up my face because of her speechlessness. "You'll be seeing a lot of him. He's a really nice, great guy. Nanny and poppy met him last week end." She looks very confused so I continue on with a brief version of our history.

"Last weekend someone slipped something into my drink at a party of his but he found me before anything happened. I didn't know this at the time and was scared, which is why I ran to Pennsylvania. I spoke with nanny and poppy and they helped me deal with everything, that's until Tristan showed up. He explained exactly what happened and then persuaded me to take a trip with him on his sailboat. So that's where I was all week."

Still confused she shakes her head hoping to make sense of my story. "Okay, I don't know where to start. So you were drugged with something?"

"Yes, some sort of date rape drug. But nothing happened. Tristan rescued me before I was raped." We both shiver. "I was so disoriented when I woke up, I ran. I ran from everyone. I thought I was raped and I needed time to deal before I'd have to come back here. I knew mom and dad couldn't help me so I went to the only place where I knew I'd receive the love and understanding I needed."

Thomas comes in to my room and asks, "Are you guys coming or not? We're hungry."

"Now would be a great time for you guys to start learning how to make your own meals." Bethany replies tartly.

"We'll be right there. I promise." I say soothingly to take the bite out of her response.

"Okay. Whose car is in the front of the house?" He asks.

"Oh that's mine." Bethany looks at me disbelievingly. "Another long story. Needless to say Tristan bought it for me." The shock on her face is comical triggering my laughter until it hurts my ribs. "Don't make me laugh, it hurts too much."

"He bought you a car?" Bethany questions flabbergasted.

"Who's Tristan?" Thomas asks simultaneously.

"Tristan is my new boyfriend who you'll meet soon, I promise and yes he bought me a car after mine was totaled." Bethany runs to the front window to look. Serena is already there looking as well.

"Kaitlyn it's a BMW. You can't afford that." Bethany states simply.

"I know but it's paid in full and along with the insurance for the year."

"Is he rich or something?" She questions.

"You could say that. His family owns Chance Industries." She looks at me perplexed.

When the business name triggers her recognition she stutters her response. "You... you don't mean Tristan Chance? The Tristan Chance.

A LITTLE DEATH BY CHANCE

Only the hottest richest guy around in this area. The one who is always in the tabloids?"

Shyly I answer her. "Yes, the same one. But he is nothing like that. Or well he isn't any more according to him." She is thunderstruck. "Okay time for breakfast. What do you guys want?"

"Kaitlyn! I need the details now. Don't leave me hanging. That's not fair." Amused I walk away to prepare their breakfast.

During breakfast, a bouquet of flowers is sent to the house for me from Tristan. The card was sweet and perfect.

> To the one who saved me,
> Thank you for an amazing week. You made me
> feel again. You're perfect in every sense of the
> word. Can't wait until I see you next. Don't
> make me wait too long.
> Yours always,
> TC

After reading it I think it would be best if I kept it hidden from everyone. My mother comes out of her room shortly after the flowers were delivered and looks like yesterday's debris. Looking at my flowers, she eyes me disgustedly. "Those yours?" I just nod. "Who did you fuck to get them?" Bethany gets ups and takes Thomas and Serena with her. Once their gone I answer her.

"Really? Is that what you think of me?"

"The only reason you receive flowers like those is when you're a good fuck for someone. You're lucky I even think about you. Where were you anyway? It's been a mess around here."

"I was at grandma and grandpas."

"Well they never said anything to me."

"Because you didn't ask them. You never do. If you weren't always drunk and thought of someone other than yourself you'd have asked. So don't blame me or them if you didn't know." Where is this attitude coming from? *I am tired of being made to feel like crap because of my parents, that's where.*

"Don't take that tone with me miss or else-"

"Or else what? What are you going to do about it? You need me whether you like it or not. If I wasn't here you would have to care for the kids and live in filth. The kids would most likely be taken away from you. So don't threaten me!"

Her eyes are blazing. As she rises, probably to attack, my father enters. She quickly sits back down. He's rushing around late for work. In all the years of drinking, he has never been late to work. He looks angrily at

185

my mother and she is about to make him more angry by making a comment when I interrupt her.

"Dad, can I help you with something?"

"No, I'm late. I forgot to set my alarm last night." He looks at his watch. "Where have you been?"

"Oh, I went to see nanny and poppy." *See Bethany I can lie when I need to.*

"That's good. How are they?"

"They're great as usual. They actually asked if Bethany, Thomas and Serena could spend the rest of the summer with them." *See lie again.* My grandparents won't mind the kids.

"That's a great idea. Would you mind taking them? Work has been so busy I won't get a chance to get away." Once their away, I will not have to worry about their safety. Then I can work on a more permanent solution.

"You can't take my kids away from me." Mom yells at me and then him.

"No one is taking your kids away. Don't be so fucking dramatic. They haven't seen John and Emily in months. This will be good for them. Will you be staying with them Kaitlyn?" He eyes my mother with disgust. "Anyway you do nothing around here so life just got easier for you."

"No Sophia is leaving for law school soon. We're spending the remainder of the summer in the Hamptons with Lara. Medical school starts soon."

"No, you can't go. Who will clean the house and do the laundry?" Mom snips.

"Guess you'll have to if you want a clean house and clothes." Dad replies nastily.

The tension is starting to escalate. The kids are upstairs, hopefully too occupied to hear any of this. Quickly I think of something to say easing the tension. "Dad you're going to be even later if you don't leave now."

"Yeah right." He bumps unwittingly into me and I wince in pain at being jarred. He doesn't even notice. "Okay good bye." The new car in front of the house next to his did not even register to him.

As the door shuts behind him, I don't have time to move before my mother hits me in the ribs. I double over gasping at the shooting piercing pain. She grabs a handful of my hair as I start to rise and drags me behind her. The pain in my ribs is excruciating but somehow I manage to get her to release me. She attempts to come at me again but this time I am ready. I push her with such force she bangs into the wall.

Stunned, I advance on her having the upper hand. In a threatening voice I explain things to her. "You ever touch me again and I'll have you arrested so fast you won't know what hit you. Do. You. Understand. Me?"

She is seething but does not answer.

Backing away from her, not daring to turn my back on her, she leaves the room. I notice Bethany is watching. "How long have you been there?"

"Long enough. When do we leave?"

"Are you sure you're okay with this. I only want what's best for the three of you. Being here is no longer safe. But it's also the summer before your senior year."

"Your right, it isn't safe here anymore. Don't worry about me. I still keep in touch with some friends in Pennsylvania from when Serena was born and nanny and poppy took care of us. I may actually be able to enjoy the rest of the summer and act my age."

"Okay I'll call them now. Then I have to call Tristan to let him know our plans. Maybe we'll leave tomorrow the latest?" She agrees. "Can you keep an eye on Thomas and Serena for a little while today. I have to meet Sophia and explain some things to her."

"Okay but if we're leaving tomorrow I want to see my friends."

"Agreed and thanks for everything. I mean it."

A little while later I call Sophia and make arrangements to pick her up for lunch. When I pull in front of her house, she comes running out with her mother in tow.

"What the hell is this? Where did you get this?"

"Tristan." I smile broadly.

"Tristan let you borrow this?" Mrs. Duncan asks suspiciously.

"No, he bought it for me. Long story short, my car met a horrible end and he felt he was to blame so he replaced it with this." They both are shocked silent.

Mrs. Duncan comes around first not knowing what to say. "How are you doing, honey?"

"I'm okay. Actually better than okay. My father agreed to let Bethany, Thomas and Serena stay with my grandparents for the rest of the summer. I'm going to take them later today."

Sophia starts to push me towards the car rudely. "Mom when I get back I'll tell you everything she tells me. Okay?"

"Yes fine. See you two later."

We decide to go to the diner and after placing our orders she attacks with the questions that have building since I ran from Tristan's party. "What happened? And start at the beginning."

I start at the very beginning from when Tristan first entered the candy store up until this morning with my mother. Along the way she only interrupted twice, which is surprising because she usually interrupts more. By the time we finish our meal most of her questions have been answered.

We head over to Starbucks and both order venti caramel

Frappuccino's. Taking two seats by the window, she starts with more questions. This round of questioning focuses on the sex with Tristan. She wants the juicy details, which I provide.

"I'm jealous. Danny wants to take things slow. But I guess it gives us something to look forward to."

"So things are good with him?"

"Yeah, they're great but he's on the road touring. Tristan was able to get a temp guitarist but Danny doesn't know if he fits yet with the other members. Their first hit is getting a lot of radio play."

"I know, we heard it driving back. It's crazy how things have changed so much in a week. You're dating a musician and I'm dating Tristan. If you had told me this was going to happen I would've thought you were crazy." We both giggle.

"I'm so happy for you. Last night he seemed so different. Is this since you started dating him?"

"Yeah, he even said as much. Sophia he is so gentle but so demanding at the same time. He pushes me to the edge then tells me to not jump. I'm only allowed to when he says so. Is that normal?"

"I guess he likes control. Some guys are like that. I once dated some guy who tried that with me but I didn't like it. Do you like it? That's the question you should be asking. It's not for me to say if it's normal or not. That's what matters."

"Yeah, I guess you're right. But I'm so naïve, I don't know what is normal."

"Don't worry about what's normal. Do what feels right. The way he reacted when you ran, I don't think he would ever intentionally hurt you."

"That's just it, I trust him implicitly. If I didn't I don't think we would've slept together. He keeps referencing some other things that has me nervous but excited as well." Sophia's eyes bug out. "I love him Sophia. Me. I get it now what you and Lara have been trying to tell me all these years." *Crane to Starbucks, table four please, to lift the jaw off the floor.*

"Oh, sweetie I'm so happy for you. You deserve someone who will treat you well and Tristan is that guy."

I am glad I was able to talk with her. She helped to give me insight and perspective. I could not talk to Tristan about this, although I'm sure he would have liked me to instead of Sophia. After finishing our drinks, I drive her home and we say our goodbyes. Things are right in our world once again.

CHAPTER SEVENTEEN

Tristan

Today is the first day of my future and all I can really focus on is Kaitlyn. Her father broke her rib "accidentally." It feels like we won't have a chance if she does not confide in or lean on me especially with something like this. Dad and I drove into work together this morning. He wants the transition seamless. He accompanies me to every meeting and offers his expertise, when asked or needed. The cancer is getting to him though because by noon he is exhausted. In my new office, his old one, he lies down.

This is the longest amount of time we have spent in one place so far. Sitting at my desk reviewing the numerous messages is a challenge especially discerning priorities from less urgent ones. It is difficult to prioritize. Jane, my assistant, is ordering us lunch. When it is delivered, we sit to have a working lunch meeting. She graciously declines my offer of extending her lunch for a real nonworking one. She says there is always work to be done. I know we will work well together.

"Tristan, you never cease to amaze me. The way you have tackled the day thus far is good. Offering the employees the opportunity to meet you was a good call."

"Thanks, I want to know each and every employee under me. I know it's a lot to remember but I feel we can get them to be more productive if I show an interest in them. I was also thinking of starting an annual employee barbeque at the house. What do you think?"

"I think that's a great idea. They deserve it."

"In the past have you ever pursued offering employees' stock options to help encourage better productivity?"

189

"No, we haven't, but that's not a bad idea."

"Sorry dad, I have so much I want to improve or change, with no offense to you, my mind is going off on tangents."

"Well, you're doing a good job today but there is something else going on that you aren't telling me. Your heart doesn't seem to be here, your mind definitely. Is everything okay with Kaitlyn?" How does he do that?

"Actually last night she fractured a rib. She-" He cuts me off with his concerned question.

"She fractured a rib how?" I briefly explain to him what she told me. And he confirms what I already know. "Her and her siblings should not be in that environment. I had Tim investigate her parents."

"I know, so did I. Her father is a hardworking man but her mother is a different story. Kaitlyn refuses to leave. She feels responsible for the children. I don't know what to do to convince her to move in with me. I have-" My cell phone interrupts us and speak of the devil, it's Kaitlyn. "Dad it's Kaitlyn I have to take this."

"Go ahead son, I'll rest right here." He lies down and appears to be sleeping almost immediately. I walk to the windows and look out across the city. This office view is amazing.

"Hey Angel, how are you feeling today?" She hesitates in answering me.

"Hi baby. How's your day going?" She says excitedly but ignores my question.

"My day is going better now that I'm speaking to you. How's your day going?"

"Thank you for the flowers they're beautiful." She is ignoring my question. I know her well enough now to know she is evading. Something must have happened last night or this morning. "Good news, I'm bringing Bethany, Thomas and Serena to my grandparent's house today. I spoke with my father and told him how they wanted to visit and he agreed." She brought Christmas to my door early and I cannot contain my delight.

"That's great. I'll have Jane call a car service to drive you. Then I can see you when you return. This is perfect. How long will they be staying?" I hear her smile through the phone.

"I'll drive them. We don't need a car service. They'll be there for the remainder of the summer. We'll figure out when I should pick them up once we get there." She should not be driving that distance by herself.

"Then I'll go with you if you won't take a driver. I should-" She interrupts me.

"Tristan, you can't just drop everything and leave now. You have major responsibilities. I'll be fine. I've done this drive so many times I could drive there blind folded." Oh she is feeling better by her cocky attitude.

"Fine, when will you be back?"

"Not until very late. I'll crash at home then tomorrow I'll meet you at the loft if that's okay with you."

"If that's okay with me of course it's okay. I can't wait. But why can't you just come straight from their house?"

She sighs. "Because I need to clear some things up with my mother first."

"Okay but I get you for the rest of the summer, right? Christmas has come early." She laughs at me.

"Yes, you do. I'll call you later when we're leaving and then when I get there. How's that sound?"

"It sounds good for now although I would really like someone to drive you. It's a long drive to complete in one day. You were injured yesterday and I don't want you so tired you fall asleep at the wheel. Please reconsider and humor me. Let me get someone to drive you."

"Thank you, but no. I have to do this. I won't see them for the remainder of the summer and I'll miss them. It has always been just us to rely on each other. Now it will be me at home with my parents."

"No, you'll be at the loft with me. I'll not have you staying there without your brother or sisters as a buffer."

"Well, I guess you're right especially after this mo-" She stops abruptly mid-sentence.

"What happened this morning Kaitlyn?" My father stirs awake at my suddenly angry tone.

"Don't worry, I took care of it."

"Kaitlyn?"

"It was nothing."

"Dammit Kaitlyn this is what I'm talking about. How are we to have a chance if you don't let me in?"

"Fine. My mother lost it and physically attacked me but I'm fine." I try to interrupt her but she ignores me and finishes. "She accused my father and me of taking her kids away from her." *Well she deserves it.* "So before he left my father accidentally bumped into me causing me to wince and my mother caught on I was hurt. She took advantage of it as soon as he left. She hit me in the ribs. While I was down she grabbed my hair and dragged me not far because I regained the advantage. I pushed her back and threatened her with the police. She's backed off for now."

"She... she hit you! That's it. Your stuff is being moved today while you're gone. I'm not compromising on this Kaitlyn. Don't ask me. I tried it your way twice and look what happened to you. No more." My voice is low and menacing. She has me feeling like a failure. Both times I listen and trust her and she has been hurt. No more.

191

"Tristan be reasonable. I can't just move in with you. I–"

"No compromising Kaitlyn. We tried it your way. No more end of story. Drop it."

"Listen here Tristan Chance, no man will tell me what I can and cannot do. When I get back we can discuss it rationally. Until then don't you dare send any one over it to get my stuff. It will just piss my parents off and cause me more problems."

"No." I hear dial tone. She hung up on me. Holding the phone away from my ear, I look at it astonished she would actually hang up on me.

"What happened?" My father inquires.

"She hung up on me." He tries to holds back his laughter.

"It's nice to see a woman who isn't awed by Tristan Chance. I think she just put you in your place, son. I like her style it's very similar to your mother's. Your mother is the only one who can do that to me." He chuckles. I gape at him.

"She hung up on me?" I'm stuck on her hanging up on me. "Was I being that unreasonable?" I ask him.

"Well, it depends on what happened."

"Her mother attacked her today but Kaitlyn was able to get the upper hand. She handled the problem for now but she shouldn't have had to handle it. I'm supposed to help her." His face is so serious now.

"Oh I see. Son, think about your response. Were you angry because Kaitlyn handled it or because you didn't?"

"I'm glad she handled it but she shouldn't have to. Dad, no one should have to live like that. I know this happens the world over but not to someone I love–" Oh I love her and it frightened me that something could happen to her.

"You love her son. Now think about your response from her point of view. She is an independent young woman. You're telling her what to do. Maybe you should try a different tactic?"

"You think I overreacted. But dad, her mother hit her. She's dropping the kids off in Pennsylvania and then there's no buffer. Then what?"

"I see your concern. How do you think it makes her feel? She knows it's not safe but she has no other option." Trying to interrupt him, he halts me with his hand. "Stop and listen to me. She can leave at any time but she won't, not at the expense of her sisters and brother. You can't expect her to."

"I understand but it doesn't help me now. What do I do dad?"

"Give her tonight. Then take her out to dinner tomorrow and discuss it like adults. Don't dictate to her. Instead involve her in the decision maybe lead her to your way of thinking."

"Okay, I'll try once more but so help me if something happens again. "I'll lock her up and throw away the key."

This feeling of helplessness sucks when someone I love is in potential danger. What is the sense in having all this money and power if I can't do anything about her situation? Her grandparents probably don't know what has happened and knowing Kaitlyn she won't tell them. They need to know so they can change her mind and intercede on her behalf. It's time to call them before I change my mind.

"Hello."

"Hello Emily, its Tristan Chance, Kaitlyn's boyfriend."

"Hi Tristan, how have you been?" Amazing how chipper she is. "What can I do for you?"

"I've been good. I was wondering if you'd spoken to Kaitlyn yet today."

"Yes as a matter of fact we did. She'll be driving the kids here tonight. Why is everything okay?" Her question is laced with concern.

"Well it depends on what you mean by okay...?" I don't mean to be so vague but I am starting to feel guilty about this call. But someone needs to help her and those kids.

"Tristan you're scaring me what happened?"

"Well last night Kaitlyn stopped a fight between her parents but not before she was injured. She was hit in the ribs, breaking it. I'm sorry to tell you this but... this morning Pamela attacked her." I rush on hoping to lessen the blow. "Fortunately Kaitlyn was able to handle her. But it just proves it's no longer safe for them in that house."

"Kaitlyn didn't say anything to us. John, Kaitlyn has a broken rib..... Yes they caused it.... Tristan hold on John wants to talk to you." I knew he would. Emily and John are good people and are not to blame for their daughter's actions but they can help their grandchildren.

"Hello Tristan. What happened exactly?" The story is quick to tell and he is not happy. "That's it Emily! I want those kids until Pamela can get her act together. We've turned a blind eye to her drunkenness long enough, hoping she'd get better. No more." Emily is talking in the back ground but I cannot hear it. "Tristan, thank you for calling us. I know Kaitlyn would never have told us. I was surprised when she called this morning asking if the kids could come for a visit. We should have figured something was wrong then. We have failed those kids but no more."

"It's not your fault. Kaitlyn didn't even call me when it happened, she called Sophia. Needless to say I was a bit angry with her. This morning after she told me what happened with Pamela, she and I had an argument because I want her to move in with me but she's refusing because of her brother and sisters." This sinks in before I continue. "I agree with you the kids can longer stay there. Maybe if you broach it with Kaitlyn, she won't feel so responsible. She won't live her life until she knows the kids are okay."

"Yes of course Tristan. We'll talk to her when she gets here. You're a good influence on her Tristan. Thank you. We'll talk soon."

"Great, thank you and good luck I know how stubborn she can be. Good bye." I ask Jane to get the newest handheld gaming systems for the kids, an iPad for Bethany and to wire some money to the Kiplings.

"Great dad, they're going to try and take the kids. Thanks for the advice."

"No problem son. Now let's get back to work. There's nothing else you can do for her until you see her tomorrow."

We handle business the rest of the day. Out of everyone we met, there are a few people I think no longer have the company's best interest at heart and need to be replaced. Their files are being sent over. Both employees are managers, one in Entertainment and the other in Research and Development. These departments will be pet projects of mine. The remainder of the day, dad and I review documents in the office. With the exception of Kaitlyn's situation, the day has been quite productive.

--- --- --- ----

Kaitlyn

Telling Tristan what happened this morning was not one of my smarter moments. He was so angry I think it's because he's scared for me and if I am honest with myself he has every right to be. I am scared to be home alone with my mother. What is to stop her from coming into my room at night drunk? She can make anything look like an accident. But he cannot just come into my life and dictate how I should live it. I am still in charge of my own life regardless of what he thinks but I am grateful that someone like Tristan cares so much for me.

After speaking with my grandparents earlier, they agreed the kids could come and spend the rest of the summer with them. They were delighted about it. When I spoke with the kids they were ecstatic. I know they feel the tension in the house which is not healthy for them.

Bethany and I decided to leave tonight instead of tomorrow. So here we are in my new car driving to Pennsylvania. The car drives like a dream. The short distance I drove it from Tristan's house home did not do it justice. I swear it purrs like a kitten- mind you I am not a car fanatic.

Thomas and Serena are having fun in the back seat with their new Nintendo 3DS systems Tristan had sent over. Bethany loves her new iPad. She can still stay in touch with her friends. Tristan was so happy with the new plans for the remainder of the summer he brought Christmas to the kids early this year. We called Tristan before we left to thank him for the gifts.

The drive here has been uneventful. It is déjà vu seeing my grandparents waiting for us on the front porch. They rush down the stairs to embrace Thomas and Serena and then Bethany and me. After grabbing the luggage from the trunk, my grandfather lifts his eyebrow at my car.

"Tristan I assume?" I can't help but laugh.

"Yeah, he sort of got his way after certain circumstances were out of our control."

"I like that boy. He's good for you and it seems for this family."

"He seems overly obsessed with the idea he needs to take care of me. He forgets I have been taking care of myself for years now."

"Kaity, give him a chance to do it. He's very fond of you." He puts his arm around my shoulders hugging me to his side and I inhale sharply at the pain. "What's wrong?"

"Nothing."

"Really, why did you gasp? It sounded like I hurt you. Did I?"

"No, I hurt myself on the boat. Nothing to worry about."

"Really what happened?" I try to think of a plausible lie but this is the human lie detector we're talking about. I have never been good at lying especially to my grandfather. So I opt to tell the abridged version of the truth.

"I got hurt while mom and dad were fighting." There plain and simple.

"What happened?" Surprisingly he is not as angry as I would have expected. So I give him the version I gave to Tristan.

"We need to do something about this now. I can't have you constantly protecting your siblings and putting yourself in danger. Your parents should not be acting like this in front of them. Your grandmother and I have sat back for far too long."

"Poppy what do you want to do? Do you really think anything will change?"

"I don't know but we need to do something. You're an adult now and should not be stuck at home caring for your siblings. Maybe if your grandmother and I force your mother's hand by threatening to take the kids away she will go get help."

"I don't think that will work. It will probably only make her mad."

"Well, let's try and see what happens."

So we decide he is going to speak with my parents tonight or tomorrow. The kids will stay with them indefinitely. He will use my ribs as leverage against them. I am nervous about how they will respond but my grandfather promises it won't affect me. He will call me after he speaks with them. As I bid my farewells, Bethany holds me tightly whispering to me to watch my back with our mother.

With music blasting and air conditioning that actually works, I feel great and life is almost perfect. I have a boyfriend who is crazy about me. My grandparents are taking the kids indefinitely. They love being with our grandparents. I start medical school in a couple of weeks. It is good to finally be me and all this happened once Tristan came into my life.

Bethany is going to think about whether or not she wants to transfer to another school senior year or graduate from home. Thomas and Serena will be enrolled in the school district there in Pennsylvania starting September. I cannot blame Bethany for feeling torn. I did promise her I would protect her no matter what.

My drive back to New York is uneventful. Tristan was right about me being tired. I feel exhausted. The last couple of days have taken their toll on me. Usually this ride does not bother me. When I finally pull into the driveway at two in the morning, my father is not home yet- big surprise there. The house is dark indicating my mother is asleep.

Boy, that could not be further from the truth because when I walk into the house she starts in on me from the dark. The lights are out except for the candle next to her chair casting an eerie glow to the room. Almost like a portent of things to come.

"You good for nothing piece of shit! I should have aborted you like I wanted to but I listened to your father. That fuck. Where the fuck is he? He's never home to see the piece of crap you are." She slurs her words and when she turns on the light her eyes are blazing with anger.

"Hello to you too mother. I see you're fit this evening. What, did you not have enough alcohol to drink tonight?" The sarcasm is a side effect of tiredness otherwise I would have ignored her.

"I'm sorry are you talking to me?" She stands to her feet wobbling slightly.

"No I wasn't. I was just going to bed. Have a good sleep." I start to walk past her and mutter to myself. "I'm sure you'll pass out soon enough." She stops me with her derogatory statements. Her voice is like nails on a chalkboard.

"Don't you dare walk away from me!" She fires off questions like a machine gun. "Who's Tristan and why is he sending you flowers? Why are my parents insisting your father and I physically hurt you?" She does not even remember this morning. "They said you have a broken rib because of an argument we had last night. Why do you insist on telling such lies? They are forcing us to either get help or their taking our children. Because of you. Because of you!" The last sentence felt like a whip against my skin it was filled with such hatred.

"Are you kidding me? The only time I lie is when people ask me about my home life. I am so tired of yours and daddy's problems. You've screwed me up to levels I only now understand. And Bethany, well

Bethany isn't that far behind. Luckily Thomas and Serena have Bethany and me as buffers. You have no idea how vile the stuff you spurt from your mouth is when you're drunk. And then you don't remember it afterwards."

It seems everything I say only incites her further. I have to just get to my room and lock the door then she can sleep it off. As I try to walk past her again, she grabs my arm and yanks me back in front of her. She slaps my face with such force my head whips to the side and I taste blood in my mouth. *That hurt, I'm seeing stars.* Then she grabs my hair and throws me to the floor. *Where did she get the strength?*

She starts to beat me as she yells. "Because of your lies, my parents are taking my children away and won't give them back until I get help. Your father has moved out. And now I have no one because of you." Out of the corner of my eye I see spittle flying from her mouth. Rising from my position on the floor, she pushes me against the wall and punches me in the already fractured rib, fully breaking it. Except this time I think it punctured a lung because I have difficulty breathing. With the wind knocked out of me, I take a swing at her and miss. I inhale very sharply and painfully before my next punch lands in her stomach forcing her to let go of my hair. I drop to my knees to catch my breath which is not happening. Next thing I know she hits me with something across my back and head repeatedly. In the fetal position trying to protect myself from the blows that keep coming, I recognize the wooden lamp that usually resides on the table next to her chair in her hand. When I try to crawl away she kicks me in the stomach multiple times. There is a shooting pain across my abdomen that was not there a moment ago.

Somehow with a surge of adrenaline and the will to survive, I manage to knock her to the floor but not before she hits me in the head again causing me to pass out. But before I pass out I watch her fall back, hit her head on the table with the lit candle and knock both the candle and the table to the floor.

When I come to briefly my phone is ringing and the living room is engulfed in flames. I smell something burning but cannot focus on what it is actually. I cannot feel a thing but I attempt to crawl away from the flames. My unconscious mother is not far away and I reach to pull her away from the flames as well. I am not sure if I have even moved before I pass out again. *Tristan I'm sorry I should have listened to you and come right to you.*

CHAPTER EIGHTEEN

Tristan

Ever since John called me I have had a terrible feeling. He spoke with Kaitlyn's parents and gave them an ultimatum. Either they get help or they willingly give up custody of their children and assault charges will be brought against them. He has been trying to contact Kaitlyn to let her know her mother did not take the news well. She threatened them and Kaitlyn.

As I pull in front of her parent's house, there is an eerie orange glow coming from the living room window. Dialing 911 as I run towards the house, I yell in to the phone "There's a fire," and I drop my phone not hanging up. I barge into the house. Kaitlyn is on the floor closest to the door out of immediate danger. I bend to pick her up and remove her from the fire when I see her mother, *oh God*, covered in flames. I look around the room for something to put the flames out. Maybe I should take Kaitlyn out first but if I do and her mother does not make it Kaitlyn will ultimately blame herself.

Ripping the curtain from the rod, I snuff the flames so I can drag her outside. The fire trucks are starting to arrive as I roll her around extinguishing the rest. I run back into the house for Kaitlyn. By this time the fire has spread to the upstairs. I gingerly pick Kaitlyn up and carry her to safety. The EMTs have arrived and are taking care of her mother. Kaitlyn is starting to come to.

"Tristan?"

"Yes, Angel it's me."

"I'm so sorry I didn't listen to you. I should have come to the loft instead of coming home. I'm so sorry." She starts to cry. The EMTs from the second ambulance have come over to her pushing me out of the way. Her eyes have not lost contact with mine throughout the assessment. She has minor first degree burns, possible punctured lung and internal bleeding. *What the fuck happened in there?* As they load her into the ambulance, she starts to call out my name.

"I'm here Angel, I'm not going anywhere."

"Sorry sir but you can follow us in your car."

"I'm her husband." I answer without thinking.

"Okay sir let me get her settled and you can sit up front."

"Baby, I'm right here. Don't worry I'm not letting you out of my sight."

"Tristan, I'm sorry." She keeps apologizing over and over as the tears stream down her face.

As we drive to the hospital, I call John to let him know what happened. "John, there's been a fire."

"What? Where?"

"The fire was in the living room and Kaitlyn and Pamela were in there. When I arrived Pamela was surrounded by flames." I don't have the heart to tell him more. "They have medevac'd her to the hospital. She's in critical condition. I'm riding with Kaitlyn now. She has only just now regained consciousness."

"Tristan, I'm on my way."

"I'm sending the helicopter to come get you. It's the fastest way. I think the kids should come as well. I don't think it is going to be good."

He is silent for a few moments. "Okay where do I go?" I tell him where to go and the helicopter should be there shortly. We hang up but not before John tells me he will call Kaitlyn's father. I don't want him anywhere near Kaitlyn. She has suffered enough because of these people. During the ride to the hospital her blood pressure bottoms out and she loses consciousness again. *Oh God please let her be okay?*

Once in the hospital I'm ushered to the waiting area to call my parents, Sophia and Lara all of whom arrive a short time later. Sophia and Lara are crying. Mrs. Duncan is with them.

"Tristan, what happened?" Mrs. Duncan asks concerned.

"I'm really not sure. All I know is that by the time I got to their house the living room was engulfed in flames and both Kaitlyn and Pamela were unconscious."

"Oh God. Is Kaitlyn okay?" Sophia asks crying.

"I don't know. They took her back there and I haven't heard anything yet." Overhead we hear "Code Blue ER."

"Oh God please not Kaitlyn." My father grabs me by the shoulders and shakes me.

"Tristan, look at me." His face is blurred by the tears unwilling to fall. "She's a fighter. There are many other unfortunate patients in there. Don't think the worst."

I barely whisper unable to find my voice. "Please keep reminding me of that."

"Okay son let's see if we can find something out." My father starts throwing his weight around to get answers and within five minutes the doctor attending to her case has asked for her next of kin.

"We can't get a hold of her father, her grandparents and siblings are in route now. What do you need?" In a no nonsense voice I answered his questions.

"I need a family member to sign consent for surgery. Who are you sir?" The doctor asks.

"I'm her fiancée. I'll sign. What exactly am I signing for?"

My father whispers everyone's thought. "Son, are you sure about this?" Curtly I nod.

"She has a punctured lung, ruptured spleen, and swelling on the brain. She needs emergency surgery for the spleen and the lung. The brain swelling we're going to watch and reassess after surgery."

"Is she conscious?"

"She has been in and out of consciousness. She keeps asking for Tristan. Would that be you?"

"Yes. May I see her before surgery?" The doctor seems hesitant but allows a quick visit while they prep the operating room. He escorts me to her room in the emergency room. When I see her, there are so many wires and tubes I am afraid to touch her. Her left hand is free. Bringing it to my lips, she wakes briefly.

"Tristan?" She whispers.

"Shhh… Angel I'm here. No talking. Save your energy you're about to undergo surgery. You're pretty banged up. I'm not supposed to be back here but you know me I won't let that stop me from seeing you." She smiles wanly at me. "Listen to me and listen good. When you get out of here, I am going to punish you for scaring me like this. I love you too much so don't you dare leave me. I need you." A tear escapes and falls. She lifts her hand to wipe the next one away.

"I love you too. I'm not going anywhere." She closes her eyes. I move the hair away from her forehead and lean forward to place a kiss on her nose. She smiles back at me with her eyes still closed. "I love you Tristan."

"Baby, no more talking." They arrive to take her away from me and I follow holding her hand as long as they allow it. My father and mother follow and envelop me in their arms when they take her from me. I feel so helpless right now. That night all those years ago comes crashing to the forefront of my mind. The pain in my heart is almost unbearable. The same fate cannot befall her as Tara. I need something to dull the pain.

"Son, she's a strong girl. She'll pull through this fine. Then you can take her home and coddle her." My mother's words are comforting but empty. I won't believe them until she wakes up from surgery.

"Thanks mom. I need to see how her mother is doing." *Even though I don't care.* Kaitlyn will want to know when she wakes up. The unit clerk on this floor is very helpful and was able to find Pamela was in critical condition. The doctors are not saying more but when they are finished with her they will speak with me of her prognosis. Now we wait. I hate waiting. I have never been a man of patience.

Time is something we all take for granted, always putting off what we can do today, tomorrow. We always feel we have plenty of time to live. But sitting here in the hospital hoping Kaitlyn pulls through surgery, I realize I have squandered my time. The time I spent with Kaitlyn has been too short but it was well spent. She makes me feel things I have long since abandoned. These emotions scare me but with her by my side I can conquer them. *Kaitlyn I need you to be okay.*

With this last thought, John and Emily trailed by the kids have arrived. Mrs. Duncan takes Thomas and Serena for something to eat so I can talk to John and Emily.

"Tristan, how are they?" John asks. He has aged since I last saw him. Concern and fear are etched on his face, deepening his lines.

"Emily, John, Kaitlyn is in surgery for a punctured lung and ruptured spleen. There is swelling on her brain as well." Emily loses control and breaks down. John is visibly shaken.

"Wh... What about Pamela?" John asks holding back his tears.

"The last I heard, she was in critical condition. The doctor said he would find me when he knew more. Here he is now."

Pamela's doctor enters the waiting room and pulls us to the side. She is not expected to survive. She has third degree burns over three quarters of her body. The only thing they can do is control her pain. She has not woken up and they don't think she will either. John, holding Emily up, follows the doctor. When they return Emily is a basket case and John is pale. They feel the kids should not see her like this. They don't want their last memories of her to be like this.

When the kids come back, John and Emily take them to the chapel to explain what is happening. Bethany returns with John wanting to see her mother.

"Bethany, I'm sorry to meet you like this. Kaitlyn has spoken so much about you. She loves you deeply. I know your sister fairly well and I don't think she would want you to see your mom like this."

"I need to see her."

"Think about it. This will be the last memory you have of her. Is that really what you want to remember?"

"I don't care. I need to see her. Kaitlyn is in there because of her! I need to tell her it is all her fault. Kaitlyn never did anything to her except love her even at her worse." The tears she is shedding could fill the ocean. The hatred she has for her mother runs so deep I don't think anyone ever knew how deep. "Why couldn't Kaitlyn just let the bed burn so many times?"

"Bethany, honey, please don't say that. Your mother loved you all. She has a problem." The hurt John is trying to hide slices through me. "She never meant any of those hurtful things she said and Kaitlyn knows that." John hugs her to him and quietly sobs.

It has been almost seven hours since they took Kaitlyn to surgery. Dad has been dealing with the company's issues since business opened an hour ago.

"Dad, I'm sorry you have to deal with all this."

"I wouldn't have it any other way. You need to be here right now. We'll handle things. Don't you worry." I start to dial the office when the surgeon makes an entrance. Everyone stands expectantly.

"She came through surgery. There was some extensive bleeding. It was difficult to find the source. It was the kidney. It was tough there for a time. She's in ICU now in critical but stable condition. We've medically induced a coma to help with the brain swelling."

"What are we looking at? When should we know if the swelling is a bigger problem?"

"The next twelve to twenty-four hours are critical and telling."

"Will she be okay?" Bethany asks quietly.

"I really can't answer that."

"Thank you doctor for everything."

"Yes, thank you." John says with gratitude.

He looks to Bethany and says, "She is a strong woman. She fought in surgery. I have a gut feeling she will be fine but it is still too early for my professional medical opinion." Bethany nods grateful. "I'll check on her again before I leave."

"When can we see her?" Bethany asks as we all forgot to ask.

"She is only allowed two visitors at a time. Give the nurses about thirty minutes to get her settled. Mind you there are many wires and tubes. She's pretty bruised as well."

"Okay. I want to see her first."

"Fine sweetheart. Why don't you and Tristan see her while I get your grandmother?"

"I'll go with you to keep an eye on Thomas and Serena." Mrs. Duncan says.

"Thank you. Kaitlyn has wonderful caring friends." John replies.

"Are you ready?" I ask her taking her hand in mine, squeezing it reassuringly.

"Tristan, we're right here." My mother says to my retreating back.

As we walk to the ICU Bethany looks up at me. "You know in the short time you have been with her, I have never seen her happy like this. That's a really nice car you bought her."

"Thank you. I really needed to hear that just now." I hug her to my side in a brotherly fashion. "How do you know she was happy?"

"Yesterday you were all she could talk about. She went on and on about how wonderful your trip together was. When I first saw her, she was so relaxed with no worry in her eyes."

"It was nice and I'm grateful we had the time together." We arrive at the room and look at each other uncertainly. Taking a deep breath together and squeezing each other's clasped hands, we enter. I hear her gasp in surprise as she sees Kaitlyn's swollen face.

"Oh, Kaitlyn." She whispers and cries. Grabbing Kaitlyn's hand gently she brings it to her lips and kisses it. I brush her hair away from her face and kiss her nose. "Tristan, what exactly happened?"

"I don't know. But when I got to your house they were both unconscious. They are the only two who really know what happened?"

"She has always protected us no matter the cost to her. If it wasn't for her, I think my parents would have either killed each other or one of us."

"I know she told me. Your sister is very special and means everything to me." I look at Kaitlyn and speak directly to her in a demanding voice. "You hear that Kaitlyn you are everything to me. Dammit I love you, don't you dare check out on me now." It is probably my imagination but I swear she squeezed my hand. "That's right Angel, you hear me. Don't leave me. I will find you wherever you go and drag you back here to me."

Bethany looks at me and a tear escapes. "Kaitlyn, it's me Bethany. You need to wake up and help me help Thomas and Serena. They need us right now."

"You hear that Angel. I'm not the only one who needs you. Dammit you better wake!"

At some point Bethany leaves only to be replaced by Emily. I get up reluctantly to leave but Emily halts me from doing so.

"No Tristan, you stay. Everyone out there agreed you should be here with her. We will take turns coming in to visit but you're staying."

"Thank you but I couldn't ask that of you."

"You didn't ask. John, Bethany and I all see how much you care for her. I would even venture to say you love her." I nod. "You hear that Kaitlyn sweetheart, this fine young man loves you. Now open those beautiful eyes of yours. The kids are fine just very worried about you. So you need to get better and wake up because they want to see you." Emily kisses Kaitlyn's cheek.

"You see Angel everyone wants you to wake up. Now wake up before I get angry at you." I whisper in her ear. "Just think what we can do when you wake up. There is still so much I want to teach you."

Emily must have overheard me because she smiles fondly at me and leans over to place her hand on my head. Hopefully she did not understand my innuendo. "Tristan, you are good for her. I'm going to let John come in and see her. Take care of her until I come back."

"Of course, I'll see you later."

Some time passes before John arrives and he has been crying. Something must have happened. He motions for me to come to the door. "Kaitlyn, Angel, I'll be right back. I'm just outside your door." I kiss her nose. "What happened John?"

"Pamela passed away. Her body just couldn't take it anymore. We knew it would happen but I had hoped Kaitlyn would have been able to say goodbye. Then maybe Pamela would have been able to tell Kaitlyn how much she did love her despite the way she has always acted towards her."

"John, I'm sorry. I don't know what to say."

"Thank you. I'm glad Kaitlyn has you. She will need you in the coming days." He claps me on the back. I embrace him.

"How do I tell her, John? Their relationship from what Kaitlyn has told me was tenuous at best."

"I know but they both loved each other. I know Pamela was difficult to live with but she did love those kids. She had a problem. Now she's with God and no longer suffering."

"I'm sorry John."

"Let's wait until she wakes up to tell her about Pamela. How is our girl doing?" He asks walking in the room.

"She still hasn't woken up yet." I resume my position at her side. "Kaitlyn, your grandfather is here. Now wake up for us."

He looks her over surprised by her face and tries to hide his remorse. "Hey Kaity. It's time for you to wake up. Everyone is worried about you." This time I know for sure she squeezes my hand.

"John, I think she can hear us. She just squeezed my hand."

"That's right girl you fight your way back to us."

"Kaitlyn, wake up for me Angel. Wake up now." Her eyes are fluttering like she is fighting to open them. "That's it Angel open those beautiful eyes for us. Show me how much you love me. Please baby." I plead with her and her eyes flutter faster than they were. I know she can hear us. But then her eyes.....

ABOUT THE AUTHOR

Kimber Swan is a penname. She lives in New York with her husband, two boys and two Shih Tzus. When she is not writing, she can be found nursing patients, completing her Masters in Nursing, hanging out with her family and friends or reading a good book. Reading has always been a lifelong love of hers since she was a child. Tristan and Kaitlyn's journey has been a story in the making for the last ten years. Thank goodness for traffic.

Dear Reader,

Tristan and Kaitlyn's story is only just beginning. Watch as their loves grows and matures. What happens when Kaitlyn wakes ups? How does her mother's death affect her? *A Little Death by Chance* alludes to Tristan's troubled past. *Second Chances* and *Last Chance* answer all these questions and more.

This story has been ten years in the making. Their journey has taken on a life of its own. This is truly their story. I may have wanted the story to go one way but Tristan and Kaitlyn insisted it be written this way. I don't know how their story will end. They keep changing storylines on me.

As a new Indie writer I deeply and truly thank you for taking the chance and purchasing this book. I hope you enjoyed it as much as I did by writing it. Hopefully you will continue on in the series. Please leave me a review and tell your friends about it. There is no better publicity then word of mouth referral.

If you liked the story please check in at these different sites for updates and release dates.

Visit my website http://kimberswan73.wix.com/kimber-swan#!home/mainPage.
Email me: kimberswan73@gmail.com
Follow me on Twitter @Kimber Swan73
Like my Facebook page and leave a comment

Again thank you and please continue on with the series. I hope to hear from all my readers.

Sincerely,
Kimber

COMING SOON FROM THE
CHANCE ENCOUNTERS SERIES

SECOND CHANCES

Followed by

LAST CHANCE